Summers' Horses

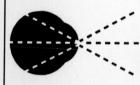

This Large Print Book carries the
Seal of Approval of N.A.V.H.

SUMMERS' HORSES

RALPH COTTON

WHEELER PUBLISHING
A part of Gale, Cengage Learning

Detroit • New York • San Francisco • New Haven, Conn • Waterville, Maine • London

Copyright © Ralph Cotton, 2011
Wheeler Publishing, a part of Gale, Cengage Learning.

Wheeler Publishing Large Print Western.
The text of this Large Print edition is unabridged.
Other aspects of the book may vary from the original edition.
Set in 16 pt. Plantin.

LIBRARY OF CONGRESS CATALOGING-IN-PUBLICATION DATA

Cotton, Ralph W.
  Summers' Horses / By Ralph Cotton. — Large Print edition.
    pages cm. — (Wheeler Publishing Large Print Western)
  ISBN 978-1-4104-6553-5 (softcover) — ISBN 1-4104-6553-5 (softcover) 1.
Horse stealing—Fiction. 2. Large type books. I. Title.
PS3553.O766S86 2014
813'.54—dc23   2013038476

Published in 2014 by arrangement with NAL Signet, a member of Penguin Group (USA) LLC, a Penguin Random House Company

Printed in the United States of America
1 2 3 4 5   18 17 16 15 14

For Mary Lynn . . . *of course*

PART 1

CHAPTER 1

Colorado Territory
Will Summers followed the big spotted cur up the last stretch of trail to a clearing on the mountainside. He guided a string of six horses and a sorrel mule on a lead rope behind him. The mule brought up the rear of the string at a gangly, uncooperative pace.

Summers looked back over his shoulder as one of the horses chuffed and grumbled at the worrisome mule. These were all good horses, he told himself, eyeing the rope respectively. All six, and the one he was riding. He patted a gloved hand on the withers of the silver-gray dapple beneath him.

On the string: *Three dark bays, an Appaloosa mare soon to foal, a paint horse and a black Morgan cross . . . ,* he accounted to himself, as if taking inventory. *Seven fine horses . . .* He turned forward in his saddle and rode on.

From a window in a weathered cabin, Layla Brooks watched Summers and the animals disappear and reappear brokenly through the trees, filing along at an easy pace.

The first living human I've seen in weeks, she reminded herself. The thought of it caused a lump to move into her throat. She kept her eyes from welling and took a breath. She trembled slightly. When she recognized Summers, she'd eased the hammers down on the shotgun in her hands and leaned the gun against the wall. *Of all people . . .*

She gave herself a thin, tight smile and touched her fingertips to her hair. All right, she had no brushes, no combs, she told herself. She looked down her front at the soiled, grease-spotted gingham dress she wore. *Quick . . .*

She stripped the dress over her head and tossed it aside. Picking up her denim trousers from across a stool, she shook them out and wiggled into them. She pulled a loose woolsey shirt over her bare breasts and smoothed it down — *Lee Persons' shirt,* she thought for a moment.

She touched her tangled hair again, this

time with both hands, and looked all around in desperation. *The water bucket . . . ?* She hurried across the floor to the big wooden bucket, hearing the sound of horses' hooves make the turn in the trail and head upward to the cabin. *Is there time? Yes, there has to be,* she said to herself.

When he reached the turn in the trail, Summers stopped and looked at the cabin thirty yards away. A thin curl of smoke rose and drifted above the stone chimney. The yard looked clean enough for the time of year. Firewood filled much of the side yard, some split and stacked, some lying strewn around a chopping block where an ax stood, its handle up.

Looking to the right of the yard, Summers saw the plank grave marker standing at the head of a freshly turned mound of earth.

Through the wavy dusty window glass, Layla peeped out and watched him ride over to the grave, leading his string of horses and mule behind him. The big cur anticipated Summers' path, and loped ahead of him.

"Take your time, Will," Layla said to herself, seeing Summers stop his horse and his string and look down at the mound of earth. She dipped water up from the bucket with both hands and let it run down her bosom.

"L. Persons," Summers murmured, reading the crudely carved pine grave marker. "So long, Lee." He took off his battered Stetson and held it at his side, the lead rope in the same gloved hand. Across the grave from him, the spotted cur plopped down on his bony rump and scratched an ear. Summers turned in his saddle when he heard the front door of the cabin swing open.

"Who's there?" Layla called out from the front porch. She stood with a towel raised to the side of her wet hair. "Is that you, Will Summers?"

Summers turned his horse in Layla's direction. "Yes, ma'am, Layla," he said. "It's me." The cur sprang to a stand and loped across the yard, leading him. "I brought Lee the mule he asked for." His hat still in hand, he gestured it back toward the grave and said respectfully, "I see he won't be needing it now."

Layla stopped drying her hair for a moment and looked over at the grave. Then she raised the towel again.

"No. He won't need it now," she said. "I will, though. I'll be moving back down to Prospect." After a moment's pause, she said,

12

"How much for the mule?"

Summers considered the question quickly. "Lee paid for it in advance, Layla." He pulled the string forward until the mule stood nearest to his side. "So, here it is, delivered as promised. It's all yours."

"Oh, *really?*" Layla said skeptically. She put a hand on her hip, the damp towel hanging from it. "Lee Persons never paid in advance for anything in his life. So, let's try again." She gave him a sharp, knowing smile. "How much for the mule, Will?" she repeated. "I'm not a charity case."

Summers looked her up and down, her wet hair hanging to her shoulders, Lee's old shirt open deep down the front and clinging to her wet breasts. He looked away, but his eyes kept drifting back to her.

"How long has he been dead?" he asked.

"It's been weeks since he died," Layla said. "I'm going to say ten weeks at the least." She stared over at the grave as she spoke. "I wrapped him and laid him in the springhouse until the ground thawed. I finally buried him three days ago." She paused, then added, "I'm past grieving him."

"I see," said Summers. He put on his hat and crossed his wrists on his saddle horn. "Ten weeks . . ."

"At the least . . . ," Layla pointed out quietly, her hand still on her hip. "I woke up in the night because the fire had gone out. I found him lying there, dead, eyes wide open. He was clutching his chest."

Summers shook his lowered head. At the edge of the porch, the big cur had plopped down again and sat staring back and forth between them as if following the conversation.

"He was a good man, Lee Persons," Summers said. He considered it for a second, shrugged and added, "Good enough anyway."

"Yes, he was," Layla said. "And now he is dead and buried," she said bluntly, trying to get past the subject of Lee Persons and on with whatever came next.

Summers sighed; he looked away again, then set his gaze back on Layla. Long shallow skiffs of snow still clung to shadowed rock ledges and low spots up on the steep hillsides.

"Ten weeks, huh?" he said, giving her a curious look.

"Ten weeks, Will," Layla repeated, staring knowingly back at him. "How many times are you going to ask me that?"

"That's all." Summers gave a shrug.

"Good," said Layla. "Now, how much for

14

the sorrel mule?" she asked again.

"I hate to take money from you, Layla," Summers said.

"Then don't," she said. She stared at him.

"What I mean is I hate to charge you anything, Lee dying and all," Summers said.

"I *want you to,* Will," Layla said bluntly. "Do I have to spell it out for you?"

"*Jesus . . . ,*" Summers whispered, looking down at his crossed wrists. After a moment he shook his bowed head and swung down from his saddle.

"No, Layla," he said. "I just didn't want to take advantage."

"Get yourself in here," she said, gesturing toward the door.

"Yes, ma'am," said Summers.

Atop a high ridge overlooking the Persons' cabin, Arlo Hughes, Dow Bendigo and his half-breed brother, Tom "Cat Tracker" Bendigo, sat atop their horses and watched the man and woman from the shelter of trees and rock.

"Fine-looking animals," Arlo Hughes said in a hushed tone.

The other two men offered no reply.

In the fading evening light, the three watched Will Summers take his rifle from its boot and untie his saddlebags. He threw

15

them over his shoulder, carried his Winchester repeater and followed Layla Brooks into the cabin.

At a height of two hundred feet, both man and woman looked small; so did the short stretch of turned earth in the front yard. Along the hitch rail, seven horses and a mule stood at rest, some of them shaking off trail dust.

"I expect your pa will want to hear about this right away," Hughes said to Dow Bendigo. He started to turn his horse back to the narrow trail. The half-breed sat staring at the pair, knowing his brother, Dow, wasn't finished with the matter.

Dow Bendigo stepped his horse over in front of Arlo Hughes, stopping him.

"Wait a minute," Dow said without taking his eyes off the cabin below them. "What's your hurry anyway? Me and Tom are still looking. Right, Cat Tracker?"

The half-breed made no reply.

Hughes stared at Dow Bendigo, noticing that his mouth hung slightly agape as he stared at the cabin.

"Like I just *told you*," Hughes replied with clear deliberation. "Your pa will want to hear about this, *first thing.*"

"My pa can wait," said Dow. "What do you think those two are doing in there right now?" His voice sounded rushed and shallow.

Hughes stared at him. "What do *you think* they're doing in there? Because if you can't figure it out —"

"That's not what I mean," said Bendigo, cutting him off. "I mean right this very minute . . . they just walked inside the door. Where do you figure their hands are *right now*?"

"Damn, Dow," Hughes said in disgust. "Let's get going before you need some time to yourself."

"I don't need no time to myself, Arlo," said Dow Bendigo. He turned to him, red-faced, wearing an angry scowl. "It'll be dark before long. We could ride down there and peep in some through a window, couldn't we?"

"We *could,* but we're not going to," Hughes said firmly.

"Why not?" said Dow. "It would give us more to tell Pa about when we get there."

"You've got plenty of explaining to do as it is," said Hughes. "You lost more money playing poker than some men make in a season. It was *cattle money* at that —"

"Forget how much money I lost," said Dow, cutting him off. "Besides, you was supposed to keep me in line, remember?"

He gave a scornful grin. "Anyway," he said sheepishly, nodding down toward the cabin, "I'd like to see those two going at it . . . you know."

"Yeah, *I know,*" said Hughes. "I'm riding on up to the cliffs. You two can do what suits you." He gave the half-breed a glance. "I'll let your pa know that you're both watching the woman get her belly rubbed. He'll be overjoyed to hear that." He looked at Dow and added, "After all the money *you* lost gambling." He heeled his horse away toward the thin path.

"Damn it, wait up, Arlo," said Dow, jerking his horse's reins and pulling it around beside the older gunman. "I just thought it would be fun, is all."

"Fun?" questioned Hughes, the two riding along. "Did you see who that was with her?"

"No, who?" said Dow.

"It's that horse trader from south of here, Will Summers," said Hughes. "Ever heard of him?"

"I've heard of him, but I've never run into him," said Dow.

"You don't want to run into him either, if you can keep from it," said Hughes. "Least-wise, not peeping through a window at him, especially while he's occupied with a woman like Layla Brooks."

"Do I look scared of him?" asked the young gunman.

Hughes turned and looked him up and down appraisingly.

"No," he said. "Do I?"

"You sound like it," said Dow.

Hughes stopped his horse and sat staring at the younger gunman.

"Let's get something straight here and now, Dow," he said. "I'm not afraid of Will Summers, nor should you be. But he *is* a man to be left alone. He's not a man to trifle with."

"So you say," Dow Bendigo returned. "All I know is he's a horse trader. I haven't seen a horse trader yet that I would cross the street for."

Hughes turned forward in his saddle and stepped his horse around Dow's horse, blocking his path.

"You don't know about Summers, do you, Dow?" he asked over his shoulder.

"I suppose not," said Dow Bendigo. He spit and ran a hand over his mouth. "But I'm betting you're going to tell me about him."

Hughes shook his head. He was used to young Dow Bendigo's haughty attitude. He was used to Tom's stonelike silence. It was his job to try to keep the pair out of trouble, as if anyone could perform such a feat.

"You ever hear of the Peltry Gang, Dow?" he asked.

"Yep," said Dow Bendigo. "The Peltry Gang is a bunch I've heard lots about. My pa knew them. Goose and Moses Peltry are a couple of bad sonsabitches is what I've heard."

"Not *are,* Dow," said Hughes. "They *were.* Will Summers is one of the men who killed them and their whole gang."

"No kidding?" Dow turned attentive. The half-breed watched the two with uninterest.

"No kidding," said Hughes. "He stuck their heads on a stick and rode them around as a warning to the remaining members."

"He did all that?" said Dow.

"He did," said Hughes. "You can ask Lucian Clay when we get up to the cliffs. He rode with the Peltrys. He still harbors some ill feelings toward Summers and the others over it."

"Who are the *others*?" Dow asked.

"Along with Summers, there was a school-teacher from Rileyville named Sherman Dahl and a lawman from the same town named Abner Webb," said Hughes.

"Abner Webb . . . ," Dow said studiously.

"There were others," said Hughes, "but that's all the names that come to mind offhand —"

"Hold it," said Dow, cutting him short as recognition came to him. "You're talking about what the folks around Rileyville call *Webb's Posse*?"

"That I am," said Hughes. "Is it coming to either of you now?"

The half-breed only looked away and spit.

"Damn right it is," said Dow. "So this horse trader rode with Abner Webb and the Teacher."

"Some say he's the one who led the posse," said Hughes.

Dow grinned and said, "Well, he's not leading a posse now. He's lying between Layla Brooks' knees."

"You're not paying any attention to what I'm telling you, are you? You need to leave this man alone," said Hughes.

"I'd like to," Dow Bendigo said with a grin. "But all I can think of now is how easy it would be for the three of us to slip in and steal that string of horses out from under his nose while he's tacking Layla to the mattress."

"That's what I thought," said Hughes. He shook his head and let out a breath.

"Look at it this way," Dow chuckled. "We take the horses home with us, it'll make up for the cattle money I lost. The old man will forget all about it."

"You're playing with fire, messing with your pa the way you do," Hughes warned. "Warton Bendigo is another man not to take lightly."

"You worry too damn much about too many things," said Dow. He jerked his horse around toward his half brother. "What about you, Tom?" he said. "Are you game for taking them horses — maybe getting a little poke at Layla Brooks to boot?"

Tom Bendigo didn't answer. He knew it made no difference what he said. Dow had made up his mind. There would be no stopping him.

CHAPTER 2

Darkness had set in by the time Will Summers rose from beneath a thin cotton blanket and sat up on the side of the bed. Beside him, Layla Brooks drew the blanket up above her naked breasts and snuggled under it. She heard the sound of a match striking and saw the flicker of its flame, which Summers held beneath the globe of the oil lamp sitting on a nightstand beside the bed.

"Why are you getting up?" she asked.

"The dog's at the door," said Summers. "I best let him out."

He adjusted the glow of the lamp.

Layla rose onto an elbow and looked at him in the shadowy circle of soft light.

"Where did you get the dog?" she asked. "I never knew you to travel with a dog."

"I don't," said Summers. "I caught him on a trade from Marvin Brannerd. Got the mule out of it too. I haven't found a buyer for him yet. It's doubtful I will. A big dog like him can come and go as he pleases. Luckily, the trade was already square. I figure the owner just wanted to get rid of him."

"What's his name?" Layla asked.

"I don't know," said Summers. "He doesn't have one right now. I think he once belonged to an army sergeant."

"Why do you think that?" Layla asked. The big spotted cur stood watching them, his tongue lolling.

"Brannerd said he used to wear a leather collar with the name Sergeant Tom Haines tooled on it," Summers said.

The big cur's ears perked up. He stepped forward in anticipation then stopped. He stared at the two expectantly for a moment. Then he relaxed.

"Did you see that?" asked Layla.

"I saw it," Summers said. "He heard me call his owner's name. He's done like that before when Brannerd said the name out loud."

"Maybe it's not his owner's name," said Layla. "Maybe it's *his* name."

"I doubt it," Summers replied. "That's a long name for a dog."

"Maybe so," Layla said, giving up the notion. "I do believe a dog should have a name," she added.

"That'll be up to his new owner, soon as I find him one," said Summers.

The cur turned restless at the closed front door, looking toward the bed. He scratched a big paw down the doorframe and gave a whine as Summers stood up, lamp in hand, and walked toward him.

"All right, settle down, ol' buddy," said Summers, crossing the floor in his bare feet. "I'm coming."

"*Buddy,* huh?" said Layla, watching from the bed as Summers loosened the latch and swung the big pine door open. "Buddy could be his name."

"I suppose it could," Summers said. "I call him whatever comes to mind." He looked out across the dark sky and saw lightning flicker on the horizon. Following the blue-yellow streak, thunder rumbled like distant cannon fire.

Storm building, he told himself, staring off above the black silhouette of hill and tree line.

The dog raced out across the plank porch and bounded out into the pale moonlight. Summers could only make out a high wagging tail until darkness engulfed the animal.

"I know, let's name him," said Layla, rising on her side as Summers closed the door, bolted it and walked back toward the bed.

25

The circle of soft lamplight spread around her.

"I don't think so," Summers said quietly.

"Why not?" said Layla. "It'll be fun."

Summers stopped and looked at her for a moment, recognizing the voice of a woman who had been alone for some time, not talking to anyone. She had wintered here with a dead man, waiting to bury him when the earth would finally allow it. She was still edgy from the experience, he reminded himself.

He put the lamp back on the nightstand and sat down on the side of the bed.

"Name him, then, if it suits you," he said.

"Can't we name him together?" she asked.

Yes, he thought to himself, the edginess was still there in her voice.

"All right," he said, going along with her, "we can name him together. How about Victor? That's a good, strong-sounding name."

"*Victor?*" She gave a slight laugh. "That's not a dog's name."

"Why not?" asked Summers. "You were all set to think his name was Sergeant Tom Haines."

"That's different," she said.

"Different how?" Summers asked.

"Because," she said, "it just is. Anyway,

I've never heard of a dog named Victor."

He slipped under the covers and reached over to put out the lamplight.

"No," she said, "leave it on awhile, please."

He heard the slight desperation in her voice and understood. She needed to talk.

"All right," he said "It's on." He adjusted under the covers and faced her, lying on his pillow in the dim lamplight. "Where are you from, Layla?"

"That was good, Will Summers," she said. She looked at him with a slight smile. "You sound like you couldn't care less where I'm from."

"I do care, Layla," Summers said. "It's just that I never got around to asking you before now."

She drew a circle on his chest with her finger and said, "All those times in town . . . ?"

"We were always busy doing other things, remember?" Summers said.

She nodded. "I remember." She paused for a moment, as if revisiting her fondest memory of their time together, and then she answered his question. "I'm from Missouri. I started out from there anyway." She studied his face for a moment, then said bluntly, "What do you care where a dove like me comes from?"

27

"I never thought of you as just a dove, Layla," said Summers. "Nobody is ever just one thing. We all started out somewhere, and we all had things happen along the way." He reached up and brushed a long strand of hair from her forehead. "If you don't want to talk about it, I understand."

He was weary from the trail, as well as their time together earlier, and he almost wished she would decide not to talk; but he knew better. Once she started, there would be no stopping her, and he couldn't blame her for it. She needed to get all of the aching loneliness out of her bosom.

"No, I want to talk," she said. She settled down beside him in the bed and rested her face on his chest.

Summers drew a patient breath and relaxed, feeling her fingertip begin to draw lazy circles on his flesh once again. She had been twelve years old when she'd left Missouri with young Uncle Fray and Aunt Melanor Turnbaugh. Both her parents had died from the fever in the wilds near Springfield. They traveled with a wagon train, slowly making their way west. Her uncle had sought comfort with her — as he called it — while his young wife suffered the final agonizing weeks of a particularly harsh pregnancy.

Summers listened and commented just enough to keep her talking.

She had turned thirteen by the time the Turnbaughs' baby was born; by then she was pregnant herself.

"When Aunt Melanor found out about it, she didn't seem at all hurt or even surprised," Layla said quietly against his chest. "I often think she knew it was happening." She shrugged slightly. "I lost the baby. It was so small, Uncle Fray buried it alongside the trail in a match tin. No prayer; no nothing. I can't remember if he even stopped the wagon."

Summers stroked her hair as she spoke.

"The next town we came to, Uncle Fray traded me to a tent saloon owner," she said. "That's where I started."

Jesus . . . Summers began rubbing her shoulders. There was more to come, he knew it.

"What made you and Lee Persons decide to take up?" he asked, prompting her along. He would keep her talking until she ran out her string.

"Like you said, Will, Lee was a good man," she replied. "He treated me good. I figured with him I could get out of the business and —"

"*Shhh,*" said Summers cutting her off.

29

From outside, he heard the dog let out a long vicious growl.

"What's got into him?" Layla said, springing up from Summers' chest.

"I don't know," said Summers, "but I better find out." He swung up out of bed, grabbing only the big Colt hanging in its holster from the head post. The dog had flown into a growling, snarling rage, as if it had something or someone held at bay.

"Will, your pants!" said Layla, jumping up from the bed naked. She grabbed Summers' trousers from a chair and pitched them to him on his way to the door.

Summers caught the trousers but didn't take the time to put them on. Whatever it was the dog was facing off with, it called for his immediate attention.

"Stay here. Bolt the door," he said over his shoulder. Barefoot, he stepped out into the darkness and heard Layla already dropping the thick iron bolt into place behind him.

He turned toward the horses in the barn as he bounded down from the porch, trousers and gun in hand, and ran to the sound of the snarling dog.

On his way through the darkness, he stopped cold in his tracks when he heard the dog let out a loud, painful yelp and fall silent.

He recognized the sound of someone scurrying through the trees, and he stepped forward quietly, not daring to call out to the dog for fear of giving away his position to whatever might lie in wait.

As his eyes grew more accustomed to the faint purple light of a quarter moon, he made out the limp, shadowy form of the cur lying in the path between the barn and the tree line. He stooped down and felt of the big dog's wet muzzle; the dog whined weakly and tried to raise his head at the touch of his hand.

"Easy, ol' buddy," he whispered. He ran his hand up over the dog's head and felt something wet and warm between his limp ears. *Blood?*

In the trees he heard the sound of horses moving quietly away from the yard, deeper into the trees.

Horse thieves! he told himself. He ran toward the tree line, his trousers still in hand. In the trees he looked all around, but he only saw distant shadows disappearing from sight. He turned back toward the barn to gather himself a horse, if there were any left there. But before he could even begin to run through the darkness, the hard blow

31

of a rifle butt reached out of nowhere, stabbed him in the back of his head and sent him crashing to the ground.

He realized what had happened in the split second before the world turned black and mindless around him.

Standing over Summers, Dow Bendigo struck a match and lit the thin twisted cigarette hanging from his lips. He smiled and looked at his half brother in the orange glow. Tom Bendigo stood with his rifle in both hands; Summers' Colt, hat and trousers lay strewn at his feet. In the distant night, lightning twisted and curled as the storm drew closer.

"Damn, Brother Cat Tracker," Dow said to Tom Bendigo, "you damn near knocked his brains out. Why so angry?" He grinned and took a drag from his cigarette.

Tom Bendigo made no reply. Instead he levered a round into his rifle chamber and pointed the tip of the barrel down at the back of Summers' bloody head.

"*Whoa,* hold on, Tom," said Dow. He shoved the half-breed's rifle aside. "We don't need to go making all that noise, spoil such a beautiful night as this. Drag him off and tie him to a tree." Reaching down, he picked up Summers' battered Stetson. He nodded at Summers' trousers lying on the ground. "Take his pants too."

"We best go ahead and kill him, Dow," Arlo Hughes cut in, making his way over to Dow and Tom. "He'll be right down our shirts soon as he's up and around."

"Carrying one of these pines tied to his back?" said Dow with a dark chuckle. "I've never noticed before now what an old woman you've turned into, Arlo. Does Will Summers really have you that spooked? He's just a horse trader."

"Forget who he is," said Hughes. "We shouldn't leave anybody living, free to announce what we've done."

"He didn't see any of us," said Dow. "Hell, he didn't see *anything*." He drew on the cigarette. "We could invite him to dinner someday. He wouldn't know the difference. I do like that notion."

"It's a bad idea," Hughes warned.

"Yeah, what about the sound of a rifle shot this time of night?" said Dow. "There's no telling who it might draw in."

As they talked, the three men failed to take notice of the big spotted cur, who had dragged himself forward and up onto unsteady paws. The dog meandered off into the darkness, his head beginning to clear a little from the swipe of Dow's pistol barrel.

33

Tom Bendigo and Arlo Hughes looked at each other in consideration.

"I might agree with you about a rifle shot," said Hughes. "But we can cut his throat."

"We're not killing him, and that's that," Dow said firmly. "I want this big man hunter to know that somewhere there's a man walking around who knocked his head off, stole his horses and took his woman . . . and there ain't a damn thing he can ever do about it." He looked at Tom. "Now drag him away, Cat Tracker." With the toe of his boot he kicked the loose trousers from the ground and over across Summers' back.

"What about Layla Brooks?" Hughes asked as Tom began dragging Summers away. "If we kidnap her, she's sure to recognize us."

"Layla Brooks is a whole other matter," said Dow. "When we finish with her, you can cut her damned heart out for all I care."

"Your pa won't like that," said Hughes. "You know how strongly he feels about that dove. He's made no secret of it."

"Dove . . . ?" said Dow. He spit in contempt. "Call her what she is, Arlo. She's a saloon whore. Always was, always will be. Far as I'm concerned, we'd be doing my pa a big favor, killing her."

"Jesus, Dow," said Hughes. "I hope you're not about to get us all into big trouble."

"Don't worry about it, Arlo," said Dow. "I'm not going to get you in trouble." He grinned to himself and added wryly, "I might get you *killed,* but I won't get you in trouble." He turned and walked toward the string of stolen horses, which stood deeper in the thick trees.

CHAPTER 3

Layla stood with vigilance at the front window of the cabin, Lee Persons' shotgun in her hands. She stared out into the darkness toward the barn, and beyond it into the shadowy trees. The first rays of morning glowed pale and white on the distant horizon.

Her eyes widened as she saw a flickering torch bob into sight and move toward the cabin above the sound of horses' hooves.

Will! God, I hope that's you.

But a sickness stirred deep in her stomach as she watched the Bendigo brothers and Arlo Hughes ride into sight, the one they called Cat Tracker leading Will Summers' horses on a lead rope behind him.

"Hello the cabin . . . Hello, Layla Brooks," Dow called out, holding the torch above his head as he reined his horse back and forth just in front of the porch. The torch cast a flickering circle of light on the rocky front yard. "Get yourself out here, woman, and say howdy."

This was not the time to show fear, Layla told herself. She summoned up her courage, walked over to the door and unlatched it. She opened the door a crack, just enough to hold out the shotgun barrel and give the three a look at it.

"Howdy, Dow," she said. "Now, what the hell are you doing here? Where's Will Summers?"

"Will Summers?" said Dow. "Never met him."

"Your Indian brother there is leading his horses, Dow," she called out.

Lightning streaked closer and thunder rumbled ominously along the hill line.

"All right, you've got me," Dow said, stopping his horse a few feet back from the porch, respectful of the big double-barreled shotgun staring out at him. "Will Summers is out there in the trees . . . tied to one of them. We knocked him cold and stole his horses. How about that?"

Layla assessed the situation quickly. She didn't like the way Dow was acting, cocky, confident. She knew what kind of rage Warton Bendigo would fly into if any harm came to her. Whatever these men had in mind, they had no intention of Warton

37

Bendigo ever finding out they were to blame.

"I don't believe you," she said, stalling as she tried to plan her best move. "Will Summers would never get caught by the likes of you."

"Oh yeah?" said Dow. He pitched Summers' battered Stetson hat to the ground. "I thought you might say something like that. Here's his hat to prove it."

After a moment's pause, Layla said, "All right, then, you caught him off guard and stole his horses. You're a big man. What is it you want from me?" She went straight to the point.

So did Dow. He grinned at Hughes and his brother, Tom.

"We want the same thing Will Summers was getting before we rode in and took his horses," said Dow.

"We were *talking,* Dow. You want to talk?" asked Layla.

"We want more than *talking* from you," Dow called out.

"That won't happen, Dow," Layla said flatly.

"Oh, it will happen, Layla," Dow said confidently. "Unless you want me to send Arlo here back to cut your boyfriend's throat."

Layla took a deep breath to keep herself from panicking.

"Your pa would skin you and your brother alive if he knew you were out here acting this way," she called out.

Dow ignored her words and said, "We *are* coming in. You might just as well put down the shotgun and get ready to give us a little party." He swung down from his saddle as he spoke.

Layla slammed the door and bolted it. There was no way she was letting them inside the cabin. She ran back to the window, swung its thick wooden shutter closed and peered out through a shooting port.

"Stay away from me, Dow. I'm warning you!" she shouted, loud enough to be heard through the window shutter and the wavy pane of glass.

Dow looked over his shoulder at Arlo Hughes, who still sat atop his horse a few feet away from the half-breed.

"Go kill the horse trader, Arlo," he said. "Show her we mean business."

"Right," said Hughes. He stuck his rifle into its boot and drew his Colt. He started to jerk his horse around toward the woods. "Now you're making sense —"

Before he got his words from his lips, a blast of blue-orange fire from the double-barrel exploded through the shooting port. Shards of glass, wood and buckshot blasted out, lifted Hughes from his saddle and flung his body ten feet, blood looming in a red mist behind him.

Dow and Tom Bendigo quickly jerked their horses farther to the side, out of the narrow shooting port's firing range.

"I'll kill the lot of you," Layla screamed from inside the cabin. Powder smoke curled and drifted through the broken window glass.

Dow grinned in the thin moonlight and looked at the mangled remains of Arlo Hughes lying on the ground, a dark circle of blood still spreading beneath him.

"By God, Cat Tracker, I believe she means it," he said to his brother. He called out to the broken window, "Does this mean we've caught you in a bad mood, Layla?"

"Get away from here, Dow, I'm warning you," Layla called out, attempting to turn the shotgun barrel far enough to one side to get an aim at the two.

"Give it up, Layla. Throw out that shotgun," said Dow. There was a strange cheeriness in his tone. "You can't hit us from that angle."

"Don't bet your life on it," Layla replied, knowing he was right, but willing to play her hand to the last card no matter how weak her chances.

"We don't have to bet on it. We'll just go cut your horse trader's throat." Dow grinned. "Now you think about it."

Will, I'm sorry! Tears came to her eyes. She'd already thought about it. She had given herself to so many men that two more wouldn't matter, she'd thought. But this was different. These men meant to kill her, she was certain. As rotten and hard as life could be, she still wasn't ready to give it up. Not like this, she told herself.

She kept a firm grip on the shotgun. She had one more shot, and then she would have to reload. She wasn't sure she could reload in time to keep these two from breaking the door in if they wanted to.

"What say you, Layla? Are you going to throw out that scattergun and let us in?" Dow called out. "Or you want to watch one of us ride away and kill your horse trader?"

She thought about the Manhattan Arms five-shot pepperbox derringer she had tucked away inside a possibles box atop the mantel. It wasn't much, but it was all she had.

They wanted the shotgun out of her hands; she would have to comply.

She watched Dow turn to his brother.

"Go kill him, Cat Tracker," he called out loud enough for Layla to hear.

"No, wait!" Layla shouted. She ran to the mantel, jerked the small wooden box down and snatched the derringer from inside. "I'm coming!" she called out.

She had reasoned it out in her mind. This was the best move, for herself and for Will Summers. She'd give up the shotgun and get them in close enough for the small gun to do some damage. It was risky, but she didn't have a choice.

The sound of the door bolt caused the two brothers to look at each other confidently and swing down from their saddles. Dow eased up on one side of the door, Tom on the other.

"Here it comes," Layla called out from the slightly opened door. She held the shotgun slowly forward, butt first. "I'm taking your word that you're not going to —"

Dow snatched the shotgun roughly from her and tossed it over to his brother's waiting hands.

"You stupid whore," he said. "Our pa must be out of his mind, wanting to take up with the likes of you."

He slung the door open wide, grabbed her and threw her backward. She fell atop a large wooden kitchen table. She had no time

42

to pick herself up before he was standing over her, holding her down, one gloved hand grasping her throat. He pressed his body down atop her.

The half-breed stepped inside and watched stone-faced from a corner of the cabin, the loaded double-barrel shotgun in his hand.

"When we're through with you, you're dead. You'll never get the chance to tell our pa," he said, his hot breath down close on her face.

She'd been right, she told herself. That made this easier. She jerked the little derringer up in her hand and pulled the trigger only inches from Dow's chest. Two shots bored less than two inches deep into his left shoulder. But the pain was enough to make him turn her loose and stumble backward with a loud yell. She aimed at the half-breed, who had raised the shotgun and taken quick aim at her. She fired the next three shots as quickly as she could pull the trigger. Two bullets whizzed past Tom's face, causing him to duck slightly to the side. The third bullet grazed the side of his throat and threw off his aim.

"Kill this whore!" Dow raged, seeing Layla roll away and off the table, her pale naked legs flailing as the big shotgun belched a blast of fire and buckshot into the table where her head had been a split second before.

She hit the floor, feeling blood stream down her cheeks from where a few hot stray beads of buckshot had struck her face. She lay addled for a moment, not knowing how bad her wound might be. She could see nothing but a black wet swirl in her left eye, and the pain of it sliced deep inside the front of her brain.

"Whoa! That took some bounce out of her bustle," Dow said. He managed to chuckle even with the small derringer bullets in his shoulder. Stepping over and standing above Layla, he saw her consciousness fading as he kicked the empty derringer from her hand. He stooped and grabbed the front of her shirt and ripped it away.

The half-breed stood staring without expression.

"As if this whore ever wore a bustle in her life," Dow added, jerking at the waist of her denim trousers. He peeled them down off her and tossed them aside. He caught Tom's questioning stare and gestured a hand down at the naked woman.

"Hell yes, I'm going to, Cat Tracker," he said, seeing the blood run down from the tiny bullet hole in his brother's throat. "And so are you. How many times does a man get the chance to saddle-break the woman who might have become his stepmama?" He laughed at his bizarre joke as he loosened his belt. Tom turned and walked out onto the front porch.

Will Summers came to with a jolt at the first sound of the shotgun blast. But as soon as he jerked his hands forward, he felt the bite of rope around his wrists and realized he was tied to a tree. He struggled against the taut cord until he collapsed, the blow of the half-breed's rifle butt still throbbing and pounding at the base of his skull.

"Layla . . . ," he murmured, hoping to keep himself conscious. With his head bowed and his eyes barely open, he still caught a glimpse of his trousers lying in a heap on the ground beside him. He thought of the small folding pocketknife he'd carried with him for the past two months.

"Help — help me . . . ," he stammered, pleading to no one in particular. Above him a darker sky had moved in low and boiling. Treetops swayed along the hill line.

He stretched his leg out and reached with his bare foot toward the trousers lying just out of reach. He dug his toes in the dirt in an ill-fated attempt to drag the pants closer to him. His effort grew so intense that after a moment he collapsed and lay panting against the tree, his shoulders feeling as if he'd wrenched them from their sockets.

But when he heard the shots of the small pistol, accompanied by the second blast from the shotgun, he feverishly renewed his efforts. This time he hooked his big toe under his trousers to get a good hold on them and dragged them across the ground.

"Come on . . . ," he pleaded with himself. When he had the trousers up onto his lap, he wiggled a foot into one pocket and whipped the pants around until they fell close enough to his side for him to grab them with his tied left hand.

Get the knife. . . . Get the knife! he demanded of himself.

Moments later he had the knife out and gripped it in his sweaty right hand. He took a long deep breath, found the length of rope binding his hands together and began slicing it. . . .

On the front porch, Tom Bendigo stared off into the trees, where only a moment earlier he'd heard something rustle through the brushy ground cover beneath a building wind. Lightning drew closer. His rifle stood in its saddle boot where he'd left it, but as he kept his eyes on the trees, he eased his Colt from its holster and cocked it at his side.

Dow stepped onto the porch beside him, hitching his belt.

"I'm all through, Brother Cat Tracker," he said with satisfaction. "Too bad she was knocked out. She missed the whole thing."

Tom only gave him a questioning look.

"What the hell?" said Dow with a dismissive shrug. "I didn't want to take all morning." He grinned, looked at the gun in Tom's hand, then out toward the woods. "What's out there? What are you looking at?"

Tom's only reply was to uncock his Colt and start to lower it back into his holster.

Dow nodded at the Colt and said, "Don't forget to put a bullet between her eyes when you've finished up with her. Nobody is ever going to know what we did here but you and me."

Tom just stared at him.

"Go on, Cat Tracker," said Dow. "Get you some." He gave his half-breed brother a slight shove toward the open door. "Don't make me start thinking there's something *odd* about you."

The half-breed walked inside the open door and looked over at the woman lying naked and bloody on the dirt floor. The thin light of an oil lamp flickered on the timber mantel above the hearth. He walked over and gazed down at her for a moment, his hand on the holstered Colt. Then he started to raise the gun, cocking it on its way up.

Dow stood in the open doorway and shook his head.

"Huh-uh, Cat Tracker," he said. "You ain't killing her until *after* you've done her." His hand went to his Colt; his finger wrapped around the gun butt. "Now get it done, so I'll know we're both together — up to our chins in this thing."

Tom stared at him harshly. Then he eased the Colt down and turned back to the woman.

"That's more like it," said Dow.

But as soon as Tom shifted away from his brother, he heard a vicious growl joined by a terrible scream. In the open doorway with his back to the yard, Dow had not seen the big cur race across the yard from out of nowhere and launch himself up over the porch in a long bound, his fangs bared for a death battle.

Tom jerked around just as the weight of the cur struck his brother full force from behind and took him to the floor. The dog's wide-open jaws locked shut on the back of

Dow's head. With Dow on the floor beneath him, the big cur shook Dow's head back and forth as if it were that of a rag doll.

Dow struggled, screaming long and loud, but to no avail. Blood flew as the dog growled, slashed and ripped at his scalp.

"Get it off me! Get it off!" he bellowed between a scream and a sob.

The half-breed drew his Colt and cocked it. But he hesitated for just a moment. The faint trace of a smile came to his face. Then he fired at the dog.

Careful not to hit Dow, he hit the floor a foot from where the dog stood, furiously mauling the downed gunman.

Without looking up, the cur turned loose of his helpless victim, spun and raced out the door and across the yard. The half-breed gave chase, but only until he stood on the front porch. He fired shot after shot, each bullet falling short by mere inches, until the dog disappeared into the shelter of the trees.

"My God, he's eaten me alive, brother," Dow sobbed, sitting up on the floor, holding up his ripped scalp to the back of his head with a bloody, trembling hand.

Tom only nodded. He stooped down beside his sobbing brother, picked up his mauled hat and examined the tooth marks in it.

"Help me to my feet, damn it!" Dow shouted through sobs. "You've got to get me to a doctor, fast! That dog is mad! Did you kill him? Did you shoot that lousy cur?"

Tom only shook his head as he helped his brother to his feet and over to the front door. He leaned Dow against the doorjamb and put his hat on his head in an effort to hold the badly ripped scalp in place. Blood ran down from beneath the hat brim.

"Lord God, Tom, hurry," said Dow. "Kill that whore and get me out of here! I'll bleed out if we don't get to a doctor! He's ruined me!"

Leaving his brother in the doorway, Tom turned with his smoking Colt still in hand and stepped back over around the table. Having fired five shots at the cur, he started to aim his sixth shot down at the woman. But she wasn't there.

He looked all around, noting that the back door stood open a few inches. He walk to it and looked out, catching no sign of the woman.

"Come on, Tom, *damn it,*" Dow shouted from the front doorway. "Get me out of here! I can barely stand. . . ."

The half-breed looked back and forth one last time. Then he walked to the front doorway and helped his slumped brother out front, down off the porch and up onto his horse. Atop his own horse, Tom looked around one last time as he lifted the lead rope to Summers' horses. Grabbing hold of the reins to his brother's horse as well, he gigged his horse forward, back toward the rocky trail.

CHAPTER 4

Morning light managed to seep in, blue-gray under the looming clouds, as Will Summers finished cutting through the rope binding his wrists and pulled himself up from the tree. He felt drops of sharp, cold rain lash in on the wind. Thunder jarred the earth beneath his feet.

He moved quickly, pulling on his trousers and running barefoot toward the cabin. He'd heard the raging cur, the man's screams and the pistol shots, followed a moment later by the rumble of many horses' hooves. His horses!

With the pocketknife still open in one hand, he reached down and snatched up a fist-sized rock from the ground.

Out in front of the cabin, he slid to a halt and examined his surroundings. A stir of dust still loomed in the air above the rocky trail the horses and riders had taken. Arlo Hughes lay dead in the dirt, his face blown away by the shotgun blast. His Colt lay in the dirt beside him; his spooked horse stood a few yards away, a rifle poking out from its saddle boot.

Big mistake, fellows, Summers commented to himself, staring after the lingering trail dust, watching it swirl away on the wind.

A silver-gray dapple, three dark bays, an Appaloosa mare soon to foal, a paint horse and a black Morgan cross. Seven in all . . . , he reminded himself.

Riding hard, he could get all seven horses back. He could be on those thieves in minutes, storm or no storm — provided Layla Brooks was all right, he had to stop and remind himself. But hell, that went without saying . . .

On his way to the cabin, he grabbed Hughes' Colt from the dirt and checked it quickly. He snatched the horse's reins and led it to the hitch rail by the porch.

Seven horses! Damn . . .

He'd lost horses before, but never this many.

Seeing the open door, he bounded up across the porch and inside. But once inside he looked all around and saw that Layla wasn't there.

"Layla . . . ?" he said, quietly at first, gripping the Colt tightly in his right hand. He saw the rear door standing slightly open and walked to it. He opened the door farther and shouted for Layla, this time letting his voice bellow across the rocky, brush-strewn yard.

"Will, over here . . . ," Layla called out weakly. Her trembling voice was accompanied by the barking of the big cur. "I — I can't see you . . ."

Summers' eyes followed the sound of Layla and the barking dog to a spot among the trees. He hurried toward the cur, dropping the rock on his way. The rain continued to lash against the ground as the storm moved in across the hillsides.

The cur met him at the tree line, whining and circling close to his legs as Summers pressed on a few yards deeper into the woods. Summers glanced down at the bloody pistol-barrel welt on the dog's head and the streak of red on his hip, evidence of the bullet that had grazed him. The cur limped slightly.

"Oh, Layla," said Summers, seeing the woman's bloody, buckshot face appear from around the edge of the tree. He ran forward and kneeled down to her; she collapsed into his arms.

"I'm — I'm all right, Will . . . ," she said weakly against his chest. "They shot me . . .

in the face. I can't see."

"You hang on, Layla," Summers said, feeling the rain upon them. Scooping her up into his arms, he tried to take on a hopeful tone. "We'll get you tended to in no time. You'll be just fine. Don't worry about a thing."

"Are you . . . all right, Will . . . ?" she asked, barely conscious.

"I'm all right, Layla," said Summers, hurrying toward he cabin, the big cur running, limping and whining alongside them.

Inside the cabin he laid her down on the bed. The dog stayed near the edge of the bed while Summers hurried to a bucket of water sitting on the cupboard counter. He took a clean cloth from a shelf inside the small cupboard, dipped it into the water and wrung it between his hands.

The dog stood staring, watching every move as Summers returned to the bed and began wiping blood from the small buckshot wounds on her cheek and chin. He winced as he took note of the small wound in her left eye. The entire white of her eye had turned bloodred. Fresh blood seemed to surge up out of her tear ducts and trickle down the side of her face.

Careful . . . , he cautioned himself, touching the tip of the wet cloth near the corner of her eye. This wouldn't do, he told himself. A wound like this might not be fatal like a gunshot or a stab wound, but it was beyond his capabilities.

"We've got to get you to town, to the doctor, as fast as we can," he murmured aloud.

"What . . . about your horses?" she asked dreamily.

"They don't matter," Summers lied. "You need a doctor."

The urgency in his voice caused her to stir. She raised her left hand limply and felt around in his direction, searching for him.

"Will, I — I can't see you," she said, weak and trembling.

"I'm right here, Layla," said Summers. "Can you see me now?" he asked, leaning over her far enough for her to see him through her right eye.

"No . . . ," she said. "Just a blur . . ." She found his forearm and gripped it in fear and desperation. "Am I going to be . . . blind, Will?"

Summers had no answer. He touched the cloth to the bleeding. It had slowed a little; but he saw nothing indicating that her vision was improving.

"Will, am I?" she asked, sounding more desperate this time, gripping his forearm tighter.

"I don't know, Layla," he replied, realizing this was no time to offer her false hope. "I need to get you to town as fast as I can."

"What about . . . your horses, Will?" she repeated, her shock and fear affecting her reasoning.

"Forget the horses," Summers said, knowing she was half out of her head. "Right now, the only thing I care about is getting you to the doctor in Wakely."

"Buddy . . . saved me," Layla said, her eyes closed, blood still trickling down her left cheek. "Is he . . . all right?"

"Buddy?" Summers said.

"The dog . . . remember . . . ?" said Layla, her consciousness slipping away as she spoke.

"Yes, now I remember," said Will, having forgotten what she'd named the big cur. He looked at the dog. The animal sat staring at Layla with a look of concern in his eyes, his wet tongue lolling.

The big cur gave Summers a short, whining bark, as if inquiring about the woman's condition. Summers looked at the swollen welt across the dog's head, the streak of blood on his hip from the bullet graze.

"Good dog," he said.

The dog stared back at the woman and gave a low, soft whine.

"He's all right, Layla," said Summers. "Now take it easy. I'm going to get you bandaged up some and take you to Wakely." Outside, the rain lashed sidelong in the wind.

As if understanding him, the big cur loped over to the open door with a limp and looked back restlessly toward the bed. He barked in urgency.

"Stay put, Buddy," said Summers. "We're going to have to look you over too."

But the dog would have none of it. He turned a restless full circle, then bounded out across the front porch, through the rain, limping toward the rocky trail.

Moments later, Summers walked out carrying Layla in his arms. He'd wrapped her in a blanket. Stepping down from the porch in the rain, he made his way to the horse and eased her up into the saddle. Before stepping up himself, he looked off through the rain in the direction the gunmen had taken. He knew the storm would already have washed out their tracks. But there was nothing he could do now anyway. Any reckoning he had coming with the men who did this would have to wait. For now the most pressing matter was getting through the storm — getting Layla to Wakely, to the doctor.

*But seven horses! A silver-gray dapple,
three dark bays —*

Put them out of your mind, he said silently,
cutting himself off. He turned the horse and
rode away through the brunt of the storm.

The Bendigo brothers stashed the string of
horses in a stand of trees alongside the trail
outside Wakely. The weather had moved
across them and rumbled off to the east an
hour earlier, taking with it any sign of their
horses' hoofprints.

They rode into town through a back alley
leading to the rear of the doctor's office.
During the stormy ride, dark blood from
Dow's torn and shredded scalp had soaked
upward around his hatband. But now the
blood had gelled and dried, clinging to both
his hat and his raw head wounds. The
pounding of his horse's hooves had beaten
in perfect rhythm with the pounding pain in
the back of his sorely mauled skull.

"I . . . will . . . kill that mangy . . . son of a
bitch," he said in a pain-ridden voice as he
and Tom reined their horses down at a hitch
rail behind the doctor's office.

Tom didn't say a word as he stepped down
and took his brother's reins from him, hitching both horses to the rail. He offered Dow
a hand, intending to help him down from

his saddle, but his proud half brother refused it.

"I'm not some milksop! I don't need your help!" Dow shouted angrily. He swung to the ground and stood holding on to the saddle horn for a moment, letting the pain and wooziness subside.

The half-breed only stared, keeping himself from revealing a slight smile at the sight of Dow's beaten and battered state.

Dow walked with deliberation, approaching the doctor's back porch. But when he stalled before attempting to climb the seven stairs to the door, Tom stepped in without a word, taking his brother's arm and looping it over his shoulders.

Inside the large, whitewashed clapboard house, Dr. Leonard Chase looked up from his desktop with a start when he heard the loud knocking on the rear door.

He walked quickly through the house, fearing that whoever was there would break the door in if he didn't answer fast enough.

"I'm coming!" he cried out, reaching for the door. "For God's sake, stop all the infernal pounding. It's not locked —"

His words stopped short as he swung the door open and recognized the Bendigo brothers. Staring into Tom's stoic face, he fell silent, stunned for a second as he always was when in the half-breed's presence.

Tom only returned the silent stare.

"Doc, I'm . . . hurt, bleeding bad," Dow said in a strained voice as Tom stepped forward, leading him inside the house.

The doctor noted Dow's pale face, his bloody hatband, his battered forehead. He saw the tiny bullet holes in the left shoulder and the blood that soaked his shirt.

"I'll say you are," the doctor replied, moving aside and gesturing the two toward his treatment room down a hallway. "Take him right to the bed," he said, instructing the half-breed.

"What happened to him?" the doctor asked the half-breed cautiously, always afraid that something he said would set Tom "Cat Tracker" Bendigo into a rage.

"He's not . . . talking, Doc," said Dow, seeing Tom's caged expression. The movement of his face caused him greater pain, yet he winced and forced himself to go on. "I got attacked by a wolf . . . up the other side of the main pass at Whiskey Bend. "He nearly . . . ate me alive."

"A *wolf*?" the doctor said with a dubious look.

"Didn't I say *wolf*?" Dow asked, heated and irritated.

Tom helped his brother sit down on the edge of a small bed in the recovery room.

"Yes, you did," the doctor submitted. He wasn't going to question the small bullet holes. "If you got attacked up the other side of the main pass, I take it you rode through the storm last night." As he spoke, he stepped over to Dow and examined him closely.

"See . . . I didn't really come here . . . to give you a report on the weather," Dow replied sharply. "My damn scalp . . . is ripped to pieces! I've got two bullets in me!"

"I understand," the doctor said with patience. "Let's get this hat unstuck and take a look-see. Then I'll deal with the bullet wounds and get your head sewed up."

Gripping Dow's hat brim firmly with both hands, the doctor gave a slight twist. It clung tightly to the thick dried blood and shreds of scalp.

"This might hurt a little," the doctor said, knowing how bad it was going to be.

Dow groaned at the increased pain caused by the twist of the hat.

As the doctor worked the brim back and forth, the pain became so unbearable that Dow could no longer restrain his moans. He let out a long, loud scream as the doctor tore the hat loose from his mauled and mangled head.

"Mother of Go-o-o-o-d!"

"There we are," the doctor said with satisfaction beneath Dow Bendigo's long, tortured cry.

The half-breed stared on with the ever-so-slight trace of a smile on his stone face.

Inside the Big Bear Saloon two blocks away, Albert Knox and Bertram "Blue Hand" Berger turned at the bar and looked out over the top of the batwing doors toward the sound of the scream coming from the doctor's office.

"The hell was that, Blue Hand?" asked Knox.

"One of them wagon train women spitting out another flat-headed baby is my guess," said Berger. "So it sounds like anyway." He raised his frothing beer mug and took a deep swig. "They spit another one out ever' eight or nine weeks." He wiped a hand across his froth-streaked mustache.

"You mean months," said Knox.

"Huh?" said Berger.

"You said eight or nine *weeks.* You meant eight or nine months," said Knox.

"Had I meant months, I would have said months," Berger replied in a testy voice. "Wagon train women breed faster than most

63

varmints."

"That sounded like it was almost a man's voice to me," Knox said, still looking out toward the doctor's office.

"There's no such thing as *almost* a man's voice," said Berger. "It's either a man's voice or it's not." He took another swig of his beer. "No man I ever knew would scream like that unless an Apache was working on him with a skinning knife."

Knox considered the matter as he tossed back a shot of whiskey and swigged beer behind it.

"Think we ought to go see what's going on over there?" he said.

"Why?" Berger shrugged. "She's spit it on out by now, loud as she was."

"I'm saying it ain't a woman having a baby," said Knox. "To tell you the truth, it sounded like Dow Bendigo to me."

"Dow ever heard you say something like that about him, he would walk around you with a skinning knife," Berger said with a dark chuckle.

"Forget I said it," Knox replied in earnest. "I meant nothing by it anyway."

"It's forgotten," said Berger.

Knox looked relieved.

"Let's walk over there," he said. "If it's a wagon train woman, she might name it after us. She might even name it after *both* of us." He grinned.

Berger set his mug down and turned with Knox toward the batwing doors.

"She can name it after *you.* I don't want nothing named after me as long as I'm on this earth," he said. "Besides, what if it's a girl?"

"So what?" said Knox. "They can still name it after us, far as I care."

CHAPTER 5

Dow Bendigo held a shaky hand toward the doctor, warding him off as he tossed back a drink of laudanum from a blue medicine bottle. He chased it with a long swig of whiskey. The doctor held a C-shaped needle between his bloody fingertips. He'd had no trouble getting the derringer bullets out of Dow's shoulder and bandaging the small wounds. Now he was ready to deal with his torn and mangled scalp.

"All right, sawbones," Dow gasped, amber rye running down both drooping tips of his mustache, "sew me up good and proper."

"As you wish, sir," the doctor replied.

Tom "Cat Tracker" Bendigo had tied his bandanna a little more snug than usual around his neck, letting it serve as a bandage for the bullet graze. He stared stone-faced from a few feet away as the doctor flipped a dangling piece of scalp back onto Dow's head with a soft plop.

Dow grunted, but he sat still, letting the whiskey and the powerful drug take hold.

Cutting a sidelong glance at his brother, Dow said grudgingly, "You don't have to watch every damn move, Cat Tracker."

The half-breed didn't so much as nod. Instead, he stepped forward, lifted the whiskey bottle from his half brother's hand and took a long swig. When he slipped the bottle back into Dow's hand, he turned, walked out of the room, down the hall and onto the back porch. As soon as he opened the rear door, he saw Berger and Knox walking up to the string of horses.

Knox and Berger turned, startled at the sound of the door closing. Their hands instinctively went to the guns holstered on their hips.

"Damn, Cat Tracker, you surprised us!" said Berger, relieved at the sight of the half-breed, but still keeping his hand on his gun butt. He gestured toward the string of horses at the hitch rail. Dow and Tom Bendigo's horses stood alongside them.

Tom only lifted his square chin an inch — a greeting that could easily be interrupted as slightly veiled contempt.

"Is this you and Dow's string?" Berger asked.

Tom turned his face slightly toward the

horses, then back to Berger.

"His same outgoing self, I see," Knox whispered to Berger.

"Shut up," Berger warned him from the corner of his mouth.

The two stepped forward toward the porch.

"Well, I'll be danged," said Knox to the half-breed, starting all over. "I told Blue Hand here that I thought I heard Dow —"

A curious look from the half-breed caused him to cut himself short.

"He heard him *cuss,* that is," Berger put in quickly. He stretched his neck a little as if trying to catch a look around the big, silent half-breed. "What's going on in there anyway?" he asked.

Tom Bendigo kept on staring at the two edgy gunmen. Then he spit, just before he turned and walked back inside, leaving the rear door ajar behind him.

"By God . . . ," Berger said quietly. "That's as much of an invitation as we'll likely get from him." He walked forward to the porch.

Knox moved along beside him, glancing over his shoulder at the string of horses.

"Somebody's lying dead somewhere," he whispered to Berger.

"You'll keep your mouth shut if you've

got any sense at all," Berger warned as they stepped up onto the porch.

"Oh, I will," said Knox under his breath. "This son of a bitch always gives me the willies."

"He's got a stare that could stop a steam engine," Berger whispered, stepping inside.

Dow Bendigo eased his Colt from his holster and cocked it at the sound of several men advancing through the hallway. The whiskey bottle still hung in his left hand.

"I start shooting, you best commence jumping, sawbones," he said in his whiskey and laudanum slur. The Colt wagged loosely in his limp hand.

The doctor stepped back and looked toward the half-breed, who walked into the room first. As Tom moved to the side, Berger and Knox entered the room and immediately stopped cold.

Laying eyes on Dow's flailing Colt and the doctor's bloody fingertips, which were busy stitching up Dow's head, Berger raised his hands chest high.

"Whoa, Dow!" he said. "It's us. Don't shoot."

"Hold on a minute, sawbones," Dow said, wagging his Colt at the doctor.

"I'm almost finished. Just another stitch

or two and I'll close it off," the doctor said, a length of thread looping between his needle and Dow's half-sewn scalp.

"Close it off in a minute," Dow demanded, his head bobbing a bit from the affects of the powerful mix of drug and alcohol. "Go scald a cat or something."

The doctor shrugged, leaving the needle and thread to hang down the side of Dow's head.

"As you wish, sir," the doctor murmured. He turned and walked away. "I'll go draw some fresh water to help clean you up."

"You do that," Dow said, turning toward the half-breed. "Cat Tracker, go with him. Keep him company," he instructed.

Tom gave the slightest nod of his head and fell in just behind the doctor, who tried to pick up a water bucket on his way out of the room. The half-breed reached out a hand and stopped him. The doctor's face turned ashen with fear, but he walked on straight ahead and out the back door, the big half-breed shadowing him.

"Lord God, Dow, what happened to you?" Berger asked as soon as Tom and the doctor left.

"What does it look like?" Dow said.

"What does it look like?" Berger repeated, not knowing what to say. He shot a glance at Knox. Dow was drunk, belligerent and armed. "Jeez, I don't —"

"I was attacked by wolves," Dow said, cutting Berger off.

"*Wolves?*" questioned Berger. He and Knox looked at each other again. They dared not say anything about the bullet holes in his shoulder.

Dow stared squarely at him and cocked the big Colt in his limp hand.

"Are you going to say everything I say, Blue Hand?" he asked pointedly.

"No," Berger replied somberly.

"Good." Dow nodded and uncocked the Colt. "A wolf came upon me up above the main pass at Whiskey Bend — likely to have eaten me alive."

"Whose horses are those out back?" Knox asked before he could stop himself.

Dow stared at him with red, drunken eyes and handed Berger the bottle of whiskey.

"Watch your language, Albert," Dow cautioned.

"Yeah, watch your language, Albert," Berger said, trying to avoid trouble. He swirled the whiskey around in its bottle. "Everybody knows that horses just have a way of showing up on a string now and then. Right, Dow?" He looked to Dow for support.

Dow just stared at him flatly, a drunken blaze in his eyes. He reached out impatiently and snapped his fingers toward the bottle even as Berger raised it to his lips.

Berger lowered the bottle and Dow snatched it from him gruffly. Albert Knox looked on, wanting a drink, but not about to ask for the bottle.

"There might be a man coming here looking for those horses after Brother Cat Tracker and me ride on," Dow said. He turned the bottle up and took another long drink, then lowered it and let out a whiskey hiss.

"*Might* be?" Berger asked. He lowered his voice and continued. "You mean you left a man *alive* who can identify you?"

"No, we didn't." Dow glared at him. "I said he might be coming. I didn't say he is for sure. And even if he *is* coming, he can't identify us."

"All right, that's more like it," Berger said with a nod.

"But if he is alive and he does come looking, I want you two to make sure he doesn't leave Wakely without a wooden box nailed shut around him." He looked back and forth between them. "Both of you understand?"

"Yep, sure do," said Berger. Knox nodded in agreement.

"Good," said Dow. He held the bottle out for Knox, who accepted it eagerly. But before turning it loose into Knox's hand, Dow held it back for a second.

"One more thing," he said. "My pa is never going to hear a damn word about any of this, else Brother Cat Tracker is going to cut your tongues out and feed them to you like they're sausage. *Comprende?*" He let go of the bottle and stared into Knox's eyes.

"Not a word," Knox said, feeling the skin crawl on the back of his neck.

"What about this doctor?" Berger asked.

"He's not going to say anything," Dow said confidently.

"How do you know he won't?" said Knox, wiping a hand across his lips.

Dow and Berger both stared at him.

"Oh," said Knox, "never mind."

Sheriff Giles Croce had seen Albert Knox and "Blue Hand" Berger leave the saloon. It was part of his job to keep an eye on War-ton Bendigo's men when they were in town, so he grudgingly picked up his shotgun from against his desk and removed his hat from a wall peg. He'd also heard the scream come from the doctor's office.

What the hell's going on?

He watched through a window as the two

73

gunmen made their way from the saloon to the doctor's big clapboard house. When they cut around toward the rear of the building, he sighed to himself and walked out onto the boardwalk.

Time to see about this . . .

He made a wide circle around the doctor's house, being careful to keep out of sight. Not long after he found a good vantage point, he caught sight of Tom Bendigo walking along behind the doctor, piloting him into the barn.

"Damn it . . . ," Croce murmured to himself. He hated dealing with the half-breed.

Inside the barn, Tom Bendigo swung the big door only half shut behind him.

"Wh-what are we doing?" the terrified doctor asked, stopping abruptly.

Without reply, the big half-breed shoved the small doctor forward. The doctor slammed against the opposite wall.

"Pl-*ease*!" he cried out.

Tom Bendigo grabbed him roughly and swung him around. The doctor identified a cruel, wild look of satisfaction in the half-breed's dark eyes, and he noticed the long knife gripped tightly in his strong right hand.

Tom Bendigo cocked his head with a curious look as he touched the sharp point of the blade to the center of the thin doctor's chest.

This is going to be slow, the doctor thought to himself. Slow and painful, then a much welcome darkness, he hoped, just when the half-breed twisted the blade deep into his heart.

"Our Father . . . ," the doctor began to whisper frantically to himself, feeling the first spread of sharp burning pain as the point of the big gleaming blade slowly press into his chest, ". . . hallowed be thy name . . ."

But his death chant stopped as he heard the metal-on-metal click of two shotgun hammers cocking in unison.

"All right, Injun, fun's over," he heard Sheriff Giles Croce growl. "Take your pigsticker out of the good doctor's ribs and drop it."

The pain in the doctor's chest withdrew, yet the blade remained poised there as the half-breed considered the sheriff's order. The doctor dared not open his eyes.

"Don't even think I'm going to ask you again," the sheriff said calmly, firmly.

The doctor felt the blade pull away; the force with which the half-breed held him relented. He opened his eyes in time to see the big knife hit the straw-covered floor at his trembling feet. He saw the sheriff's free hand lift Tom Bendigo's Colt from the holster on his hip.

The half-breed stepped aside, his hands chest high in a show of submission. The tip of the cocked shotgun had moved along with him. The barrel came to a rest on his breastbone, only inches beneath his wide chin.

"You doing all right, Dr. Chase?" the sheriff asked calmly.

"I — I —" The doctor swallowed a tight knot in his throat and struggled to reply.

"That's all right, Doctor," said Sheriff Croce. "You can tell me later."

Croce turned his eyes back to the half-breed. Tom stared at him, his dark gaze wild with smoldering rage.

"Shame on you, Tom 'Cat Tracker,' " said Croce. He worked a lump of tobacco in his jaw and spit sidelong to the floor. "Why were you about to kill the only sober doctor this town has ever had?"

The half-breed only stared at him.

"Where is your brother Dow?" the sheriff asked, his finger still on the triggers of the shotgun.

Tom Bendigo only cut a glance toward

the big clapboard house.

"I could've guessed as much," said Sheriff Croce. He looked at the doctor and said, "Don't you have some patients you need to go see, for, say, the next day or so? I've got a feeling things will look better to you here after the dust settles."

"I — I'm certain I do," the frightened doctor said. He stood trembling, a spot of blood on the center of his chest where the tip of the big blade had been.

Sheriff Croce stared at him expectantly for a moment, waiting for a reaction from the doctor. "Well? Is there anything keeping you?"

"Oh! No, Sheriff," the doctor responded.

He hurriedly ran toward a buggy horse standing in a stall at the far end of the barn. He led the horse out of the stall, threw a riding harness on its muzzle and a blanket over its back. After a moment, Sheriff Croce and the half-breed watched him ride away, the horse moving in a fast trot, looking around in confusion at the empty buggy sitting outside the barn.

When the doctor had ridden out of sight, Croce turned to the half-breed with a sigh. He nudged the big stoic gunman with the tip of his shotgun barrel to get him started out of the barn and back toward the clapboard house. He reached down to pick up the knife and shoved it down in his waist beside Tom's Colt.

"After you, Tom 'Cat Tracker,' " he said, his shotgun still cocked and pointed at the back of the half-breed's head.

On the way to the doctor's house, Croce spotted the string of horses standing at the hitch rail. As he walked past them, he looked down at the file marking on the front of their dusty hooves.

"I'm starting to get a *really* bad picture from all of this . . . ," he murmured, shaking his head.

CHAPTER 6

In the doctor's office, Dow and the other two turned their attention toward the sound of the rear door opening and closing. They saw Tom walking toward them down the hallway, his hands and holster empty. Behind Tom, they set eyes on the shotgun, and Sheriff Giles Croce, who carried the weapon at port arms in front of him.

"Don't do something stupid, Dow," Croce said, peering around the big half-breed. "I don't want to have to tell your pa he's got both sons lying on ice here."

"You always were a kind and thoughtful fellow, Sheriff," Dow said with a drunken grin. Looking back behind the two, he asked, "Where's my damned doctor?"

"I sent him visiting," said Croce. "Your brother, Tom 'Cat Tracker' here, was about to cut his heart out for dinner."

Dow grinned flatly. "Either call him Tom or call him Cat Tracker, Sheriff," he said on his half brother's behalf. "But don't call him Tom 'Cat Tracker.' He says it sounds like you're calling him a *tomcat* tracker."

"I'm not the one who named him," the sheriff said dismissively. He took a step back from the half-breed and looked at the four men. "Tell me what's going on here, Dow," he said firmly.

"Just what you see, Sheriff," Dow said. "I've been getting my scalp sewn back on. You've gone and run my doctor off before he's finished. Now I have to finish it up myself."

"He wasn't finishing nothing but his time on earth when I found him," Sheriff Croce said. He gave Tom a stern look. Then he looked back at Dow and said, "What happened to your head anyway?"

"Wolves, is what happened to me," Dow said. "Up in the pass, one caught me by surprise. Damned near ruined me." The needle and thread dangled down the side of his stitched head as he spoke.

"Wolves, huh?" said Croce, making no effort to hide his skepticism. He looked at the blood and the two small holes in Dow's shirt. "Wolves are starting to arm themselves out there?"

"The bullets were an accident I don't care to talk about," Dow replied. "But it was wolves that did the rest of this to me. It looks like somebody will have to clear Whiskey Bend of them before folks can travel through without getting eaten alive."

"Duly noted," said Croce. He eyed Dow with suspicion. "Now, what about the horses out back?"

"What about them?" Dow asked.

"Whose are they?" Croce asked, noticing Dow grow more defensive now that he'd touched on something the young gunman wanted to hide.

"They're mine," Dow offered with a slight shrug.

"They've got a dealer's marking filed on the front of their hooves," Croce said. "I saw it on our way here."

Dow grinned. "You don't miss a thing, do you, Sheriff?" he said. "No wonder my pa keeps you in tobacco money and pocket change."

The sheriff ignored his remark and looked from one face to another as he saw the gunmen stifle a laugh at his expense.

"Saying you got them from a horse dealer?" Croce asked.

"Yep, that's what I'm saying," Dow replied.

"Have you got a bill of sale?" Croce asked.

"Hell no, not a lick," said Dow. "He was

in a big hurry to get going." He grinned and looked around at the others.

"No doubt because of the wolves," Croce said in a sarcastic tone.

"No doubt," Dow replied. "Anyway, he said I wouldn't need paperwork. Said the file markings would grow over in no time." He shrugged. "I sized him as an honest stock dealer. I hope I wasn't taken advantage of."

The men chuckled.

But the sheriff saw no humor in it. He kept the shotgun cocked but was careful not to point it directly at anyone.

"Here's what you and your brother are going to do, Dow," he said. He glanced around and added, "All four of you, for that matter. You're going to stand up and get out of here, right now."

"Whoa, Sheriff, hang on," Dow said. "My pa is not going to stand still for you acting this way. It's not what he pays you to do."

"Warton Bendigo pays me to protect his interests any way I see fit to in this town," said Croce.

"Does that include running his sons out of here?" Dow asked. "Me with my head still needing sewing?"

"I'm not blind, Dow. I saw the two Xs filed on those horses' hooves and shoes" said the sheriff. "*Dos Equis* is Will Summers' marking. Everybody knows that."

"You know, come to think of it," Dow said, "I believe that was the man's name who sold them to me —"

"Those are Summers' horses?" Croce asked, his voice becoming wary.

"They *was* Summers' horses, Sheriff," said Dow. "You can see for yourself they're mine now."

"Huh-uh," said Croce, shaking his head. "I don't like how this is sounding. You all get out of Wakely. I don't want you here if Summers shows up wanting his horses back."

"Summers *is not* coming here, Sheriff," Dow said, giving him a look. "Do you get what I'm saying?"

"Are you for *damned* sure?" Croce asked.

"*Pretty damned* sure," said Dow.

"Pretty damned sure won't cut it," said Sheriff Croce. He kept the shotgun poised, ready to put it into play if need be. "I want you out of here, and your brother too. If I have to, I'll take the whole story to your pa and let him sort though it."

"You don't want to do that, Sheriff," Dow said, his voice full of warning. He stood up, the needle and string still dangling from his scalp. The half-breed stood beside him, even

83

without his gun or knife. The other two Bendigo gunmen just stared, not sure what move to make. The sheriff worked for Warton Bendigo, the same as they did.

"Hey now," Berger offered, "let's all cool down here." He looked at Dow and said, "Your pa won't have to hear about nothing if you go on and do like Croce says, right, Sheriff?"

Croce stood firm. "I've said all I've got to say on the matter."

Knox stepped forward and looked Dow and Tom Bendigo up and down. "Come on, Dow, Tom. The sheriff here is just doing what's best all the way around. You two light out with the horses. If Summers *is* alive, and shows his face here, we'll stop his coach for him."

Dow thought about it for a moment and seemed to cool down. He chuffed and looked at Knox and Berger with the trace of a smile.

"Stop his coach?" he said. "I like that."

"Yeah," said Berger, playing on Knox's remark. "We'll not only stop his coach, we'll derail his whole damned train."

"Not here in Wakely, you won't," said Croce. "I'll stall him here as long as I can. But I won't have him shot down on my streets." He jutted his chin. "It's bad for business."

Dow looked at the sheriff. "And my pa?" he asked pointedly.

"If I say Warton Bendigo will never hear about it from me, he won't," said Sheriff Croce. "Now both of you get those horses and get them out of here . . . before I change my mind."

"I've got to get somebody to finish sewing my head," Dow said, gesturing at the needle hanging from the length of thread.

"I'm sending a gal over from the saloon," said Sheriff Croce. "She's Doc Chase's apprentice. She'll fix your head up well enough to travel."

"A whore for an apprentice? What else will she fix up for us, Sheriff?" Knox asked with an oily grin.

The sheriff ignored him and looked at Dow and the half-breed.

"I don't want to see either of you here a half hour from now," he said.

It was just after noon when Will Summers rode up the main street into Wakely, cradling Layla Brooks on his lap. Ahead of Summers and the woman, the big cur scouted forward, his nose sniffing back and forth in every direction. The dog had rejoined them on the trail, having tracked the gunmen

85

toward Wakely through the downpour.

Sheriff Croce set eyes on the man and woman riding double and rose from a wooden chair on the boardwalk out in front of his office. He picked up his shotgun from against the wall. Cursing Dow and Tom Bendigo under his breath, he walked toward the doctor's house, where Summers had reined over to the hitch rail.

Layla had managed to sleep for the past hour in Summers' arms. She awakened as he sat her from his lap into the saddle and steadied her with one hand as he started to swing down. He stopped for a moment as she gripped his forearm tightly.

"Will? *Will!*" she shouted, on the verge of hysteria. "I — I can't see! Everything is dark and bleary!"

"Easy, Layla," Summers said. Hoping to calm her, he patted her hand on his arm. "We're in Wakely now. We'll get the doctor to take care of you. You're going to be all right."

She eased her grip on Summers, allowing him to swing down from the saddle and lower her into his arms. As he carried her toward the front yard of the doctor's clapboard house, he watched the big cur lope along the all but deserted street. The large animal meandered his way almost to the front doors of the saloon before turning back and trotting toward him.

Beyond the dog, Summers saw the two men step out of the saloon and stare toward him from the boardwalk. When he directed his gaze in the direction of the sheriff's office, he saw the single figure walk toward him with the cradled shotgun.

Summers stopped for a second, stricken by a sudden sense of caution.

Sensing a change in Summers' mood, Layla turned her head back and forth, struggling to see, but she found nothing more than a dark swirl of broken sunlight and shadows.

"What's wrong, Will?" she asked.

"Nothing," Summers replied. He walked on, into the front yard and up onto the front porch. As the big dog bounded up behind him and stood watching restlessly, Summers reached out and opened the front door.

"Hello the house," he called out, stepping inside the foyer. He waited for a moment and when he heard no response, he called out again. "Hello the house. We need the doctor."

On the porch behind him, Summers heard the dog growl low and menacingly.

"Hush up, Buddy," Summers said, catching a glance of three men slowly approaching. Turning back to the house, he started to call out for the doctor again, but before he could, he saw a young woman walking toward them down the long hallway, wiping her hands on a small towel.

"The doctor is off making his visits," the young woman said to Summers, stopping, looking more closely at Layla as she spoke. "I'm Vera Dalton, from the saloon. But I help the doctor some."

Summers looked her up and down quickly.

"Begging your pardon, ma'am," he said. "But we've got to see the doctor. She's been shot in the face by a shotgun. There's a piece of buckshot dug into her eye." He gestured a nod toward Layla's face, partially wrapped in a bloodstained cotton cloth.

"Take her right in here," the young woman said. "I'll see what I can do for her 'til the doctor gets back." She gestured Summers and the woman toward the surgery room, which she had only finished cleaning up an hour earlier.

Summers wasted no time. He hurried into the room and laid Layla down on the small bed. As soon as he had turned to the young woman beside him, he heard the dog begin to growl more intensely on the front porch and sensed that the three men weren't far from the house now.

"Go settle your dog, mister," said the young woman. "I'll take good care of her."

"Will, don't leave me," Layla called out in a weak voice. "I can't see you . . ." She sounded as if she was on the verge of passing out.

"Go on," the young woman whispered. "That's most likely the sheriff coming to see what's going on."

Summers stepped back and slipped away, out of the room, down the hallway, through the front door and onto the front porch.

In the street, ten yards from the porch, the sheriff turned to Knox and Berger as the two approached him from the saloon.

"I thought I made myself clear," said Croce, tipping the shotgun barrel a little toward them. "*Nobody* is killing *nobody* in my town."

"You made it real clear, Sheriff," said Knox. "We just figured we'd best tag along a ways, see to it everything's straight up."

"Don't forget, we work for Warton Bendigo too," said Berger. "His interest is our interest." He thumbed himself on the chest.

Croce could see the two had been drinking steadily since Dow and the half-breed left town two hours earlier. *Getting their bark on . . . ,* he told himself.

"All our *interest* is the same here," said Croce. He swung the shotgun up easily, leveled it and cocked it at their chests. "Except *yours* is about to run out."

"*Whoa*, get ahold of yourself, Sheriff!" Berger shouted, suddenly sobered by the sight of the two big, gaping gun barrels.

"No, *you* get ahold of yourselves," said Croce. "Get ahold of your horses, get ahold of your drunken asses and get out of here."

From the front porch, Summers stood watching, the dog growling at his side. He couldn't hear every word, but he didn't need to — not to know that something was amiss here.

As he stared ahead, the two gunmen raised their hands chest high and backed away. Crestfallen, they turned and walked off, looking back over their shoulders at the sheriff and his aimed shotgun.

When the two had gotten a safe distance away, the sheriff turned toward the porch and looked at Summers and the growling dog.

"Keep that cur in hand," the sheriff called out.

"I've got him, Sheriff," said Summers, who had already reached over and taken a firm hold on the loose nap of the big cur's neck to keep him from bolting after the two gunmen.

"I'm not tolerant of dogs running loose, threatening my townsfolk."

Summers offered no comment. The cur settled a little, but kept his hackles up, staring past the sheriff toward the two men as they approached the saloon.

"I'm Town Sheriff Giles Croce," the sheriff offered. Before Summers could reply, Croce said, "You'd be the horse trader, William Summers. I've heard of you, and seen you here and there dealing your horses."

"Pleased, Sheriff Croce," said Summers. "I've heard of you too."

Croce nodded, lowered the shotgun, walked into the front yard and stopped again at the bottom of five wooden porch steps. He placed his empty hand on the step railing.

"Who's the woman you carried in there? What's wrong with her?" he asked.

"Her name is Layla Brooks," said Summers. "She's been beaten, shot in the face . . . and misused," Summers added in a lowered voice in spite of the fact that there was no one around to hear him.

"*Misused?*" questioned Croce. "You mean she's been . . . ?" He let his words trail.

"That's what I mean, Sheriff," said Summers. "They used a shotgun on her. I brought her here hoping the doctor can save her eye." He studied the sheriff's face closely as he spoke. He saw no sign of deception or guile. Yet he did see a deeper hardness come to the already hard-set face.

"Sonsabitches," Croce said quietly. "What kind of low poltroons do a thing like that?"

"You tell me, Sheriff," Summers replied, easing his words, testing the man standing before him.

"The kind that need to have their necks stretched and twisted sideways," Croce said without hesitation. He stepped up onto the porch, keeping a respectable distance from the dog, whose low rumbling growl seemed to rise as he drew nearer, then fall quieter when he took a cautious step back.

"Is your dog always so unfriendly toward law officers, Summers?" Croce asked pointedly.

"He's not my dog, Sheriff," Summers said. "I took him on a trade. He's with me until somebody wants him." He turned the subject away from the dog and asked, "Has anybody been through here with a string of horses?"

Croce shook his head, but said nothing.

What was that . . . ? Summers caught the

sheriff's response but let it pass for the time being.

"I suppose your woman can identify the men who did all that to her," Croce said.

Summers decided to say no more for now. Instead, he stared into the sheriff's eyes with a guarded expression, letting him steer their concern back to Layla.

"I don't know, Sheriff. We'll have to ask her, first thing," he said.

CHAPTER 7

Inside the big white clapboard house, Sheriff Croce and Will Summers waited in the kitchen, seated at a wooden table, cups of strong coffee in hand. The big cur had quietly slipped in with them. He lay on the floor, his head lowered onto his crossed paws, watching every move, hearing every word, as if understanding them.

When Vera Dalton walked in, her right hand closed, a bloodstained towel in her left, Summers stood up and gave her an inquiring look. The cur stood up too.

"She's all right," said the young woman, before he could even ask. "She's starting to wake up from the chloroform."

"What about her eyes?" Summers asked.

Vera gave him a grim look. She held out a fist and opened her hand, revealing a tiny metal object on her palm.

"I took this piece of broken buckshot out of her left eye," she said. "It was buried down in the white, away from the pupil, lucky for her. The doctor will have to tell you if she's going to see out of it again. I can't say."

"And her other eye?" Summers asked.

"She caught some burnt powder in it," said Vera, sounding as knowledgeable as any doctor Summers could remember talking to. "But I think it'll be all right after some healing."

Summers let out a breath of relief. He looked at the sheriff, then back at Vera Dalton.

"Can I see her?" he asked.

"Yes, I think she'd like you to be there when she wakes up," Vera said. "She whispered your name some while I was working on her."

Seeing Summers begin to follow the young woman out of the kitchen, Croce set his coffee cup down and stood up.

"I'll just go along with you, Summers," he said, "see if she can tell me anything about who did this to her."

Vera took note of the dried blood on Summers' bare head.

"It looks like you could use some attending to yourself," she said.

"Yes, ma'am," said Summers. "Now that I know she's going to be all right, I suppose I could use some cleaning and bandaging myself."

Vera followed him and the sheriff down the hallway, into the room, where they found Layla struggling to sit up on the edge of the small bed.

"There, now, you need to take it easy," said Vera, hurrying over to Layla and taking her by the arm to keep her from falling backward. Layla's left eye was bandaged over; her right eye looked cloudy, red and sore. A wide bandage covered a buckshot wound in her right cheek and another on her chin.

"Will . . . ?" she said, her right eye looking dreamy and out of focus.

"I'm right here, Layla," said Summers, stepping forward and stooping down to her, taking her hand between his. "I'm not going anywhere. Not until I know you're all right. You keep still like this woman tells you."

Layla saw Sheriff Croce as only a blurry lurking shadow behind Summers. Fear came to her voice when she spoke.

"Who is this with you, Will?" she asked.

"It's the town's new sheriff," Summers said.

Before he could say more, the sheriff stepped forward and introduced himself.

"I'm Sheriff Giles Croce, ma'am," he said.

"I want you to know I'll be after whoever did this to you. I won't stop until somebody hangs for it."

Will Summers listened; the sheriff sounded sincere. But there was something about Giles Croce that Summers didn't trust. He just couldn't pin down what it was.

"Do you feel like talking yet?" Croce asked Layla Brooks, standing over her and Summers, his shotgun still cradled in his arms.

"I'll try," Layla replied in a weak voice.

Summers gave her hand a squeeze and turned it loose.

As the sheriff spoke to Layla, Vera Dalton stepped away and returned with a damp cloth and a small pan of clean water. She gestured for Summers to sit on the wooden chair beside the bed.

"Let me clean the dried blood off so I can take a better look at your head," she said quietly to Summers.

While Vera Dalton attended to the welt on the back of his head, Will Summers watched and listened to the sheriff question Layla Brooks. Summers noted that the lawman asked her three times if she could identify the men who had beaten, raped and shot her. Each time her answer remained the same.

"I told you, Sheriff," she said, "I can't

remember anything that happened."

Croce let out a patient breath and looked at Summers for help. Vera placed a wet folded cloth on the back of Summers' head and had him raise his hand to hold it in place for her.

"I remember everything that happened, Sheriff," said Summers. "But I never saw either man's face. They knocked me out. When I woke up they had tied me to a tree and gone to the cabin. I never saw their faces."

"But you know there were two or more of them?" Croce asked.

"Judging from the tracks, there must have been three of them," said Summers. "But the only one I saw was the one lying dead in the yard. Most of his face was blown away. His own mother wouldn't recognize him."

Sheriff Croce looked back at Layla, who sat staring blankly at him though her cloudy right eye.

"How did he die? Did you kill him, ma'am?" the sheriff asked.

Layla looked completely baffled. She shook her head slowly.

"I — I guess so, Sheriff," she said. Tears of pain and frustration came to her red and puffy right eye. "I just can't seem to recall any of it."

Sheriff Croce shook his head slowly and looked down at the floor for a moment.

"So, neither of you can identify whoever did this," he said in conclusion.

Summers only stared at him.

"We know there were at least three men," the sheriff continued. "One of them is dead, with his face blown off. The others have lit out to God knows where." He paused, then looked at Will Summers and said, "You're not giving me much to go on, Summers. I don't even know which direction to start looking."

"The storm washed their back trails anyway," Summers said flatly. He wasn't going to count on help from Sheriff Croce.

"Even the weather was in their favor," said Croce.

"They've got my horse, and a six-horse string I was leading," said Summers. "Each horse has a double X filed on the front of its hoof, even my own. The string also have the markings filed on their front shoe."

"I know that you always use the *Dos Equis* marking, Summers," said Croce. "Everybody knows it. Trouble is that mark will soon grow over on their hooves, and the shoe can be changed. Then you've got nothing to prove the horses are yours."

"I don't plan on it taking me that long to find them, Sheriff," Summers said.

The sheriff straightened his stance and looked back and forth between Layla and Summers.

"My job is to help, and I wish I could," said Sheriff Croce, "but I need more to go on."

Will Summers stared at him. Behind Summers, Vera stepped back with the cloth and pan of water in hand. His head still throbbed a little in pain, but it felt better overall now that she had washed away the caked blood.

"Sheriff Croce," he said, "it sounds like your job is to convince me I don't stand a chance ever making this right."

"I'm just being honest with you, Summers," Croce said. He looked down at Layla Brooks and said, "Ma'am, if you start to remember anything, you come straight to me and tell me about it, you hear?"

Layla only nodded.

"If I can be of help to you, Will Summers, you let me know," the sheriff said. "Right now I've got to ride a few miles out and shove a few ragged-assed land squatters off of some grazing lands." Touching the brim of his hat in a parting gesture, he turned and walked out the front door.

When the sheriff was gone, Vera turned to

leave the room with the pan of pinkish bloody water in hand. The big cur raised his head and watched her.

"I'll just go throw this out," she said.

The cur lowered his head onto his paws as she turned and left the room. Summers sat quietly until the front door opened and closed. Then he leaned in closer to Layla and took her hand.

"You can't remember anything about the men who did this to you?" he asked quietly.

She tried to focus on his watery image.

"I have no memory of any of it, Will," she said. "Don't you believe me?" She gripped his hand tightly in spite of her weakened condition.

Summers heard the hurt in her voice. After all she'd been through, who was he to question what she could or could not remember?

"If you say that's how it is, of course I believe you, Layla," he said.

"I — I don't think the sheriff believed me," she said, sounding worried. "You saw him . . . Did he look like he believed me?" she asked.

Summers realized the disadvantage of Layla not being able to see the sheriff's reaction to her words. He patted her shaky hands for reassurance.

"I'm sure he believes you, Layla," he said. "Not that I think it's going to make much difference."

"What do you mean, Will?" she asked, her right eye still trying to focus more clearly on him.

"I mean it doesn't matter much what this sheriff believes or doesn't believe," Summers said. "If these men ever pay for what they did to you, it won't be from his doings."

When Vera walked back into the room carrying the emptied water pan, Summers let go of Layla's hand and stood up.

"You'll need Dr. Chase to take a look at her eyes as soon as he gets back to town," she said.

"When do you think that will be?" Summers asked.

"I don't know," Vera said. "It could be a day or even two. He keeps supplies in his buggy in case he stays away overnight."

"Nobody knows where he went?" Summers asked, finding it unusual that a town doctor would leave without telling someone where he was going.

Vera gave a slight shrug.

She looked at Layla and said, "Wherever he is, you need to stay here and wait for him. That was the first time I ever took buckshot out of a person's eye. I'm not a doctor. Not yet anyway."

Layla looked up at her with her cloudy vision.

Vera offered a thin smile and turned to Summers.

"I'm just the doctor's apprentice. I can do most of what a doctor does. But right now I'm still a saloon dove," she said with a flat, wry smile. "I'm usually the one lying on my back."

"You did good," Summers said, ignoring her self-deprecating comment. He reached inside his trouser pocket, took hold of three gold coins and handed them to her.

As Vera took the money, Summers asked, "Where does the doctor keep his horse and buggy?"

Vera gave a nod toward the back of the house.

"That's his barn," she said. "He keeps his rig and animal in his own barn, so if he leaves late in the night, everything is close at hand."

"Will?" said Layla, sounding a little shaky. "Are you leaving?"

"I'm just walking out back," Summers said, turning toward the rear door. The cur sprang up from the floor in spite of his soreness, shook himself off and fell in beside

Summers.

From a dusty saloon window, Knox and Berger spotted Summers and the dog. Man and canine walked the short visible distance between the rear of the house and the weathered barn standing a few yards off to the side.

"There he goes," Knox murmured, "and Sheriff Croce is off somewhere taking care of business." A harsh look spread across his round, bearded face.

"We're just asking for trouble if we kill him now, after Croce warning us not to," said Berger. He stood with his hand resting on the butt of his holstered Remington, his fingers tapping restlessly on the gun's black handles.

"Yeah . . ." Knox spit in contempt and ran a hand over his lips. "If it wasn't for Croce being on Warton Bendigo's payroll same as us, I'd shoot him full of holes, then go ahead and kill this horse trader.

"It would appear to be the right thing to do," Knox said, staring out the window after Summers and the cur made their way inside the barn. "We did sort of give Dow our word that we'd kill this man for him. He's counting on us doing it, even though he heard Croce tell us not to."

"Knowing Dow, he's not going to like us *not* going ahead and doing it for him," said Berger, "no matter what Croce told us."

"I feel bad about it myself, to tell you the truth," Knox replied. "I don't like giving my word in matters like this and not following through."

"Agreed," said Berger. "This sheriff has put us between a rock and a —"

"Hard spot," Knox finished for him.

Someone let out an angry curse from across the saloon, interrupting their conversation, and the two gunmen directed their attention toward four poker players who sat around a battered table bowed over their cards. A chair scraped the floor loudly as a big gunman named "Flat-Head" Logan Mc-Corkle tossed his cards into the middle of the table in disgust. He stood up and stomped away to the bar, a dark scowl on his face.

Berger gave a tight little smile and looked at Knox. The same smile was on his own bearded, moon-shaped face.

"Are you thinking what I'm thinking?" Berger asked under his breath.

"About getting 'Flat-Head' Logan to kill Summers for us?" Knox asked.

"Yep, that's it exactly," said Berger. "Flat-Head is always asking me to put in a good

105

word to Warton Bendigo for him. This is a good time to see how serious he is."

"Yeah," said Knox. "The sheriff can't say a damn word to us if Flat-Head kills Summers in *his* town."

"No, sir, he sure can't," said Berger. He stepped toward the bar. "Come on, Knox, I feel like buying you and me both a drink," he said over his shoulder.

"Make it a bottle," Knox said, walking along with him.

At the bar, Berger gave a gesture to the bartender for a bottle and glasses as they stepped up on either side of the big, rugged gunman.

"What do you two want?" Logan asked, still brooding over his poker losses.

"We want to buy you a drink, Flat-Head," said Berger, picking up the bottle as soon as the bartender set it down in front of him. He filled McCorkle's glass, grinned and then poured one each for him and Knox. "Then we want to talk a little business with you."

"Business . . . ?" Logan looked back and forth at them while he wrapped his big fingers around the shot glass. In spite of the changing weather, he still wore his bulky, full-length bearskin coat. A large, battered Montana-crown Stetson hung from his shoulder by a strip of rawhide.

"That's right," said Berger. The three lifted their glasses and threw back their shots of rye. "Knox and I would like to see you riding with the Bendigos, next time we ride over into Wind River and bring back some cattle."

"I'm not rustling any more cattle. It's hard work," said Logan.

"Then forget the cattle," said Berger. "We'd like you riding with us next time we turn over a train or crack a bank teller's head." He grinned and added, "Am I getting through to you yet?"

"You're all over me," said Logan. He reached a big hand from inside his coat sleeve, picked up the bottle without an invitation and poured himself another drink. "We can go do it right now, far as I'm concerned."

"That would be fine by us," Berger said, "but Warton likes us to see that a man ain't shy about maiming and killing before we take him on. We need to see some proof. You understand, don't you?"

"Shy . . . ?" Logan gave him a hard stare. "Watch my drink for me," he said.

The two stood staring as the big gunman walked to the card table, overturned it and shouted at a miner who sat stunned, chips, cash and cards strewn all over him.

"You cheating son of a bitch!" Logan raged. He grabbed the man with both hands, yanked him up from his chair and hurled him into a potbellied wood stove twelve feet away.

Seeing the miner try to pull a pistol from his boot well, Berger and Knox both flinched as a big Smith & Wesson streaked from inside Logan McCorkle's bearskin coat and began blazing in his hand.

A tense ringing silence set in as Logan calmly walked away from the miner's sprawled and bloody body, back to the bar, the Smith & Wesson smoking upward along the sleeve of his coat.

Picking up his glass and downing a shot of rye, the gunman set the empty glass down hard onto the bar.

"Is that enough *proof?*" he said grimly.

Berger and Knox stood as if awestricken. Finally Berger blinked as if to get his mind started.

"It's one hell of a start," he said.

CHAPTER 8

Will Summers had heard the gunshots from the saloon a moment earlier, but when no other shots resounded, he dismissed the matter. Gunshots from a saloon were the least of his concerns, he reminded himself.

He stood at the open door and looked all around inside the barn. His eyes followed hoofprints out through the open rear doors. Whoever had taken the horse from the stall had mounted and left in a hurry, he noticed, looking down at the upturned straw and earth. If these really were tracks from the doctor's trip out of town, he hadn't even bothered leading the horse from the barn before jumping on its back and putting his heels to it.

Peculiar . . .

He walked out the rear door a few feet and spotted the buggy sitting to the side. He approached the buggy and looked down in the space behind the driver's seat. The doctor's empty supply basket and two rolled-up blankets lay on the buggy's floor. Beside them lay a black leather doctor's bag, something no doctor would leave behind when making a home visit.

He turned his attention away from the empty buggy and followed the tracks, which moved toward a trail leading out the back of town. The cur stood beside Summers, staring in the same direction, doing his best to help him figure out the puzzling events that had transpired here.

Back inside the barn, Summers shut the rear and stall doors, and he and the dog walked out of the barn, back toward the doctor's house — but both man and dog stopped short near the hitch rail as Summers looked down at the overlapping hoof-prints left where the string of horses had stood. The cur sniffed at the prints, then found something that drew his nose upward and back toward the trail. Summers thought he heard a low, rumbling growl emanating from deep down in the dog's chest. But he paid no attention right then. Instead, he kept his eyes nailed to the hoofprints.

Yep, they've been here, he said to himself, *whoever they are. They've been here and Sheriff Croce knew it.* No wonder Croce didn't bother asking him to describe the horses — he already knew what they looked like. He knew about the *Dos Equis* hoof brands, and shoe marks as well, which were imprinted in the dirt, plain as day.

Summers let out a breath in contemplation. He heard the big dog continue to growl low and steady at his side. What else did the sheriff know? Who was he trying to protect?

It didn't matter; he'd find out, Summers told himself. He took a settling breath and let it out slowly. *A silver-gray dapple, three dark bays, an Appaloosa mare soon to foal, a paint horse and a black Morgan cross . . . lest we forget,* he said to himself.

From an alleyway beside the saloon, Knox and Berger watched intently as "Flat-Head" Logan McCorkle stalked along the side of the doctor's house toward Summers and the big cur standing bedside him.

"Don't let that cur get ahold of you, Flat-Head," Knox whispered.

"Logan McCorkle's not going to let that happen," Berger said to Knox without taking his eyes off the scene unfolding before them. "You saw him in action . . . He's one cold, killing sumbitch."

Summers chastised the dog for growling,

but as he looked down at the animal, he also caught sight of a man in the big bearskin coat walking toward him with deliberation.

Summers started to call out to the man, but the dog was ahead of him. He sped straight toward Logan McCorkle, his fangs bare, his big hackles standing high and thick on his back. Will Summers saw the big bearskin coat open; he saw a hand reach inside and come out with the Smith & Wesson. Something told him the gunman wasn't drawing the gun to ward off the attacking dog.

As the cur sped along the alleyway toward McCorkle, Summers saw the gunman disregard the running dog and level the big revolver toward him instead. Quickly dropping into a crouch, Summers drew the Colt from his waist and fired as the gunman's first shot zipped past him, less than a yard from his right shoulder.

No warning, no nothing . . . The thought flashed across his mind as his first shot hit the man squarely in the center of his big fur coat. *What was this . . . ?*

Even as the gunman flew backward, his Smith & Wesson exploded again. This time the shot went high and wild as the running dog launched himself airborne, flew ten feet and drove the man the rest of the way to the ground.

Summers remained in a crouch, his Colt pointed and ready. When the wounded man turned the revolver away from him and toward the dog, Summers fired again. This time the bullet knocked the man back flat on the ground and sent his gun flying from his open hand.

The cur rolled upright, shaking himself off quickly. Staying low in his stance and barking steadily, he circled the body lying in the dirt.

"Easy, Buddy . . . get back," Summers said to the dog as he walked in closer to the downed gunman, his smoking Colt still poised and ready.

But when he saw the look on the dying man's face, Summers knew the gunfight was over.

"Who are you? What was that all about?" he asked, stopping a few feet back and staring down at the man's trembling face, the rise of steam coming from his heaving chest with each labored breath. A narrow trail of blood stretched out along the ground.

"Go . . . to . . . hell . . . ," the man managed to say in a broken, raspy voice.

"Do I know you, mister?" Summers asked, noticing that faces were beginning to appear on the boardwalk out in front of the saloon. He did not see the two gunmen slink back out of sight, into a shadowy alleyway.

"Go . . . to . . . hell," the man repeated, his voice sounding weaker, more strained.

The dog bounded forward and barked down at the gunman from only a foot away.

"That . . . damned . . . dog," he murmured. Then his face fell to one side; his eyes went blank. Summers relaxed his gun hand a little and looked along the street as townsfolk began to gather.

"Stay back. Be good, Buddy," he said quietly to the dog, as if the animal understood him.

"Lower that shooting iron, mister," a heavyset man wearing a white barkeeper's apron called out as he and the others approached Summers. He carried a sawed-off shotgun at port arms.

But instead of lowering the Colt, Summers held it more firmly. He didn't see the sheriff anywhere. Then he remembered that Croce had told him he had to ride out of town a few miles.

"This man fired first," Summers called out as the townsmen drew closer. "I have no idea why," he added.

"I believe you, mister," said the barkeeper. "I saw it from the window." Realizing that he held the shotgun as if ready to use it, he lowered it, grasping it loosely in one thick hand.

"We all believe you," said an ancient townsman, who wore a battered derby hat with a string of beads and feathers hanging from its brim. "This fellow went wild on us in the saloon a while ago. He killed a miner named Bob Bates for no reason at all."

The barkeeper stepped out in front of the others, looking Summers up and down.

"Good thing your dog saw him coming. You're lucky to be alive, mister," he said in a friendlier tone.

Summers lowered the Colt, uncocked it and shoved it down inside his waist.

The barkeeper tilted his head curiously toward Summers and said, "You look real familiar. Do I know you?"

"I'm Will Summers. I deal horses up and down the mountain range about this time every spring," Summers said.

"I saw you come through last spring," said the townsman in the feathered derby.

"So did I," said another townsman. "You're the one who rode with Abner Webb's posse, brought down the Peltry Gang, ain't you?"

"I rode with Webb," Summers said.

"You'll have to excuse me," said the

barkeeper. "I wasn't here last spring. I'm Charlie Clair. I only bought this place back before winter." He let the shotgun slump down his side. "But I've heard of Webb's Posse and what the lot of yas did."

Summers only nodded.

"Is the sheriff still out of town?" he asked.

"Yep," said Clair, "but he should be getting back most any time."

"Any of you know this man?" Summers asked, gesturing down at the body lying in the dirt.

"It's Logan McCorkle," said the old man in the derby. "Folks call him Flat-Head . . . or they used to," he corrected himself. "He was a rounder and a no-good." He grinned and added, "I would never have said that to his face. You aired him out real good."

The steam from the open wound in McCorkle's chest had stopped curling. Dark blood poured out of the gaping bullet holes.

Summers nodded again. The big cur had sidled over to him and stood looking curiously at the townsmen.

"Will some of you square this for me with Sheriff Croce when he gets back?" he asked.

"We'll tell him," Clair said with a shrug. "There's not much to square, far as we're all concerned. McCorkle went nuts, tried to kill you. The dog warned you, most likely saved your life."

"Ain't you going to stick around, tell him yourself, Summers?" the old man asked.

"I'm heading out," Summers said. "If the sheriff needs to talk to me, tell him I'll be on the south trail, headed back down off the mountain range."

He was really heading north, in the same direction his string of horses was heading. But something told him not to tell the sheriff any more than he had to.

"We'll tell him for you," said Clair. He looked at the big cur and said to Summers, "I don't expect you're looking to sell that cur, are you?"

Summers looked at the dog and considered him for a second. The dog looked back at him, as if he was waiting for an answer.

"I might just hang on to him for a while," Summers said.

Vera Dalton met Summers and the dog in the foyer of the doctor's house. She stood holding a tray with a covered plate of food on it. She'd been on her way to the surgery room, but she stood and waited for Summers and the dog to follow her. "We heard shooting . . . *twice,*" she said.

"So did I," Summers said, walking back toward the surgery room. "Thought noth-

117

ing of it at first — then the gunman came after me. A fellow named Logan McCorkle killed a miner named Bates over a poker game. Not long after, he tried to kill me in the street."

"Will, are you all right?" Layla asked, hearing him as he walked into the room. She sat on the side of the small bed staring at him through her bleary right eye.

"Yes, I'm all right," said Summers. "Buddy warned me in time. I spotted a man walking along the alleyway toward me. He jerked out a gun and started shooting. The dog went for him, threw his aim off some — enough to keep me alive."

"Is Buddy . . . ?" Layla trailed off, unable to finish the question for fear of what the answer might be.

"He's all right too, Layla. He's here with me," said Summers. "I think we need to get out of this town a ways."

"What about her eyes?" Vera asked. "The doctor still needs to look at them." She set the tray down on a stand beside the bed.

Summers didn't want to bring up the possibility that the doctor had been spooked — that he might have been scared away from town for no telling how long. Instead, he just looked at the two women.

"We'll come back when we know he's

here," he said.

Vera stared at him, sensing that something was wrong.

"You shouldn't leave," she warned him. "Eye wounds are not something to be neglected. The doctor needs to check her out as soon as he gets back."

"I understand," said Summers.

"Maybe you could ride out, and she could wait here?" Vera suggested.

"No," Summers said. "We both go, or we both stay." He wasn't about to tell Vera that something was amiss here — that Sheriff Croce had seen his stolen horses, and most likely the men who had done this to Layla as well. The sheriff had lied to them, but this was neither the time nor the place for him to explain it to her.

Vera started to speak. "I just don't see why you have to —"

"If he goes, I go," Layla said, cutting Vera off. "I'm not staying here without you, Will," she said to Summers.

Vera looked at the two for a moment, considering something.

"Okay," she said with resolve. "There's a place not far from here. It's Bob Bates' mining shack. God knows he won't be using it."

Summers gave her a questioning look.

"If you *have* to leave, at least stay close

enough for the doctor to come see you," she said.

"Thanks," said Summers, realizing she was right. "Tell me how to get there. That's where we'll stay."

"Good," said Vera. "It's less than ten miles out above the main trail, on a streambed. Bates owned a claim there. You can't miss the place once you find the stream. Just follow the water right up to the shack. When the doctor gets back, I'll send him up there straightaway."

Two miles outside Wakely, Albert Knox and Bertram "Blue Hand" Berger stopped their horses, giving their animals a rest. The horses were in need of it, as they'd booted them into a hard run on their way out of town.

"Damn," said Berger, reflecting on the gunfight, his wrists crossed on his saddle horn. "I never saw a man get himself killed so fast in my life."

"It was that dog," Knox said. "McCorkle never got a clear shot with that cur spotting him, coming at him that way. Something like that will rattle a man, throw him off."

"Oh? You think so?" said Berger, giving him a sarcastic look.

"I sure do think so," said Knox, not realizing he was being mocked by his companion. "I'll tell you something else," he said. "I don't believe it was wolves that attacked Dow. I'm thinking it was this dog, trying to stop him from stealing the horses. You saw them little bullet holes in his shirt. Somebody shot him too."

Berger continued staring at him, the same flat, sarcastic look on his face.

"Did you think of all that earlier or just now figure it out?" he asked.

"I suspected it before," said Knox. "But after seeing that big dog fall upon him that way . . . now I'm all but convinced."

Berger shook his head, turned his horse and heeled it along the trail.

"I'm *convinced* that if we don't kill this horse trader, Dow is going to have that crazy Injun brother of his eat our brains for breakfast." He glanced around as Knox heeled his horse forward alongside him.

"I don't think we ought to go back to Wakely," Knox offered. "Sheriff Croce might figure out we were behind everything."

"The horse trader and the woman have to leave town sooner or later," Berger murmured, thinking out loud.

"Yeah, but which way will they go?" Knox asked.

121

"You saw how he was looking down at the tracks around the hitch rail?" Berger asked.

"Yeah, I saw that," said Knox.

"He's a horse trader," said Berger. "He's going to follow his stolen horses as long as he can. He'll head north, toward the Bendigos, I'm betting."

"And we'll be waiting, eh?" Knox said eagerly.

Berger didn't answer. He booted his horse up into a trot and rode along, studying the jagged hill lines running high above the trail.

PART 2

CHAPTER 9

Before Will Summers and Layla Brooks had been gone three hours from Wakely, Dr. Chase rode his worn-out buggy horse along the edge of the main street. Vera Dalton, who was still inside the house tidying up, saw the doctor as he rode past a side window. She hurried out through the rear door to meet him.

"My goodness, Dr. Chase," she said. "I've been worried about you!" She walked into the barn as the doctor stepped down stiffly from the horse's back and led the tired animal to its stall.

"No more than I have myself," the doctor said with a tired, wry smile. He looked her up and down. "I take it the sheriff must've brought you over to finish treating Dow Bendigo's scalp lacerations?"

"That's only part of it," said Vera. "After the Bendigos left town, the horse trader, Will Summers, brought a woman from up around Whiskey Bend."

"Will Summers . . ." The doctor reflected on the name for a second, then said dubiously, "Not another attack by a wolf, I hope."

"No," said Vera, aware that the doctor still doubted Dow's story. "Some men stole Summers' horses, a whole string of them.

A string of horses . . . ?

The doctor made the connection, but kept silent about it for the moment, letting Vera finish.

"They beat and raped the woman; shot her in the face with a shotgun too. I had to remove a broken piece of buckshot from one of her eyes."

"A shotgun wound in the face . . ." He winced a little at the vision of it.

"It's not as bad as it sounds," Vera said. "She managed to miss most of the blast. But she took some buckshot to the side of her face. The worst was the piece in her eye. I got it out, best I could, but I told her she needed you to check on her."

"You are the best apprentice a doctor could hope for, Vera," said Dr. Chase. "But eyes are tricky. I do have a special acid solution I made just for such a wound." He considered things as he spoke, looking her up and down appraisingly.

126

"An acid solution, Doctor?" Vera asked with a concerned look.

"It is acid in name only," said the doctor. "A very mild acidic solution I have mixed and used since the Civil War."

"Boron acid solution?" she asked.

"*Boric* acid," said the doctor, correcting her. "Carefully mixed, it aids healing the eye and keeps the wound clean." He smiled at Vera's knowledge of medicine and treatment. "The woman could not have been in more caring, capable hands than yours."

"Thank you, Doctor. I'm learning, the best I can. But I knew she would need more than a saloon dove can give."

"I understand," said Dr. Chase. "Just let me tend to this horse, go wash up and I'll take a look —"

"She's not here, Doctor," Vera said, stopping him from finishing. "I sent her and the horse trader up to Bob Bates' cabin to wait for you. They're just about getting there by now."

"Bob Bates' cabin?" said the doctor, considering it. "But why?"

"I told them it's a good place to wait for you," said Vera. "Bob Bates is dead, Doctor. The gunman, 'Flat-Head' McCorkle, shot him over a card game."

"My Lord!" the doctor said. "Was there

anything I might've done for Bates, had I been here?"

"No," Vera said. "But now Flat-Head himself is dead too. He tried to kill Will Summers, but the horse trader's big dog lit into him . . . and the horse trader shot him dead."

"The horse trader has a big dog, you say?" the doctor asked, still piecing things together in his mind. "As big as a wolf, would you say?"

"As big as any wolf I've ever seen," Vera confirmed. "Why do you ask?"

"Never mind," said the doctor, hearing the barn door squeak, but Vera had already made the connection between Will Summers' big dog and Dow Bendigo's alleged wolf attack.

The two turned as Sheriff Croce stepped inside the barn, his shotgun cradled in his arm.

"There you are, Doctor," said Croce. "You're back all safe and sound." He gave a grin as he stepped closer. "I told you everything would look a little better after the dust settled. The Bendigos are gone on up to the cliffs."

"The dust might be settled, Sheriff," the doctor snapped at him, "but the stink here is getting intolerable."

"What are you talking about, Doctor?" the sheriff asked.

"Vera here just told me about Will Summers losing a string of horses to thieves, about a woman being raped and shot and about Summers' big dog." He stared coldly at Giles Croce. "Any of this sounding suspect to you, Sheriff?"

"Hold on," said Croce. "You can't go blaming the Bendigo brothers for any of this. Dow *happened* to get attacked by a wolf. They just *happen* to have a string of horses. None of this means anything. It certainly isn't proof of anything."

"No, it's not, Sheriff," said the doctor. "Not when you're swinging from Warton Bendigo's sugar teat."

"I'd kill any other man for saying something like that to me," said Croce, enraged, humiliated. His hand tightened on his rifle stock. He stepped over into the doctor's path.

"I doubt you'd kill a man for anything these days, unless you had Warton's go-ahead on it first," said Dr. Chase. "Now get out of my way. I need to gather some supplies and medicine. I've got a patient waiting for me to check on a wound one of your *owners* probably gave her."

Croce turned as the doctor shoved past

him and stomped out of the barn toward the house, Vera Dalton right behind him.

"You're wrong, Dr. Chase!" he shouted at the open barn door. "Nobody owns me! I have to do what I think is best for everybody — for this whole damned town! It's not easy! It's hard! *Damned* hard!" he ranted to the big empty barn.

Riding double on the horse that had once belonged to Arlo Hughes, Will Summers and Layla Brooks left Wakely, the dog trotting along with a slight limp a few feet ahead of them. Summers had followed the marked hoof tracks leading away from the hitch rail behind the doctor's house until they came to a fork in the trail.

"Here's where we turn up toward the miner's shack," he said, examining a thin dusty path running upward beside a narrow stream. Keeping the reins in hand, he swung down from behind Layla.

The vision in her right eye had cleared some, but she could still see only a shadowy outline of Summers as he stepped forward, his head bowed toward the hoofprints continuing on along the main trail.

"I know you want to go on after the horses," she said, almost apologetically.

Summers didn't reply right away. Of

course he wanted to go after the horses, and the men who had done this to her. But that would come in time. He reached up and lifted her down from the saddle and held her for a moment.

"This is more important to me, Layla," he said. "I'll get the horses back sooner or later. First, we're going to take good care of you."

She could see him no better up close than she could from a few feet away. At either distance, he appeared to stand behind a gauzy veil. She couldn't read the expression on his face; she couldn't make out the level of sincerity in his eyes. She had only his words to go on.

"You — you don't owe me anything, Will," she said, listening intently for any revealing inflection in his tone or delivery. "Neither of us asked for this to happen."

"*Owing's* got nothing to do with it, Lalya," Summers replied.

All right . . . , she thought, waiting for something more — needing something more.

But Summers didn't offer anything else on the matter.

"Stay here," he said gently. He turned and stepped forward, leading the horse to the edge of the stream, where the animal sank its muzzle into the cold, clear water.

131

Layla let out a breath and tried again to focus her right eye. She attempted to concentrate her vision on the short, rounded blur of the dog, hearing the sound of him lapping water a few feet from the horse, but it was no use. The blurriness was constant, unrelenting. She turned her eye along the furry outline of the horse and that of Will Summers standing beside it.

She felt warm tears run down her sore and swollen cheeks; the tear from her wounded left eye ran pink with blood.

Summers stood staring along the main trial, where the stream turned sharply against a long rise of solid rock. On the other side of the long rocky turn, the main trail continued on, carrying with it the tracks of his horses.

All seven of them . . .

Stop it, he thought, cutting himself off before he got started.

He looked back and saw Layla's face turned toward the trail behind them. He interpreted her demeanor, and realized that she didn't want him to see her crying.

"Layla . . . ," he said softly, going to her. She turned, facing him, and he saw the tears — a watery reddish smear on her left cheek beneath the bandaged eye.

"Will, I'm sorry," she said, letting him take

her into his arms. "I didn't mean to break down like this. It's not my way."

"*Shhh,* take it easy, Layla," Summers said. "You've got a right to break down some, if it helps."

She shook her head against his chest, staring at the ground through the thick fog engulfing her vision.

"It doesn't," she said, without raising her face to his. After a pause, she said, "Maybe it does . . ." She started to cry again, but she forced herself to stop. "I don't know," she said, her arms tightening around him. "What — what am I going to do, Will? I mean, if my eyes get no better? What will I do then?"

"Just keep going on, Layla," Will offered, not knowing what else to say. "That's all any of us can do. We take what life puts upon us, and we go on with it."

With his left hand, he loosened the bandanna from around his neck, shook it free of dust and wadded it in his hand.

"Here, turn your face up; let me wipe your tears," he said. He didn't want to mention the red smear on her face. It would only frighten her, he thought.

She resisted as he tipped her chin up, careful of her sore and wounded face.

"I don't want you to look at me like this,

Will," she said.

Summers played it off with a shrug, continuing to raise her face.

"I've been looking at you like *this* all day, Layla," he said. "So don't go getting shy on me now."

She managed a short, brave laugh and raised her face to him.

"Anyway," Summers said, "what kind of man would I be if all I cared about is how you look?"

"The *normal* kind?" she offered. She managed a short chuckle. "Or have I been wrong, thinking men are always out to find themselves a beautiful woman?"

"*Beautiful* can mean different things to different people," Summers offered. "There's surface beauty. Then there's beauty deep down."

"Judging from my experience, men don't bother looking for deep-down beauty," she said, "unless the surface beauty first draws them in that direction."

Summers looked at her; it was good that she was talking, taking her mind off things, for a moment anyway.

"Well, maybe you're right," he conceded. "But if a man only looks for surface beauty, surface beauty is likely all he'll ever find . . . leastwise, all he'll ever deserve."

"You're just being kind, Will," Layla said. "But don't think I don't appreciate it." She offered a sad smile.

"Kindness is not my strong suit, Layla," Summers said.

"I don't believe you," she said. "I've always thought of you as kind, well mannered . . . So did the rest of the girls."

"You're making it sound like every dove in the territory and me —"

"You know that's not what I meant," Layla said, cutting him off. "Doves talk about men, in the same way all other women do," she said. "Which one would be a good beau . . . a good husband."

"And you were all talking about me?" Summers asked. "No wonder my ears burned from time to time."

"Don't flatter yourself," she said, shaking his arm him a little, chastising him. "We didn't spend every waking hour talking about *Will Summers.*"

Will smiled, holding her against him, glad she seemed to feel better.

"I'm honored to have been mentioned at all," he said.

As he held her close, he noted the dog step back from the edge of the stream and look off toward a distant hill line. Water drizzled on the dog's wet flews; a deep, guarded growl rumbled in his chest.

Will Summers stiffened and lifted his eyes up along the hill lines.

"Easy, Buddy," he whispered down to the dog.

The dog's growl stopped; he turned his wet face up toward Summers. He gave a short whine and stood less tense, satisfied now that he'd alerted his two companions.

"What is it, Will?" Layla asked, her face still against his chest.

"I don't now," Summers said. "But I'm learning that when Buddy growls, it's wise to pay attention."

"*Buddy,* huh?" said Layla. "You've been calling him that more and more."

"Why not? It seems to fit him," Summers said. He continued to scan the hills as he walked her toward the waiting horse, which had raised its head from the water at the sound of the dog growling.

"Do you see anything out there?" Layla asked as Summers helped her up onto the saddle.

"No," said Summers, "but this is hard country to spot something in, especially if it's something that doesn't want to be seen. We'd best get on up into some cover."

He swung up behind the saddle, reached around Layla and turned the horse along the path. The dog bounded up ahead of them.

From the edge of a ridge halfway up the hill line, Bertram Berger lowered a battered pair of binoculars from his eyes, blew on a cracked lens and passed them on to Albert Knox's eager hands.

"There they go," he said. "The sumbitch is riding Arlo Hughes' horse. The woman's face is bandaged. She looks badly injured." He squinted with his naked eyes as a low rise of dust began to loom behind the tiny figures. "I couldn't see much anyway with the glass cracked."

"What were they doing?" Knox asked. He bumped his palm against the side of the battered binoculars, as if doing so might create a clearer image.

"They weren't doing anything, just watering the dog and horse," said Berger. He saw what Knox was doing to the binoculars and grew agitated. "Don't beat on them. You'll make the glass fall out."

"So what, if they don't work anyway?" said Knox, lowering the binoculars from his eyes.

"They're all we've got," Berger said. "Give them back before you make them worse." He held his hand out and snapped his fingers impatiently.

Knox handed him the binoculars. The two sat for a moment staring out at Summers and Layla riding the winding path upward toward the cover of trees and boulders.

"Do you want to follow them?" Knox asked.

"They might have already seen us," said Berger. "They might be riding up to find a good spot, and bushwhack us when we ride in on them."

"So we're not going to follow them?" Knox asked.

"We'll follow them, but not far," Berger said. "I know that hillside. The path they're on goes upstream a few miles, then stops. The only way down is to jump off the other side and try to fly." He gave a dark sinister grin. "Or else ride back down past us."

"Either way, they'll be dead," Knox replied, returning Berger's dark grin.

CHAPTER 10

Afternoon shadows had drawn long across the hillsides and ridgelines by the time Summers led the horse into the clearing out in front of the disheveled cabin. The split log–and-stone cabin stood alongside the stream at the end of the rocky mountain path.

"This has to be the place," Summers said, stopping and gazing ahead. "This path looks like it plays out underground not far ahead."

Layla Brooks had sat slumped in the saddle the last half hour of the uphill trek, but she raised her face and tried to look at the cabin with her right eye as Summers stepped around to help her down.

"I can't see well enough to know what it looks like, Will," she said, taking his shoulders and letting him lower her to her feet beside him.

"You're not missing much, Layla," Summers said. Yet, upon seeing a cloud of disappointment on her injured face, he quickly changed his appraisal and said, "But I've seen worse. It'll do until the doctor comes and checks you out."

Her right eye searched in vain across the fuzzy image of the cabin standing before them.

"Are you sure, Will?" she asked. "I mean, if it's too bad we can always camp out in the yard . . ."

"No, it'll do," Summers said. "I'm going to check inside, see how it looks for accommodations."

"I'll go with you," she said quickly, placing her hand firmly on his forearm.

"Sure," Summers said, realizing how frightening it had to be, after all she'd been through, and now not being able to clearly see anything around her. "Buddy seems to like it here," he offered to ease her fears. "He's already made himself at home."

The dog had loped ahead, checked out a dusty tin can, one of many that littered the front porch, and plopped down on his belly. He sat staring at the two, panting, his tongue lolling down the side of his mouth.

Stepping forward, Layla tripped a little over one of the rusted cans. Her firm grip grew tighter on Summers' forearm as he caught her and steadied her with his free hand.

"Careful," he said. "Sometimes these miners scatter empty airtights around as much for security as anything else."

"So they would have us believe," Layla replied.

They walked across the littered yard, up to the unlocked door. Buddy waited till they stepped past him; then he stood up and turned to the door.

When Summers swung the creaking door open, the dog stepped forward as if appointing himself in charge.

"After you, Buddy," Summers said, giving a sweeping gesture with his hand.

Inside the front door, the two stopped and Summers examined the cabin's interior. Buddy walked straight across the floor to the low stone hearth where a bear's head sat, staring out at them through lifeless eyes. Dried black blood lay in the circle surrounding the severed head. A swarm of flies rose and buzzed above the head as the dog approached and poked his nose at it, disturbing them.

"What's dead, Will?" Layla asked. She heard the flies, and smelled the soured, putrid flesh.

"It's a bear's head, Layla," said Summers.

"Let's sit you down and I'll get it out of here. I'll do some other cleaning too."

Without turning her loose, he reached out with his free hand and pulled a chair over to a wooden table, which was piled high with empty cans, eating utensils and whiskey bottles. A big, bloodstained butcher knife stood with its tip sticking into the tabletop.

"I can help, Will," she said, resisting a little as he ushered her to the chair.

"No, you take it easy," said Summers. "Quit trying to force yourself to see. You might do yourself more harm than good."

She sat down and let out a breath.

Summers stepped over, picked the bear's head up by its ear and carried it outside. The dog walked along behind him, its muzzle still probing close, examining the smell through the swirl of accompanying flies.

"Go find yourself something to do, Buddy," Summers said over his shoulder. "It looks like I'll be housecleaning for a good part of the evening."

After heaving the heavy bear's head off onto a tree-covered hillside, Summers spent the next two hours cleaning and making the cabin inhabitable for what he hoped would be a short overnight stay. When he'd finished, he stood on the front porch and gazed off into the looming purple darkness. Through the open door behind him, he listened to the crackle of split pine logs burning in the hearth.

"This will have to do, Buddy," he said quietly to the dog standing beside him.

The dog wagged his tail a little and gave a low, peaceful whine under his breath.

Summers had carried in a bucket of fresh water from the stream, sloshed it over the dried bear blood and scrubbed it loose with a stiff-bristle brush. With the help of a homemade straw broom, another bucket of water rinsed it out the front door. When he'd finished washing away the blood, he'd cleared the table, throwing cans, bottles and other debris into a dusty feed sack, which he carried out around the corner of the cabin.

While Layla sat by quietly, he'd brought in firewood and built the fire in the stone hearth. He'd found a cupboard full of airtight tins and sorted through them. He'd selected a can of red beans and a can of corn, as well as a sack of coffee beans.

While he stood on the front porch waiting for the food to heat in two small pots and the coffee to boil, he reached a hand down and scratched the dog's rough head.

"These are things that have to be done,"

he murmured, as if the dog had questioned his actions.

He stood gazing off through the darkness and thought of the fork in the lower trail, where the tracks of his horses had been led on by the hands of thieves.

A silver-gray, three dark bays, an Appaloosa mare soon to foal, a paint horse, a black Morgan cross . . . , he reminded himself.

Seven fine horses, lest you forget . . . , he thought wryly — as if a man could ever forget such a thing. He'd had the same thought countless times throughout the day.

Inside the cabin, Layla stood and walked to the open doorway, seeing only darkness beyond the flicker of shadowy firelight.

"Will," she said quietly, "are you there? I hear the coffee boiling."

Summers put the thought of the stolen horses out of his mind. He turned to the door, the big dog following suit.

"I'm coming," he said, walking inside.

She stood up, meeting his cloudy image.

"Will, you've got to let me do something to help," she said, almost pleading with him. "I'm not used to others doing things for me."

"I understand, Layla. But why shouldn't you take it easy and enjoy the help for a change?" Summers added, not wanting to tell her that there was little she could do under the circumstances.

"I — I can't, Will," she said. "Blind people are not helpless . . . They do all sorts of things."

"Your blindness is temporary, Layla," Summers said. "This is going to be over soon. Let me take care of you, best I can, for the time being," he said.

He took her forearm, helped her back to the chair at the table and seated her.

"Maybe I should be trying to learn to do things for myself, Will," she said grimly. "What if this is not temporary?"

"Come on, Layla," Will said, trying to play down the gravity of her question. "Your right eye is scorched a little, is all. It's going to be all right. You heard what Vera Dalton said."

"Vera Dalton is a dove, Will, no different than myself," she said. "I thank God she was there for me, and for everything she's done . . ." She let her words trail and shook her head slowly. "But what if she was wrong? What if I only get worse and worse until my eyes are gone?"

"Try not to think that way, Layla," Summers said. "You've got to have some faith — things are going to get better for you."

"I want to, Will. I really do," she said. "But

I'm so scared . . . more scared than I've ever been in my life."

"*Shhh,* Layla," Summers said. "Don't do this to yourself. You've got to put it all out of your mind . . . give the healing a chance."

"I know, and I'm trying to," she said. "But I'm alone out here, Will. I'm a whore who's lost her looks, maybe even lost her eyes. What's left for me?"

Summers saw her breaking down. He knew of nothing to say that could make her feel better.

"Let me get you a plate of food, some coffee," he offered. "You'll feel better with some food and hot coffee in you."

She calmed herself. She lowered her head and nodded slowly.

"Yes," she said with resolve, "some food and coffee would be nice." She thought about the small derringer she'd somehow lost in her struggle with the Bendigos. If she had still had the gun, she didn't know if she could have trusted herself with it.

At the hearth, Summers dipped beans and corn into two wooden bowls he'd found in the cupboard and scrubbed with the brush and some clean water.

"All right, then, try some of this," he said, walking to the table and setting the bowl and a cup of hot coffee in front of her. He laid a small metal spoon beside the bowl.

Layla stared down at the fuzzy image and shook her head, feeling around almost frantically for the spoon.

"I — I can't even feed myself, Will," she said in a shaky voice.

Summers quickly picked up the spoon and tapped it on the side of the bowl to get her attention.

"Allow me, ma'am," he said, trying to lighten the situation. "I've been wanting to get some practice feeding damsels in distress."

Layla closed her hand over his and forced a tight smile.

"You'll likely get all the practice you'll ever want with me," she said.

With his black leather medicine bag on the floor of the buggy by their feet, Dr. Chase and Vera Dalton traveled as fast as his tired horse and lightweight rig could take them. In spite of their haste, it was fully dark when they reached the fork in the trail.

"I'm afraid this is as far as the horse can pull the rig. These old buggy wheels will never make it," the doctor said, turning off to the side of the trail. "We'll lead the horse and leave the buggy here."

"It's a steep walk from here," Vera said,

looking around in the thin light of a quarter moon.

"Don't worry, my fine and lovely apprentice," said the doctor. "Billy Boy will ride us after he's rested a bit. Until then we best lead him and not push our luck." He reached a hand over and brushed a strand of hair from her face.

She shied away a little.

"Of course." she said. "I'll get the clean bandages and your medical bag, Doctor."

The doctor chuckled quietly and shook his head in the darkness.

"Don't worry, Vera," he said. "I won't make any demands of you at a time like this."

"I understand, Doctor," Vera replied in a strictly professional tone. She started to reach back over the seat and pick up the bag and bandages, but the doctor stopped her with a hand on her forearm.

"I meant what I said back in town, Vera," he said quietly. "You have proven yourself to be the best medical apprentice I have ever seen."

"Thank you, Doctor," Vera said. She sat quietly, wondering where this was leading.

"I want you to know that you have more than adequately fulfilled our arrangement. Owing to your hard work and the skill you have acquired, from now on you will be my apprentice, and my apprentice *only.*" He looked at her in the pale, thin moonlight. "You'll no longer have to take care of my . . . *personal needs.*"

"I don't mind, Doctor," Vera said. "It was part of our agreement. You've kept your end of the bargain. I'm learning medicine, lifting myself up a little higher every year."

He patted her shoulder.

"Indeed you have," he said, "and that's all the more reason I cannot continue to take advantage of your generosity. I must come to respect you more as a colleague than an object of desire." He paused for a moment, then said, "So I am setting you free in that regard."

Vera sat in silence, staring at the dark trail ahead. For a moment she couldn't speak.

Dr. Chase paused again; then he added solemnly, "In a few days you will no longer be my apprentice. I've already drawn up the necessary papers for you. The world will be calling you *Dr.* Vera Dalton soon enough."

A tight lump rose in her throat.

"Thank you, Dr. Chase," she whispered at length.

Higher up on a cliff overlooking the dark trail, Albert Knox awakened at the slight sound of a horse's hoof clicking against rock. He'd drunk half of the bottle of whiskey he'd taken from his saddlebags while Berger lay rolled in a blanket, sound asleep.

What's that . . . ?

Knox rolled up onto his knees, bleary-eyed, as he heard the sound of muffled voices on the trail below. He set the bottle aside, rubbed his face and picked up his rifle, which was resting on the rock ledge beside him. Listening intently, he heard the faint sound of voices. He noted that one voice belonged to a woman, the other a man. Uh-oh!

"Wake up, Blue Hand!" he said to Berger in a harsh whisper. "It's them! They're right under us!"

Berger stirred, but he only grumbled and rolled over on his other side.

"Damn it, Berger!" shouted Knox, a little woozy from the whiskey. "Wake up! We've got them trapped!"

From below, Knox heard the man's voice call out in a demanding tone, "Who's up there? Make yourself known."

"Damn it, Berger! Maybe this will wake you up!" Knox said to himself. He swung the rifle up to his shoulder and began firing round after round in the direction of the voices below.

Pulling the horse along by its reins, Vera and Dr. Chase tried to flee from beneath the blue-orange streaks of fire raining down on them. But before they had gone five yards along the dark rocky path, Vera heard the doctor let out a deep grunt and fall to the ground, the spooked horse's reins still in his hand.

"Dr. Chase!" Vera shouted, turning and seeing Chase's dark outline on the path, the horse jumping and whinnying beside him.

"I'm done, Vera!" the doctor managed to let out. Shot after shot continued to explode and slam the path all around them. "Take Billy Boy . . . !" he said in a weakening voice.

"Oh my God!" Vera shrieked. She took a moment to muster up the courage she needed, and then she grabbed the reins from the doctor's hand. She stooped down over the dark figure until she saw his shadowy face in the thin moonlight. "I've got you, Doctor," she said sobbing, clutching his shoulders. "Get up! I'll get you out of here!"

"No . . . get yourself out . . . ," the dying doctor managed to say, shoving at her hands.

Vera felt him fall limp and stop trying to

resist her efforts. She screamed and shook him. But it was no use; he was dead.

She turned with the horse's reins in hand and jumped up atop the frightened animal through sobs. She felt it bolt forward up the trail and she tried to hang on as she struggled to process the poor doctor's fate.

"What the hell are you shooting at, Albert?" Berger asked, rising into a crouch, awakened by the sharp thunderous rifle fire.

"I've got them trapped down there!" Knox said, his voice thick but excited. "I think I hit one!"

The two fell silent and listened to the sound of the horse's hooves running up the trail.

"You better hope that horse is running away without a rider," said Berger.

"It is. I'm sure of it," said Knox.

Berger asked bluntly, "Are you drinking whiskey when you're supposed to be watching the trail?"

"Maybe . . . What of it?" Knox said with a drunken slur.

"Give me a drink, that's what of it," said Berger, seeing Knox's rifle aimed loosely up at him.

Knox chuckled; he picked up the whiskey bottle and handed it to him.

"I thought you were going to chastise me," he said.

"No, sir," said Berger, "I wasn't going to chastise you." He took a long swig and handed the bottle back to the half-drunken gunman.

As Knox took the bottle, Berger said quietly, "But I have had it with you, you stupid son of a bitch."

Knox heard the hammer cock on Berger's Colt as it sprang up from the angry man's side. He saw a streak of fire explode in his face. Then blackness overtook him as the bullet struck his forehead. His body hit the ground with a thud; the next two shots he neither heard nor felt.

"Now I'll go see what kind of mess you've made of things," Berger said to himself. Lowering the smoking Colt to his side, he picked up the bottle of whiskey. He turned the bottle up, finished it in one swig, tossed it away and walked to his horse.

CHAPTER 11

Wrapped in the warmth of a small bed inside the miner's cabin, Will Summers opened his eyes at the sound of the gunfire down along the path. On the floor, the dog heard the shots too. He sprang up, hurried halfway to the door and stopped. He looked back toward the bed and barked sharply. Beside Summers, Layla tensed at the sound and rose onto an elbow, looking toward the door even though she couldn't see anything clearly.

"Will? Are you awake?" she whispered, her voice sounding scared.

"Yes, I heard it," Summers said. He rolled up onto the edge of the bed and sat for a moment, noting that the rifle fire seemed to have stopped as quickly as it had started. The following pistol shots had stopped as well.

"What do you suppose it was?" Layla

asked, scooting over and lying close to his back.

"Whatever it was, it must've done what it set out to do," Summers said. "It's stopped now."

"Do you think it could have had anything to do with the doctor?" she asked. "Vera Dalton said she'd come see us as soon as he got back to town."

Summers thought about it. The doctor might have ridden out after dark, knowing how serious Layla's eye injury was. Summers stood and stepped over to the chair where his trousers lay.

"I suppose he could be traveling up here at night, if he knows the country well enough," Summers said. "I better go see what it's about. I don't like gunshots in the middle of the night."

"Can I go with you, Will?" Layla asked, sounding frightened.

"No," said Summers, "you need to stay here. I don't know what I might run into out there."

He put on his trousers and buttoned the fly. He pulled on his boots and stamped them onto his feet. He knew she was thinking about the last time he had asked her to stay put, and what had happened to her. He grabbed his shirt from across the chair back and put it on.

"I have no way to protect myself," she said.

"I'm leaving Buddy here with you, Layla," Summers said. "He'll watch after you until I get back. I won't be long," he added.

"Please don't leave me here," she said, worry in her voice.

Summers picked up his gun belt from the bedpost and strapped it around his waist.

"You know I've got to, Layla," he said. "If it has anything to do with the doctor coming up here and taking care of your eyes, we can't risk something happening to him."

Layla fell silent for a moment.

"Come on," said Summers. "I'll lead you to the door so you can drop the bolt once I'm gone. You can feel for it and unbolt it when I get back. The rifle is on my side of the bed. It's got a bullet in its chamber; all you have to do is cock it and fire. I'll hear it and come running."

"All right," she said, realizing that what he said made sense. If the doctor was out there in some sort of trouble, they had to know, for the doctor's sake, and hers as well. "I'm going to sit at the table close to the door until I hear you call out to me."

As she stood up from the bed, the dog hurried to the front door, bouncing up and

156

down on his front paws, restless, eager to go.

Summers walked her to the door, put his hand over hers on the bolt and lifted it with her.

"Are you going to be able to do it?" he asked.

"Yes," Layla said, mustering up the strength that was required of her.

With his knee, Summers had to push the dog back away from the door as he started to open it.

"No, Buddy, you're staying here," he said. The dog let out what sounded like a groan of disappointment.

Down the mountainside on the dark path, the sound of the fleeing horse's hooves had already disappeared by the time Berger stepped down from his horse, leading Knox's horse behind him. He walked cautiously, rifle in hand, toward the dark figure lying sprawled in the middle of the narrow snaking dirt path.

"Hey there, *horse trader,*" he said in a hushed, guarded tone, "is that you? You better not make a move. I'll put a bullet straight through you."

But after a moment he began to realize that whoever lay there wasn't going to put up a fight. With less caution, he stepped closer, took a long wooden match from inside his shirt, struck it on his rifle stock and held it down for a better look.

"Jesus, Albert, you stupid sumbitch," he murmured as if Knox were still alive and with him, "you killed the damn doctor."

He stooped down over the dead doctor and, out of habit, rifled through his trouser and jacket pockets. He jerked a gold watch from Dr. Chase's vest pocket and turned it in the flicker of the burning match.

"You won't need this," he said. He dropped the watch into his own vest pocket, then searched the doctor's inside lapel pockets, took out a long leather wallet and spread it open enough to see a folded paper and a stack of dollars in it.

"You won't need this either," he chuckled. "I hear everything is free in hell." He closed the wallet and stuffed it into his own lapel pocket. Standing, he gazed up the dark path alongside the stream. He considered whether or not to slip farther up the path and see if Summers would ride down to see what the gunfire was all about.

"To hell with it," he said to himself after a moment. He'd already put too much into this. He'd ride on up the cliffs and tell Dow Bendigo that Will Summers killed Knox.

Like as not, Dow would want to ride back and kill Summers, but all that was for another day, he thought. He climbed back up into his saddle, took the reins to both his horse and Knox's horse and rode away in the darkness.

Farther up the path, Vera Dalton rode the frightened buggy horse at a dangerous speed along the meandering path. From the other direction, Will Summers rode along at a good strong clip himself, but not so fast that the sound of his own horse's hooves drowned out any chance of him hearing the racing hooves coming up toward him. Luckily for both parties, he caught a glimpse of the woman's and the horse's black silhouette against the purple night sky as they rounded a turn only a few yards ahead of him.

Veering his horse over to the side of the path opposite the stream, he raced out alongside the frightened animal and grabbed it by its bridle, slowing it down.

Seeing him beside her, Vera yanked hard for control of the horse's reins as she screamed, lashing out at Summers with her free hand.

"Ma'am, it's me, Will Summers. I'm here to help," he shouted loudly, slowing his horse, keeping a firm grip on the buggy horse's bridle until both horses slowed to a trot, then a walk.

"Oh, thank God, Will Summers!" Vera cried out as the horses came to a halt, both of them sliding a little in loose rock and dust beneath their hooves. She sat slumped, trying to catch her breath.

"Take it easy, ma'am," said Summers, keeping a firm grip on the buggy horse. "We heard shooting down there. Are you all right?"

"Yes . . . I — I think so," Vera said, struggling with her words as she gasped for breath. "But Dr. Chase is dead! Someone shot him."

"Shot him?" Summers stared down the winding path in the darkness as if he might see who had done such a thing. Then he jerked on the buggy horse's bridle and said to Vera, "Come on, let's get to the cabin, in case you're being followed."

"I've got Dr. Chase's medicine bag," she managed to say. "We were heading here when someone ambushed us from up on a hillside."

Summers shook his head in regret.

"I heard pistol shots after the rifle fire. Did either of you fire back?" he asked.

"No," Vera said, "we didn't even have a

gun with us. Dr. Chase disapproved of carrying guns." She paused, then said, "Although I suppose having one this time might have helped . . . ?" She ended her words as a question.

"No, probably not," Summers said. "But it couldn't have hurt either. Who knows?"

He looked back at the darkness above them, considering the matter, but he was at as much of a loss as she about who might have done it, or why.

"How is Layla?" she asked.

"Not good," Summers said. "She can't see much out of her right eye. It's staying red and swollen."

"I brought a solution for her eyes," Vera said. "It's something the doctor made."

"Good," said Summers. "I'll get you up to the cabin and go down and find the doctor's body."

"Go now, Mr. Summers," Vera said. "I can find my way to the cabin. I know the way."

"Are you sure, ma'am?" Summers asked.

Vera could tell by his voice that he wanted to ride down right away.

"I'm sure, Mr. Summers," she said. "If it means you might catch Doc's killer, *please* go now. I'll look after Layla while you're gone."

As Summers turned his horse, he shouted

over his shoulder to her, "Announce yourself well, ma'am. I left the dog and a rifle with her."

"I'll be careful," Vera said.

In the darkness, Summers traveled quietly, well aware that the same ambushers who shot the doctor might still be lying in wait somewhere up on the rocky hillside. In the thin purple moonlight, he stopped his horse and stepped down cautiously when he spotted the dark outline of the body lying on the narrow path.

Colt in hand, he stepped over to the dead doctor, looked all around in the shadowy darkness and stooped down to feel the doctor's wrist for pulse, just for good measure. Finding no sign of life, he turned the wrist loose and shook his head in regret. Then he noticed the way the doctor's coat lay open, the inside of his jacket and trouser pockets turned inside out, and he knew that the gunman had come down to scavenge the body for anything of value.

"You didn't deserve this, Doctor," he whispered. "I'll get you on up the hill."

He holstered his Colt, lifted the body onto his horse's back and walked the animal to a slender pine sapling beside the path. He tied the horse's reins around the sapling for safekeeping. Then he drew the Colt again and began walking up the steep hillside in the direction of a dark edge of rock skylined against the purple heavens.

Atop a steep and treacherous footpath, he stepped onto flatter ground and immediately caught the lingering scent of burnt gunpowder wafting among rock and brush.

Here's where it took place, he told himself, lowering his Colt a little, examining his surroundings, seeing nothing but the empty shadowy land beneath a quarter moon and a wide sky full of stars.

He took a few steps to his right before he almost stepped on the body of Albert Knox lying dead at his feet. Bending over the dead ambusher, Summers saw the bullet holes in his head. The smell of whiskey rose from the bloody corpse.

Peculiar . . . , he thought. He had no clue who would have ambushed the doctor, or why they would have killed this man — one of their own. But he had a nagging suspicion that it was all somehow connected to his stolen horses — *a silver-gray dapple, three dark bays, an Appaloosa mare soon to foal, a paint horse —*

Stop it, he told himself, cutting off his train of thought. He had too much going on right now to worry about the stolen horses. There was Layla . . . Her eyes needed attention. And now there was Vera Dalton too, who also needed protection until they were safely back in Wakely.

He lifted the Colt from Knox's holster, checked it and shoved it down behind his belt. He picked up the rifle lying in the dirt, checked it.

Every little bit helps . . .

When the time was right, he'd go back after his stolen horses. You can bet on it, he promised himself, staring intently out in the direction he knew the horses had traveled, on past the fork in the trail.

Layla stood up when she heard the horse's hooves coming toward the cabin. Buddy lifted himself from the floor at her feet; a long, low growl rumbled in his chest as he stared toward the littered front yard. Concerned that danger might be approaching, Layla clumsily picked up the rifle, unable to see clearly what she was doing, and fumbled with the hammer.

She heard the horse's hooves stop, and footsteps began to move across the porch. As a woman's voice called out through the darkness, an overwhelming sense of relief shot through Layla's entire body.

"Layla? Layla, it's me, Vera Dalton," Vera

called out. "Don't shoot. Let me in." She knocked hard on the bolted wooden door.

The big dog shot across the floor and lunged at the front door in a round of barking.

"No, Buddy, it's all right," said Layla, laying the rifle aside. She stepped over to the door and reached out to the fuzzy image of the iron door bolt.

She swung the door open and stepped back, holding Buddy with both hands on his thick neck, knowing that wouldn't stop him had he really wanted to attack.

But the big dog settled down when Vera stepped inside carrying the doctor's black leather medicine bag and closed the door quickly behind her.

"Vera, are you all right?" Layla said, her right eye searching hard for something to focus on. "Where's Will? Where's Dr. Chase? We heard shooting."

"Will is all right, Layla," Vera said in a rushed and breathless voice. She hurriedly turned and bolted the front door. "But poor Dr. Chase is dead." She held up the leather medicine bag. "I brought some solution for your eyes. I had counted on Dr. Chase doing this . . ." She paused and bit her lip in apprehension. "Now it looks like I'm going to do it myself."

"Where is Will?" Layla asked again, as if nothing else mattered at that moment.

"He went down to get the doctor's body and bring it up here," Vera said. She stepped over to Layla, took her forearm gently and directed her back to the chair. Buddy stepped out of the way and watched, as if convinced of the woman's good intentions.

"He's not going after the ambusher, is he?" Layla asked, her voice getting a little shaky.

"No, he said he would look around some, then bring Dr. Chase up here. I believe him." She looked at Layla pointedly. "Do you?"

Layla sat down and gazed ahead with her cloudy right eye.

"Yes . . . yes, of course I believe him," she said. She seemed to settle down some as Vera set the leather medicine bag on the table and opened it.

"Good," she said. "While we're waiting, I need to take a look at your eyes and get started with this solution right away."

CHAPTER 12

The colors of morning wreathed the eastern sky when Bertram "Blue Hand" Berger reached a stretch of flatlands leading across a wide rocky basin to a line of jagged hills. He stopped for a moment, leading Knox's horse beside him, and looked back over his shoulder. searching his back trail for any sign of followers.

Nothing . . . , he thought.

He relaxed, laying his hands on the saddle horn. The only sign of man or horse in any direction was the line of marked hoofprints in the sandy soil where Dow and Tom Bendigo had led the string of stolen horses earlier.

Summers' horses, he told himself.

He spit and gave himself a thin, wry smile, thinking of everything that had happened. *To hell with Will Summers and his damned horses,* he thought. He wished he'd killed Summers as he'd intended to do, before that idiot Knox tipped off their position and proceeded to kill the wrong damned man — the damned town doctor to boot. He shook his head and spit again in disgust.

So much for that, he thought. As far as any of the Bendigos would ever know, Will Summers killed Albert Knox.

He gazed out across the desolate but familiar land lying ahead of him. He'd made this ride many times since throwing his lot in with Warton Bendigo and his gang of rustlers and robbers. Five short miles ahead, he knew there would be water in a rock basin. There, he'd fill his canteen and water the horse. Ten miles farther on, he would find the trail leading up along the Red Cliffs. Down the other side of the cliffs, he would make his way another thirty miles across more rough up-and-down terrain before finding any water.

But once he watered the horse and himself again, he'd be almost home, or at least to the place he called home for now. *The Bendigos . . . ,* he thought, booting the weary horse forward, Knox's horse right on his side.

In the rising morning heat, atop a tired and thirsty horse, it took him nearly an hour to ride the short five miles to the water hole. The last mile of the ride, he began to see the lazy swing of two buzzards circling over-head.

What the hell . . . ?

When he got closer to the water hole, he stared through the wavering morning heat and set eyes on a dead horse lying near the water's edge. He saw three more buzzards standing atop the dead animal's bloated side, their heads lowered, feeding busily on the waterlogged carcass.

Damn it!

Riding in closer, he recognized the dead horse as the Appaloosa mare from the stolen string of horses. Between the mare's hind legs, a half-born foal lay partially submerged in bloody water.

"Dow, you fool," Berger murmured, see-ing a gaping bullet hole in the mare's fore-head.

He half circled the edge of rock basin to where the water was not dark with blood. Stepping down from his saddle, he let his and Knox's horse lower their muzzles into the tepid water.

"Drink it up, cayuses," he said to the dusty, thirsty horses. "Another day or two, this water will poison for a long time to come."

Without drinking any of the basin water himself, Berger took the half-full canteen from his saddle horn, uncapped it, took a sip of warm water and spit it out. He cursed under his breath and eyed the drinking horses with envy.

So what? he told himself. He could make it another ten miles without water. Once he turned onto the trail up to Red Cliff, he'd find water . . . somewhere.

Moments later, he pulled the horses away from the water, their muzzles still drizzling, and climbed back into his saddle. He turned the animals and rode away, still following the stolen horses' tracks in the sandy soil. As long as the two horses were watered, he'd be fine. People made too big a deal out of having water. Not him, though, he told himself. He could handle it . . .

Yet nearly four hours had passed in the scorching heat across the flatlands by the time he'd reached the trail that would lead him up toward Red Cliffs. In the unforgiving terrain, he had become so addled from his body's loss of water that he simply rode past the turn.

From beneath a darkened overhang above the flatlands, two of Warton Bendigo's men, Rowe Jolsyn and a Mexican named Chulo, sat staring down at the rider flopping limply back and forth in his saddle.

"Yep, it's Blue Hand, all right," said Rowe Jolsyn, staring down through a long telescope.

"What is wrong with him?" the Mexican asked.

"It looks like the heat's got him," Jolsyn said, scanning Bertram Berger up and down with the telescope. He saw the wild look on Berger's face close up — saw him swaying and laughing maniacally as something struck him funny in the dangerous midday heat.

"He is *loco, sí*?" said Chulo. "He does not know he has passed the turn." He reached down and started to raise a rifle from his saddle boot. "The poor bastard," he said. He shook his head and crossed himself quickly.

"Hey! What are you doing?" Jolsyn asked, giving him a puzzled look.

"We can pick him off from up here and put him out of his misery, eh?" said Chulo.

"Yes, we *could*," Jolsyn said in amazement. He laid a gloved hand over Chulo's to keep him from drawing the rifle any farther. "*Or* we could ride down there and just get to him before he broils himself like a goose."

Chulo turned the rifle stock loose with a look of disappointment.

"Whatever you say, Rowe," he murmured

with a sigh.

The two stepped their horses out of the shade and rode down a loose gravelly trail toward the lone figure below.

Berger had enough sense left to look around as he heard the two horses coming upon him from behind. Luckily for Jolsyn and Chulo, they reached him just as his hand came up gripping his Colt.

"Easy, Blue Hand!" said Jolsyn, grabbing the upraised gun and wrenching it from Berger's grip. "It's me, Rowe!" he said. "Me and Chulo!" He gestured toward the Mexican, who sat his horse on the other side of him, holding on to the two horses.

"It's a good thing . . . you showed up, Rowe," Berger said in a dry, rasping voice. "I was going to . . . shoot somebody."

Jolsyn held on to Berger's gun as he lifted the canteen from his saddle horn and handed it to him. "Don't talk, drink this," Jolsyn said.

Berger tried to take a sip without removing the canteen cap. Then he held the half-full canteen upside down and shook it, trying to get the water flowing.

Jolsyn and Chulo gave each other a glance.

"Here, Blue Hand," Jolsyn said quietly, reaching for the canteen, "let me get that for you."

Chulo watched impatiently as Jolsyn uncapped the canteen and handed it to Berger. The parched gunman raised it with both trembling hands and drank gulp after gulp as water streamed down both edges of his mouth.

"Oh God!" Berger said in a half sob as he finally lowered the dripping canteen. "I was a goner." He gasped and strangled and collected himself as Jolsyn took the canteen back from him.

"You were lost," Chulo said flatly with no sympathy for the man.

"Didn't you see where the hoofprints turn? Where Dow and Tom Bendigo's tracks led up the trail?" Jolsyn asked. He thumbed toward the hills above them.

"I saw them . . . I figured they might be trying to throw me off," said Berger, a disoriented look in his eyes.

Jolsyn looked at Chulo. The Mexican stared back at him with dark eyes and patted a hand suggestively on his rifle butt.

Jolsyn shook his head slightly. Then he turned back to Berger.

"Are you feeling better now?" he asked.

"Yeah, much better . . . *obliged,*" Berger said weakly. "I'm ready to ride on up to Red Cliffs . . . ask Dow what the hell he was thinking, shooting that mare . . . leaving her lying there poisoning the water hole."

"You might want to let it alone, about him shooting the pregnant mare," Jolsyn said. "You're still not thinking straight."

Berger just looked at them.

"Dow said it was an *acci-dent,*" Chulo said.

"An *accident*?" said Berger. "She was shot right twixt the eyes."

Jolsyn put in, "Dow said she started slipping her foal, and he didn't have time for it. While she was birthing he was shooting at her. She managed to get up and make a run for it. He caught up to her at the water hole, is all."

"Holy Mother . . . ," said Berger, trying to get a picture of it in his overheated brain. "She was foaling, and he was shooting at her?" Berger considered it. "Why'd he even tell you something like that? Why didn't he just keep his mouth shut about it?"

"You know how Dow is," Jolsyn said. He shrugged.

"Yeah, I suppose I do," said Berger, still seeing it in his mind.

"Anyway, that's the whole story on the water hole," said Jolsyn. "Now you'll forget it ever happened, if you know what's good for you."

"Jesus, Joseph and Bob . . . ," said Berger, still unable to clear the picture out of his mind.

"Come on, let's ride to Red Cliffs," said Jolsyn, turning his horse. "You'll feel better once you get there."

"Where is Albert?" Chulo asked as he and Berger turned beside Jolsyn. He eyed Knox's horse, its reins in Berger's hand.

"Damn," said Berger, lying. "Of all things, some damn horse trader shot him deader than hell."

"Uh-oh," said Chulo. "Warton Bendigo will want to hear all about this. He liked Albert Knox."

"Yeah, I know he does," said Berger, lying straight ahead. "It's a damn shame what happened to ol' Albert. He didn't deserve to die that way."

For the next two days, Will Summers did what he could to keep his mind off his stolen horses. He cleaned up around the cabin. He chopped, stacked and carried in wood, the big cur right at his heals. He prepared food and coffee while Vera tended to Layla. When he wasn't busy with chores, he watched closely as Vera washed Layla's burnt and wounded eyes with the clear solution Dr. Chase had mixed and bottled before his untimely death.

On the second day, he sat watching Vera pour a small amount of the solution into a shot glass.

"Bow your head for me, Layla," she said gently. "We don't want to use any more of this than we have to. With Dr. Chase gone, we have no way to make more once we run out."

"Tell me what to do, Vera," Layla said. "You're the doctor now."

"Keep your eye open for me," Vera said.

She held the rim of the shot glass circling Layla's injured eye. Summers watched intently as she tipped Layla's head up and to the side, letting the solution fill the blood-streaked eye.

"Is it less painful this time?" Vera asked as she held the glass in place, seeing the solution turn pinkish in the shot glass.

"A lot less," Layla said, her head lying sidelong, resting in Vera's free had. "The first couple of times it burned a little. But not much now. Now it feels soothing and cool."

"Good," said Vera. "It's starting to heal. This will keep it clean. Can you move your eye around a little, let the solution get all over it real good?"

Layla rolled her injured eye carefully.

Summers watched; so did Buddy.

Vera waited a few moments, then raised Layla's head back into its bowed position and removed the glass and looked at pinkish solution.

"It's clearer than before," she said. "I think you're coming along nicely."

"Thanks to you," Layla said, nodding slightly, holding a clean cloth up beneath her eye to catch any solution running down her cheek.

"Now, then, the other eye," Vera said. She held up three fingers a few inches from Layla's right eye. "Can you see my fingers?" she asked.

"Yes, but they're still blurry," said Layla. "Although I do see them more clearly than I could yesterday."

Summers let out a breath of relief. He stood up and picked up his rifle leaning against the table.

"I'll be out front if you need me," he said. Before turning away, he added, "Come morning, we need to get the doctor's body back to Wakely for a proper burial. The springhouse won't keep him much longer."

"Yes, you're right," Vera said. "I need to take the doctor home."

When Summers and the dog were out the

door, Vera looked closely at Layla sitting with the bandage removed from her bloody left eye, both eyes staring straight ahead.

"You and Dr. Chase were close," said Layla. "I can tell by the sound of your voice when you mention him."

"Yes," Vera said, "we were close." As she spoke she loosened the bandage on Layla's cheek and her chin to get a look at the rest of her facial wounds. "I have been his *apprentice* almost since the day I arrived in Wakely. He needed a woman, and I needed a way out of the life."

"I understand," Layla said quietly.

"I know you do," Vera said with a slight smile. "No one understands a dove like another dove." She gave the injured woman a reassuring squeeze on her shoulder. "We are sisters of circumstance."

As the bandage came off her cheek, Layla reached her fingertips up to the healing wounds, but stopped herself short.

"Tell me the truth, Vera," she said. "Is this going to leave my face badly scarred?"

"No, I don't think so," Vera said. "It will be noticeable upon a close look. But to the kind of men we consort with, I don't think it will matter."

Layla fell silent.

"Ask me what you really want to know,

Layla. Are scars on your face going to matter to *Will Summers*?" She leaned close to Layla's ear and whispered, "The answer is *no*. It won't matter at all."

"Is it that obvious how I feel about him?" Layla asked in a hushed tone.

"Yes, to me it's pretty clear," Vera whispered, examining the healing buckshot wounds. "I hear in your voice what I hear in my own when I speak about Dr. Chase."

Layla managed to smile. She laid her hand over Vera's, atop her shoulder.

"It feels good having a sister to talk to," she said quietly.

"Yes, I know what you mean," said Vera. In a quiet tone she said, "While it's just us doves here, tell me about the men who did this to you."

After a silent moment, Layla began to speak. "I can't identify them, Vera. I can't describe them . . . I don't even know for sure how many were there. I can't remember anything . . . and now with my eyes injured, I wouldn't even know if they were standing here in a corner."

Vera rubbed her shoulder, feeling her tense up.

"Take it easy, Layla. You're safe here. No one's going to harm you. Anything you can remember, you can tell in secret. I'll never repeat it."

"I believe you, Vera," Layla said. She shook her head in frustration. "But they knocked me unconscious, and it must have caused my mind to go blank. It's as if the shotgun blast wiped out any memory of them." Tears came to her sore and injured eyes.

Vera continued to rub her shoulder. "That's okay, darling. I don't blame you for not remembering it. I wouldn't remember it either. You stick with what you've told me, and you'll be all right."

"Tomorrow we're going to Wakely?" Layla asked.

"Yes, tomorrow," said Vera. "I want to get the doctor back to town and tell everyone what happened. But don't you worry; nobody is going to question what you say." She squeezed Layla's shoulder and continued rubbing it, comforting her. "I'm your doctor now. I'll see to it."

CHAPTER 13

In the early light of the next morning, Sheriff Giles Croce watched as Summers and the two women rode into Wakely. The horse trader followed ten yards behind the big dog, who scouted along the street as if he were on someone's trail. Beside Summers, the doctor's rig rolled along with the top down, the women in the front seat, the doctor's body wrapped in a tarpaulin, leaning to one side behind them in the small luggage compartment.

Heads turned along the boardwalk at the sight of women driving the familiar rig. They could make out the wrapped body lying propped up behind them.

This looks bad . . .

Croce leveled his gun belt, took his hat down from a wall peg and put it on. He walked out the door and closed it behind him.

At the hitch rail out in front of the doctor's big clapboard house, Summers stepped down from the saddle, prepared to explain to the gathering townsfolk what had happened to the doctor.

"Everybody give us some room," he said, making his way to the buggy and taking Vera's hand, helping her down from the driver's seat.

"Is that Dr. Chase?" a townsman asked anxiously, staring at the canvas-wrapped corpse.

Summers assisted Layla down and made sure Vera took her hand before turning to the group of concerned townsfolk.

"Yes," Summers said. "I'm sorry to have to tell you that it is Dr. Chase."

Reaching out, he pulled a corner of the tarpaulin away to expose the doctor's pale, ashen face. A gasp rippled across the anxious crowd surrounding the buggy.

"What happened to him?" an elderly woman named Naomi Loff asked, on the verge of tears.

"He was shot in an ambush," Summers said, "on his way up to visit a patient."

"An *ambush*?" asked a bald mercantile storeowner named Oscar Stubbens, stepping in closer. "But who would do such a thing? *Why . . . ?*" He stared at Summers in disbelief. Then he looked at Vera Dalton, who stood to the side, holding Layla's hands in hers.

Summers understood. They needed confirmation from one of their own.

"Vera, for God's sake," said Stubbens, "what happened? Were you with him?"

"Yes, I was with him," Vera said. She continued holding Layla's hands as she spoke. "It's like Mr. Summers says. We were headed up to Bates' mining shack to see our patient here." She gestured toward Layla. "It was dark. Someone shot him from a ridge above the trail. I got away."

"But who would want to kill our doctor?" Naomi Loff asked, tears flowing from her eyes.

"Maybe whoever it was didn't know it was Dr. Chase on the trail," offered Sheriff Croce. His voice towered above the others as he walked up, stopped and stared at Will Summers, his right hand on his holstered Colt. "Maybe the ambush was intended for somebody else."

Summers caught the suggestion in the sheriff's voice.

"Meaning this horse trader, Sheriff?" Stubbens asked, looking Summers up and down.

Croce stared at Summers, and Summers

met his gaze, refusing to comment.

"It's not a secret that your horses were stolen, Summers," Croce said. "I expect any horse thief in the territory figures you'd be trailing him and the stolen string by now."

"Are we going to talk about my business right here in the street, Sheriff? Because if we are, I'm going to mention a couple of things that you might not like folks hearing —"

"No, Summers," Croce said, cutting him off. "I wouldn't discuss your business out in the open." He offered a nervous smile for the benefit of the townsfolk. "What kind of a man do you think I am?"

Summers didn't answer, but his expression showed contempt.

"We'll talk in my office," Croce said quickly. "I'll want to hear everything you can tell me about what happened to the poor doctor."

Summers looked at the two women, who stood listening intently.

"Vera, take Layla inside," he said. "I'll be along when the sheriff and I are finished."

Sheriff Croce turned to the town barber, Clarence Wrenn, who stood beside Oscar Stubbens.

"Barber, why don't you and a couple helpers take the doctor's body to your shop . . .

get him cleaned up and presentable?"

"Come on, Clarence," said Stubbens. "Freddie and I will give you a hand."

A short man named Freddie Waller stepped forward from the gathered townsfolk and walked to the buggy.

"Summers," Croce said, gesturing a nod toward his office, "let's you and me talk privately, if that suits you better."

Summers felt like telling him that it made no difference to him if they talked right there in front of the town. He had nothing to hide. But he kept himself from saying it. He and Sheriff Croce were overdue for a talk. A *private* talk might be best . . .

As townsmen lifted the doctor's body from the buggy and Vera ushered Layla toward the house, Summers and Croce walked to the sheriff's office in silence.

When they reached the office door, Summers stepped aside and gestured Croce ahead of him. As Croce walked through the door, he wrapped his hand around his holstered Colt. Summers watched, poised and prepared.

"Horse trader," he said as he drew the Colt and turned to face Summers with the gun pointed at his belly, "don't you ever ride into my town and threaten me —"

Before he could get the words out of his mouth, Summers snatched the gun from his hand. Sheriff Croce found himself facing Summers' drawn Colt; he heard it cock, the tip of the barrel pressed up under his chin.

"You've run all out of threats, Sheriff," Summers said. "Now it's time you start telling me what you know about my horses and who stole them."

But Croce wasn't through yet. He stared at Summers, his head tipped back by the hard point of the gun barrel.

"Have you lost your mind, Summers?" he said. "You can't stick a gun in my face. I'm a lawman —"

"No, you're not," Summers said. "You're just a snake hiding behind a badge, hoping nobody can see through it."

"You'll go to jail for this," Croce said, still not giving up.

"That's better than where you're going if you don't tell me the truth."

"Wha-what are you talking about, Summers?" the sheriff asked, recognizing the determination in Summers' eyes.

"I saw all the marked prints behind the doctor's house. You saw them too," said Summers. "You know who stole my horses, who raped and beat Layla Brooks."

"No, you're wrong. I don't know," Croce said, his voice starting to waver as he sensed that Summers wasn't going to back down. "I saw the horses standing there at the hitch rail, but I didn't see who was —"

"So long, Sheriff," said Summers, cutting him off again sharply. "It's time to paint the ceiling."

"No, wait! Please, Summers!" Croce said, realizing without a doubt that Summers would pull the Colt's trigger any second.

Summers stared at him, keeping the big gun cocked and poised.

"Okay, I saw them," Croce said, speaking quickly. "I don't know who they are, but I did see them come to the doctor's back door. One of the men was badly injured. His scalp had been ripped off by a wolf. They got Dr. Chase to sew it on. They would have killed the doctor if I hadn't come along and stopped them. That's the truth. You've got to believe me."

"It's almost the truth, Croce," Summers said, the gun barrel still up under the sheriff's chin. "But if you hadn't known who these men were, you would have told me all this before. Now, who are they? Who are you protecting?"

Croce broke down. His voice trembled. His eyes filled with terror. "Damn it, man,

I've told you all I can! If I tell you who they are, I'll be dead anyway, as soon as they find out. So go on and kill me, if it means so much to you."

"Dead is dead," Summers whispered with resolve. "So long, Sheriff." His finger closed tighter on the Colt's trigger.

"Summers, listen to me!" Croce screamed out in one final attempt to save himself. "The doctor's whore, Vera, knows who they are. Hell, both those whores know who did it. Why don't you ask them? Or do you just want an excuse to kill me?"

Summers' trigger finger stopped tightening.

"What do you mean, *they both know*?" Summers asked. "Start making sense, Sheriff." He prodded Croce's chin with the tip of the gun barrel.

"Vera Dalton's the one who finished sewing the injured man's scalp back on," the frightened sheriff said. "The other whore knew them long before they did what they did to her."

"She doesn't remember anything, Sheriff," Summers said. "She didn't see their faces, and if she did, it wouldn't matter. Her mind's a blank about everything that happened."

"So she says. Do you believe her, Summers?" the sheriff asked. "I don't. I think she's just afraid to say anything. She knows what those men will come back and do to her. The doctor's whore is scared too . . . So was the doctor himself, for that matter."

Summers stared at the sheriff for a moment, asking himself who in these parts could instill this much fear in so many people. Finally one name sifted through to him.

"Warton Bendigo . . . ," he said aloud.

The sheriff looked as if Summers had just backhanded him across the face.

"What?" he said. "Jesus, *no*! Warton Bendigo has nothing to do with any of this! Summers, you're stepping onto dangerous ground."

"Yep, Warton Bendigo," Summers said, the sheriff's response being all he needed to confirm the matter.

"You're out of your mind!" said Croce. "Warton Bendigo is a wealthy cattleman, a land speculator and, and . . . God knows what all else. He wouldn't stoop to stealing horses, or raping a whore."

"Not Warton Bendigo himself," said Summers, "but I've met some of his men here and there. The only cattle they handle belongs to the big Mexican spreads across the border. Any speculating they do is about

189

how to rob a bank or derail an express car."

"I never said a word about Warton Bendigo or any of his men," Croce insisted, badly shaken by Summers' words. "Don't you mention my name to the man!"

"You're his *gunman* here in Wakely, aren't you, Croce?" Summers said. "He takes care of you, and you keep an eye on who comes and goes here — who might be snooping around for the banks and railroads."

"You're wrong, dead wrong, Summers!" said Croce.

"Don't worry, Sheriff. I won't mention your name when I go get my horses," Summers said. "After all, you didn't tell me it was him. You were ready to take a bullet to keep from telling me."

Croce stared ahead, sweating.

"I'm not telling you nothing," he said, "except that you're going to get yourself killed, you go messing with Bendigo or his men."

"You don't need to tell me anything, Croce," Summers said. "You don't even have to point me toward his spread. I'll just follow the prints from where I left them on the trail."

Summers opened the sheriff's Colt and dropped the bullets one after the other onto the plank floor.

Croce stared down at the bullets, then back up at Summers, his jaw tight.

"What do you think I am, a *back-shooter*?" he asked, his fear turning to anger now that he knew Summers wasn't going to kill him.

Summers eyed him sharply. He closed the empty gun and pitched it to him.

"You don't want to know what I think you are, Croce," he said. "When I come back to Wakely with my horses, if you're still pinned to that badge, I'll put a bullet through it."

Croce bristled a little, seeing Summers lower his Colt back into his holster.

"You're not coming back, Summers," he said, a short, sly grin spreading across his face. "I'll bet a month's pay on it."

Inside the doctor's house, Summers found Vera Dalton rummaging through the drawers of the doctor's oak rolltop desk. When she heard a creak on the wooden floor, she turned, startled, and saw Summers watching her.

"Oh, Will," she said, "I was just looking for something of mine . . . I thought the doctor might have placed it somewhere in his desk."

"I understand, ma'am," Summers said, with little interest in what she might have been looking for. He went straight to the point. "Who was the man with his scalp torn off?"

"I don't know," Vera said.

"Tell me the truth," Summers insisted without getting too demanding.

"I am, Will," she said. "The sheriff came and got me to attend to a wolf attack. But when I got here, the man was gone. I stayed to clean up the room and the surgical instruments . . . because, well, I'd rather be here than at the saloon."

He studied her eyes for any sign of deception, but he saw none.

"Do you know Warton Bendigo, or any of his men?" he asked.

"Warton Bendigo, no," she said. "I understand there's only one dove in the territory he has anything to do with. She worked down in McCabe until she quit and left town."

So far, so good, Summers decided.

She shrugged. "But sure, I know most or all of his men. His crazy sons too. I wouldn't be much of a dove if I didn't know that whole bunch."

Summers looked at her and let out a breath. She wasn't afraid of the Bendigos, and she wasn't lying, he was certain of it. He offered a slight smile, hoping he hadn't been too strong with his words or manner.

"I don't think you're much of a dove anyway, Vera," he said. "I think you're one hell of a fine doctor."

She stared down at the floor for a moment, gathering her emotions; then she raised her face and said, "Why, thank you, Will Summers. It is most kind of you to say so."

"Is Layla sleeping?" he asked.

"Resting," said Vera, "but I'm sure she's not asleep yet. Keeping her eyes closed is best for now. They're healing remarkably well. But you can talk to her if you need to."

"No," Summers said, "let her rest." After a moment's pause, he asked Vera in a lowered tone of voice, "Do you believe she doesn't remember anything about what happened?"

"She's very convincing," Vera said. "I can understand a woman not remembering such a thing —"

"That's not an answer," Summers said quietly, cutting her off.

Vera stared into his eyes for a moment, wanting to know why he was asking, not about to give anything up on her sister of circumstance.

Summers saw the look and said, "Is she going to change her story, if she's pressed very hard to do so?"

"You mean is she going to start remembering things if somebody tries to force her to?" she asked. She shook her head. "No, I don't think so, Will. We come from the same place in life, she and I. Doves give themselves up in the flesh. But what's inside, nobody can force us to turn loose."

Summers nodded.

"Let her rest, Vera. I'm going after my horses," he said. "Tell her I'll be coming back when I finish up with the men who stole them."

"Coming back for her?" Vera asked pointedly.

"I'm coming back to Wakely," he said. Changing the subject, he asked, "You said Warton Bendigo has two crazy sons. What do you mean by crazy?"

"Crazy enough that I should warn you to stay here and forget the horses. But I'm not going to," Vera said. "I figure I'd be wasting my breath. I only hope you're still the *Will Summers* I've heard of."

"I wouldn't know who else to be," Summers said. He nodded toward the doctor's desk. "I hope you find what you're looking for, *Dr. Dalton.*" He turned and walked out the front door toward the hitch rail.

Vera stepped over to the front window and

watched him turn his horse along the side of the house and ride in the direction of his horses' tracks. The dog lingered behind long enough to look back and forth along the street, then turned and bounded along beside the horse.

"You too, Will Summers," she murmured to herself as man, horse and dog rode out of sight.

■ ■ ■ ■

PART 3

■ ■ ■ ■

CHAPTER 14

Warton Bendigo stood up from behind his ornate Spanish desk and looked out through the window across the high rock-walled valley, which only made up a small portion of his territory in Red Cliffs. He raised a cup of coffee to his lips and took a sip from the thick steamy mug. In the distance, three riders came into sight down a rocky trail.

"Who guarded the pass last night, Chip?" he asked over his shoulder. Three gunmen stood from their chairs for a look out across the valley floor.

Chip Bryant, a tall, weather-hardened gunman, adjusted a wad of tobacco to one side of his mouth and stepped closer to the big outlaw.

"Conn Alvarez and Dade Clinton, boss," he said, wondering why Warton Bendigo asked. But Chip knew that questioning anything the hot-tempered outlaw said wasn't a good idea.

A gunman named Ed Murphy looked at the other two and then turned to Bendigo, who was still staring out the window.

"I should go say something to them, boss?" he asked.

"Who?" Bendigo asked over his shoulder.

Murphy looked at the others again, his confidence a little shaken.

"Alvarez and Clinton, boss," he offered in a hesitant tone.

"Why would I want you to talk to them?" Bendigo asked firmly. "Don't I look like I can speak for myself? Or do I need you to do my talking for me?"

Chip grinned to himself, happy to see Murphy squirming. The third gunman, Mitchell Udane, winced and shook his head a little. Bendigo was good at baiting a man. Murphy had walked into it.

"Jesus! No, boss — !"

"Oh, I don't?" Bendigo said, stopping him short.

"No! I mean, no, sir, to you needing somebody to talk for you —"

"Sit down and shut up, Murphy," said Bendigo. "I hate to kill a son of a bitch for being an idiot." He sipped his coffee as Murphy dropped down quickly into this chair. Then he spoke to Bryant.

"Chip," he said, "I want two more men

up there with Alvarez and Clinton tonight. Lots of men have been showing up. I want to make sure they're all ours."

"Sure thing, boss," said Chip. He turned to Murphy and spread his hands a little as if to say, *See, that's how it's done.*

A tense silence set in. Chip stood poised, yet patient. Murphy sat completely still, as if he'd been turned to stone by Bendigo's voice alone. Udane was fidgeting; he couldn't stand it. Finally he took a deep breath.

"Anything else, boss?" he ventured.

Now Chip winced. *These guys never learn . . .*

"Did you hear me say there's *anything else,* Udane?" Bendigo said, spinning around to face the three gunmen, his cup of coffee in hand.

Udane's spine turned to jelly.

"No, sir," he said. "It's just that I thought since nobody was saying anything —"

"You sit down and shut up too," Warton Bendigo barked. But as soon as Udane sat down in his chair, the big outlaw leader growled, "Better still, get your worthless ass out of here. You too, Murphy. I want to talk to my top man *alone,* without having to watch you two scratch your lice."

The two gunmen looked at Chip Bryant

as they stood up to leave. Chip reached out and swung open the door, giving only a sliver of a grin as they filed past him on their way out.

When the two were gone and Chip had shut the door behind them, he stood perfectly still until Bendigo flagged him forward with a broad hand, gesturing for him to sit down.

Chip took a seat and relaxed a little, strategically setting down his hat on the right side of his lap, so as to keep both his gun hand and the butt of his holstered, black-handled Colt out of sight. Bendigo took note of it; he liked it. He liked seeing a man who stayed ready for anything. He liked a man who was as tough as he was.

"Chip, are you afraid of me?" he asked gravely.

"No, sir, boss," Chip said without hesitation. "I am afraid of no man."

"Most of my men are," said Bendigo.

"Yes, sir," said Bryant coolly. "But that's them. It's not me, sir."

Bendigo nodded firmly. He stepped back over to his desk, set his cup down and picked up a fancifully engraved Colt. He cocked and uncocked the gun idly as he spoke, noting that his action didn't appear to intimidate Chip Bryant.

"I'm sure you saw the horses my sons brought through here the other day?" he said.

"Yes, sir, I saw them," said Chip.

"Fine-looking horses, eh?" Bendigo said.

"Yes, sir, they were," said Chip.

"How do you suppose they got them?" Bendigo asked, knowing that the gunman would be honest with him.

"Stole them, sir. Just like they said," Chip responded without hesitation.

Bendigo shrugged, lowering the engraved Colt and pitching it over onto a stack of paper on his desk.

"Hell, of course they stole them," he said, "just like I taught them to do. What kind of fool pays for horses when they're standing all over the place, most of them saddled and ready to ride?" He gave a short, wry smile.

Chip returned the expression. He could see the old man was trying to put himself into a better mood.

"I feel much the same way, sir," Chip said.

"We all do," said Bendigo, "even those of us who won't admit it." He raised a finger and shook it a little for emphasis. "Every man who is a man wants to *steal* a horse," he declared. "It's bred into our nature."

Chip only nodded. He sat quietly, knowing Bendigo didn't keep him here to share his philosophy on man's innate need to steal horses.

"But those two no-good sons of mine are lying to me, Chip!" he said, exploding suddenly, slamming his broad open hand down on his desktop. "I know it in my bones."

"About what, boss?" Chip asked, trading *sir* for *boss* now that it appeared Bendigo was bringing him into his confidence.

"Dow said they killed the man and woman they stole the horses from — *leave no witnesses,* just the way I taught them," said Bendigo. "But I don't believe him."

Chip stared at him, waiting for more.

"He told me they stole them from a squatter up above Whiskey Bend, where the wolf attacked him," Bendigo continued. "You saw the horses — do they look like they belonged to some ragged-assed squatter to you?"

"They looked too good to belong to any squatter I ever run across," Chip said.

"See?" Warton Bendidgo shook his finger again. "It's a damn lie! They're both lying to me and I want to know why. I want to know what they're hiding and I want you to find out for me, Chip. Do you understand me?"

"Yep." Chip shrugged. "You want me to get close to them and hear the truth on the matter."

"Yes," said Bendigo. He plopped down into his chair with a sigh. "It's not the kind of thing a father likes to ask of another man. A fellow likes to think that he can beat the living hell out of his sons — bullwhip them, pistol-whip them, whatever he needs to do to get the truth out of them. But I've done everything in the past short of setting them on fire. Nothing works. I need help here, and I need it to be our little secret."

"Nobody will ever hear about it from me, boss," said Chip.

Bendigo shook his head slowly in reflection.

"A man never knows how his sons will turn out," he said sadly. "I tried to raise them to be the toughest, meanest, thievingest sonsabitches this side of hell, the way my pa raised me. But it's hard raising boys on your own. Neither one of their mothers was worth spit in a bucket." He paused for a moment, and then added, "But I tried raising them to be just like me — that's all I knew, after all."

"And that's all you could do, boss," Chip said quietly.

"If my pa ever caught me leaving a *living witness* behind anything I ever done, he would have skinned me alive and charged folks to watch him do it."

"Times change," said Chip with regret. "I'll find out everything I can, boss. You can count on it."

"Don't let them bulldog you, Chip," Bendigo said. "They're both headstrong, and would just as soon kill a man as tip their hats. Gaining their trust will be difficult. It might take you a while to find out anything."

"I'll watch my step, boss," said Chip. "You'll be surprised how quick I'll get them to trust me."

"Dow will be your best bet to learn anything," Bendigo advised him. "The Injun won't talk unless he's doped out of his skull on peyote. Then it won't make any sense what he says anyway. The closemouthed bastard ain't worth the juice it took to squirt him into the world."

Chip watched him grow angrier as he spoke.

Finally, Bendigo settled down a little. He reached a shaky hand toward a whiskey bottle.

"Do what you can, Chip," he said. "I owe it to everybody here to know what goes on away from here, so we don't have to jump and get struck by surprise. I want to know, and I want to know fast."

"I'll get it done as fast as I can, boss,"

Chip said, standing and putting on his hat.

"Start by riding out and seeing who's riding in." He jerked a thumb toward the window. "If one of them is 'Blue Hand' Berger, he might know something about those damn stolen horses."

"I'm on my way, boss," said Chip, heading out the door.

Just outside the office, Chip saw Udane and Mitchell milling at the front door. He identified their questioning stares as he walked past them.

"Go find 'Shotgun' Holder, tell him to get over here," was all he said.

"Sure thing," said Murphy.

The two watched Chip walk to the hitch rail, gather his reins, step atop his horse and ride away.

From inside a branding pen, Dow and Tom Bendigo had both seen the three riders come down off the high trail. As the riders advanced, the brothers recognized Bertram Berger among the men. They gave each other a look and walked to their horses, peeling off their gloves and brushing ashes and the waft of burnt hair from their coat sleeves. The two shallow bullet wounds on Dow's shoulder were healing quickly; so was the bullet graze on the half-breed's throat.

"I wonder what happened to Albert Knox," Dow said sidelong, realizing that Berger was leading Knox's horse.

His Indian half brother made no reply.

As they stepped into their saddles, Dow eyed Tom up and down, an angry look on his face.

"It wouldn't kill you to say something every now and then," he said.

Tom only stared at him, his dark eyes completely flat.

"Hell, forget it," Dow said, jerking his horse around toward the distant riders. "You've never said anything worth listening to anyway."

They booted their horses out across a dusty flatland spotted with clumps of wild grass and broom sage.

Before they had gone a hundred yards, Chip Bryant galloped up alongside Dow and waved his hat. The two looked over at him in surprise.

"Didn't you hear me ride up?" Chip called out, putting his hat back atop his head as they galloped along. "It's a good thing I wasn't dogging you two," he added. "You'd have been in the stew."

Tom and Dow just looked at each other.

"Where the hell are you going, Chip Bryant?" Dow asked, slowing his horse a little as they talked.

"Where does it look like?" Chip replied. He gave a stiff grin. "I'm going along with you two troublemakers."

Dow and Tom slowed their horses to a halt and stared at the gunman, their hands close to their holstered guns.

"What makes you think you are?" Dow asked bluntly.

Chip Bryant took a breath and let it out with a cagey look on his face.

"Don't get your shirt twisted, Dow," he said in warning, his hand also close to his big holstered Colt. "I'm only following orders, doing what your pa told me to do. He wants me to warm up to you two horse turds, get close enough that you'll start telling about them stolen horses and the people you stole them from."

"Oh," said Dow, "I see . . . you're like one of them Pinkerton men."

He eased his hand away from his gun, but Tom kept his hand in the same position.

"Yeah, something like that" said Chip. "I'm what you might call a spy for Warton Bendigo. So you best start showing me some respect, else I'll tell your daddy on you."

Tom cocked his Colt, wasting no time as he started lifting it from his holster. But

Dow held a hand toward him, stopping him.

"Easy, Brother Cat," he said, keeping his eyes on Chip Bryant. "Let the man do what he's told. He's already got my attention." He grinned, then said to Bryant, "What can we tell you that'll make your job easier for you?"

Hearing Tom uncock his Colt, Chip sidled over closer to Dow and the three rode forward together, abreast, this time slower.

"For starters, what the hell really happened to your head?" Chip asked. "When your pa said a wolf jumped you, I just about rolled on the floor." He chuckled and shook his head.

"Oh, really . . . ?" Dow raised his hat from his head and let Chip see the stitches outlining the healing wounds. A small part of his scalp still lay agape where he'd left without waiting for Vera Dalton to come finish sewing it.

"Holy aces and kings," said Chip, staring at the wounds. "Looks like you got caught stiff-legging some Indian chief's daughter!"

Staring at him blankly, Dow said, "What if I told you I really did get attacked by a wolf?"

Chip sighed and let out a breath. "Then I'd have to say my ride out here was all for nothing. You're just too damn hardheaded for me to deal with."

Dow and Chip both heard Tom's Colt cock again.

"Tell him to keep that damn gun down where it belongs," said Chip. "I've had guns cocked at me since my grandparents first came to visit."

"Brother Cat, listen to him," Dow said. "Can't you see the man wants us to all three be friends?"

Tom's gun uncocked again.

To Chip, Dow said, "The horse trader we robbed had a big dog. The cur did this to me while I was fixing to kill the man's woman."

Chip nodded and smiled to himself.

"That sounds better," he said. "Why don't you tell me the whole damned mess, and I'll work it around to something your pa can *believe* when I go to tell him?"

After a pause, Dow looked Bryant up and down appraisingly. "You know, Chip, our pa is getting older — what you might call *soft under his topknot.*"

Chip listened intently.

"It hurts me to say this," Dow continued, "but there's a day coming when the best thing for that old bull will be a bullet between his horns — send him off to that much longed-for green pasture in the sky."

"Sadly, what you're saying is true," Chip agreed.

"I know," said Dow, "and when that dreaded day comes, we're going to need somebody to stand behind that bullet and make sure it sticks deep enough in his brain." He gave Chip a sidelong glance and added, "Any idea who might cotton to such a job?"

"Let me think on that," Chip said with a dark chuckle. "I'll see who I can come up with." In afterthought, he asked, "By the way, where is that string of houses?"

Dow grinned. "I took them away from here, for safekeeping."

As the three of them booted their horses up into a run, kicking up chunks of earth behind their pounding hooves, Chip glanced back toward the ranch house.

Was that fast enough? he said to himself, as if talking to Warton Bendigo.

CHAPTER 15

The Mexican, Chulo, Rowe Jolsyn and Bertram Berger rode at a steady pace, watching the three men approach. When Chip Bryant and the Bendigo brothers drew close enough to be recognized, Chulo pushed his broad sombrero up off his sweaty forehead and let it fall down behind his shoulders, hanging from its rawhide strap. He slowed his horse almost to a stop.

"What have we done to deserve such an important welcoming party as this?" he said to the other two, who also slowed down beside him, Berger still leading Albert Knox's horse by its reins.

When Berger set eyes on Dow and Tom Bendigo, his face turned ashen with fear. The Mexican and Jolsyn both noticed, but they made no comment.

"Damn, I didn't know I was so popular," Berger said, trying to sound confident.

"Who said it's even about you, Blue

Hand?" Jolsyn said, eyeing him up and down.

Berger ducked his head a little and sat in silence as the Bendigos and Chip rode in closer and came to a halt.

"Hola, amigos," said Chulo, throwing up a hand in greeting.

"Stick your greasy hand in your pocket, Mex," said Dow Bendigo. He cut his horse away from Chulo and Jolsyn, stopping in front of Berger.

"Where the hell have you been, Blue Hand?" he said in an angry voice. "Where's Albert?" He looked at Knox's horse, then back at Berger.

"Albert's dead, Dow," Berger said. "As for where I've been," he continued, using the lie he'd been rehearsing in his mind. "I've been busy fighting like a wild man, trying to save his life and mine —"

"Hold it," said Dow, cutting him off. He looked at the Mexican and Rowe Jolsyn. "You two ride on; go water your horses. None of this concerns you."

Chulo and Jolsyn looked at each other. Jolsyn started to say something, but he saw Chip Bryant shake his head slightly in a silent warning.

"Right you are, Dow," Jolsyn said. He and the Mexican cut their horses away from the four riders and booted the tired animals on toward the big timber and stone ranch standing in the distance.

As the two rode away, Dow sidled right up against Berger's horse and sat with his hand on the butt of his Colt.

"Start talking, Blue Hand," he said.

"Start talking . . . ?" asked Berger. "What do you mean?"

"I mean tell me exactly the same story you're going to tell our pa when you're standing in front of him with your hat in your hands."

"Damn it, Dow," said Berger, "I'm going to tell him just what happened after you and Tom left Wakely. I'm not going to tell him anything about the horses or Will Summers and Layla Brooks —"

Dow grabbed Berger by the front his shirt before he could even finish.

"If you so much as say her name again, I'm going to kill you, Blue Hand. Kill you and let the buzzards pick over your innards. You understand?"

"Yes! I do, Dow!" said Berger, shaken by the crazy, wild-eyed gunman.

"Now, then, word for word," Dow said, still gripping Berger by the shirt, "from right when Tom and I cut out with the string of horses."

"Okay," said Berger, speaking quickly, "but before I go over the story I'm going to tell your pa, I need to tell you what happened after you and Tom left Wakely."

Dow turned loose of his shirt. Chip Bryant listened closely.

"Will Summers and the woman *whose name I can't say* rode into town, straight to the doctor's office."

"Damn it," said Dow. "They're both still alive?"

"Yes, they are," said Berger. "The woman was in bad shape. Summers was banged up, but nothing to stop him, or even slow him down for that matter."

Chip sat taking it all in with his head lowered a little.

"We sicced a gunman named 'Flat-Head' Logan McCorkle on Summers, but that big cur warned him, and Summers killed Flat-Head deader than hell."

"That *damned dog*!" said Dow, his fists clenching tight at the thought of the big cur. "Wait 'til I get my bare hands around his neck! I'll choke him to death and watch his tongue swell up and his eyes bug out of his dog head!"

"That ain't all, Dow," said Berger. "Knox and I followed Summers up into the hill range and had him all set for an ambush,

216

but everything went wrong. Summers killed Albert." He held up the reins to Knox's horse in his hand. "I managed to save his horse."

"He'd be proud to know that," Dow said, staring skeptically at the reins in Berger's hand. "I suppose you can tell me what time all this took place," he said coolly.

"Huh?" Berger looked confused.

"I see you're wearing a watch now," Dow commented, gesturing at the watch fob hanging from "Blue Hand" Berger's vest pocket. As he spoke, he idly drummed his fingers on his gun butt.

"*Oh!* Yes, I am," Berger said, continuing to lie. "This belonged to Dr. Chase. He got himself shot in the fracas between us and Summers. He was riding with the horse trader — gone out to look after the blind whore, I suppose."

"Layla Brooks is blind?" Dow asked.

"As a bat, I hear," said Berger. "Not only blind, but she can't remember a damn thing that happened to her," he said. He offered a cautious grin.

Dow stopped tapping his fingers. He shot Tom a glance, then looked back at Berger.

"So the news in not all bad, eh, Blue Hand?" He chuckled under his breath.

"Not all of it," said Berger, finally feeling

a little relieved. "But I've got a feeling Summers is riding this way. The horses' tracks were clear. I figure he'll be back on their trail as soon as he figures out what to do with the blind whore."

Dow sighed and gave a patient smile.

"We will just have to deal with that when the time comes," he said. Again he sidled his horse over close to Berger. "I bet you are one hungry sumbitch, ain't you?"

"It's been a long, hard night. I could eat; that's a fact," Berger said, glancing off toward the ranch house in the distance.

Looking toward his brother, Dow lifted the reins to Knox's horse from Berger's hands.

"Brother Cat Tracker," Dow said, "why don't you take Berger over to the hills there and fix his breakfast?"

Berger looked scared, sensing the hidden message in Dow's words. He thought about the gun in his holster, but he knew that Dow would be just as quick to draw his gun. Seeing no other option, he jerked his horse around quickly and booted it back along the dusty trail.

Chip Bryant sat watching stone-faced as Tom gigged his horse and rode after Berger at a slower, almost leisurely pace.

From the window of his office, Warton Bendigo stared out past Chulo and Jolsyn as they rode closer to the front yard. He stood with his hands folded behind his back, watching "Blue Hand" Berger ride away from his half-Indian son in a stir of dust.

The aging outlaw leader shook his head when he saw Berger's horse take a headlong spill just as Berger turned in his saddle and began firing his Colt wildly at Tom Bendigo.

Hearing the gunshots, Chulo and Jolsyn both turned in their saddles and looked back at the stretch of flatland where the half-breed rode on through the rising swirl of dust. Berger's horse flailed its legs wildly until it flipped itself upright and whinnied loudly.

"What the hell is this?" Chulo asked Jolsyn. In the distance they saw Berger struggle to his feet and back away quickly from Tom Bendigo.

"It's nothing we want to see," said Jolsyn, turning his eyes away and staring forward.

Warton Bendigo watched with detachment as Berger held his hands chest high, pleading for his life. His half-Indian son pressed his horse forward one slow step at a time.

The half-breed aimed and cocked his Colt at Berger from twenty feet away. Bendigo saw the Colt buck slightly in Tom's hand; he saw the blast of gray smoke streak out and curl upward. He heard the pop of the single shot roll across the rocky ground as "Blue Hand" Berger fell back limply in the dirt.

Good shot, he thought.

He watched Tom step down from his saddle, walk over and stoop next to the dead man. In spite of all the doubts he had about his sons, he had to admit that at times like this, they still caused his chest to swell with pride — they were ruthless, bloodthirsty. He smiled to himself and let out a breath, watching Tom go through the dead man's pockets and lift what appeared to be a watch from his vest. He had to admit, if it came to killing one of them and letting the other one live, he wasn't sure which son he'd choose. They both had their ways.

He knew his sons wanted to take what was his. It's only natural that a young man comes to the point in his life when he's ready to kill his pa and step into the boss's saddle. Bendigo's smile faded from his face, and was replaced with a harsh, grim stare.

He wasn't giving up anything he'd acquired without a fight, he told himself. *Not to these good-for-nothing sonsabitches . . .*

When the Bendigo bothers and Chip Bryant filed into Warton Bendigo's office, their eyes immediately went to the corner where a tall, rawboned man stood staring somberly at them. The man wore a brown derby cocked jauntily to one side of his head, and a black linen suit a size too small for him, his knobby wrists showing below his coat sleeves. A double-barreled shotgun lay draped over his left forearm.

"What the hell was that about out there?" Warton Bendigo said, thumbing toward the window with no greeting for his sons. "I saw the whole thing."

"That was a personal matter," Dow said. "If you saw it, you know that Blue Hand shot first at Brother Cat Tracker. All Tom did was defend himself."

Warton Bendigo knew what Dow said didn't completely explain the altercation. There was a lot more to it, he was certain, but he also knew it was useless to try discussing the matter any further. Instead, he took a deep breath and let it out, trying to hold on to some degree of patience, or at least grasp a bit of self-control. He cocked and uncocked the ornate Colt he held by his side.

"So, Tom," he said, changing the subject, turning his gaze to his half-breed son, "where'd your shot hit ol' Blue Hand?"

Tom stared at him stone-faced for a second, then lifted his finger and tapped himself between his eyes.

"No kidding, son?" said the aging outlaw leader, stifling a proud grin. "I could see it was a good shot from here, but damn . . ."

"Old man," Dow said to his father, his eyes still locked on the black-suited man in the corner, "what's 'Shotgun' Holder doing here?"

Warton Bendigo stopped clicking the Colt's hammer, leaving the pistol cocked at his side. Dow's "old man" comment didn't go unnoticed. The offense was worth a rap in the teeth any day of the week, but he had more important matters to tend to.

"Morton and I were talking about setting up a train raid," Bendigo said matter-of-factly. "Some of us still work for a living. Right, Holder?" he asked the grim-faced man in the corner.

"Some of us work for a living," Morton "Shotgun" Holder repeated in a flat tone.

Dow wasn't buying it, but he had to let it go, for now anyway. He cut a glance to his half-breed brother. Tom didn't appear concerned that Holder was standing in the corner, a shotgun over his left arm, his right hand resting on his left forearm just over the gun hammers. Neither did Chip, Dow thought as he slid his eyes over him.

"Okay," Dow said. "So, when is this robbery? I could use a good pay."

"We haven't set it up yet," Warton Bendigo said. "First, I need to know what you and Cat Tracker might have left hanging on your back trail. You lost a bunch of money I trusted you with."

Dow shrugged. "Yeah, gambling and whoring," he said, as if that should be enough explanation to justify anything that had happened.

"I've forgotten about the money," the outlaw leader said, keeping his temper under control. "What I still can't get straight is the matter of the stolen horses. Who you stole them from, whether or not you killed him —"

"*Jesus!*" said Dow, cutting him off sharply. "Again with the damn stolen horses?" He flashed a heated look at the half-breed, then back to their father. "Is there ever going to be an end to this? I'm ready to go shoot every damned one of those cayuses just to get it settled and done with!"

"Tell me everything one more time, Dow," Warton Bendigo said, keeping his voice in a low and even tone. "I can't help myself." He gave a short shrug. "Call me an overly concerned father."

"No," Dow said stubbornly, "I'm through talking about it. I told you everything . . . We stole the horse string and killed the squatter and his woman. That's all; *that's it.* End of the whole damned story!"

"No, not yet, *boy,*" Warton Bendigo said in a strong tone, not about to back off. "Not until I've gotten the truth on it. What would Blue Hand have said that was bad enough it got him killed?"

"Nothing, damn it," Dow shouted. His temper was blowing out of control. Tom stood watching, his face blank. "All right, *old man,*" said Dow. "Why don't you ask Chip! He was there. He heard everything that was said between us and Berger."

Warton Bendigo and his sons turned to Chip Bryant with questioning stares.

"What about it, Bryant?" said the outlaw leader. "Were you able to find out anything?"

"He told me everything, boss," Chip said coolly.

"What?" Dow cut in with a look of feigned shock and surprise on his face. "You mean

224

you had Chip *spying* for you, trying to weasel his way in with Tom and me?"

Warton Bendigo ignored Dow and Tom. He looked at Chip in surprise, wondering how he could have learned anything in such a short time.

"It's like he just said, boss," said Chip. "They stole the horses and set about killing the man and woman they belonged to. They left the man tied to a tree to die, and shot the woman in the face."

Dow and Tom shot each other a smug grin, hearing Chip take their side.

"Only the man was Will Summers, and he didn't die," Chip continued. "The woman didn't die either. They shot her in the face — blinded her. But she lived through it."

Chip paused only long enough to see the stunned and puzzled look on Dow's face. Then he went on.

"The woman is Layla Brooks, boss," he said. "Berger was on his way to tell them that Summers is on his way here . . . with quite a mad-on, would be my guess."

"Why, you dirty, double-crossing son of a — !" Dow started to take a step toward Chip, and so did the half-breed, but Chip's Colt came up from his holster slick and fast. The gunman cocked it.

"Hold it right there, both of you!" Warton

225

shouted at his sons. They both stopped, not because of their father, but because "Shotgun" Holder moved forward from his corner, the double-barrel swinging up into play.

"You shot Layla Brooks?" Warton raged. "You know how I feel about that woman, and you *shot her*?" His face grew livid with fury.

"Yep, Tom shot her," Dow said, as if it meant nothing to him. "I would have, but he got to her first. Of course we both poked her until her eyes crossed." He gave a wide, cruel grin. "I can see why you liked pulling her knees apart." He shot his father a wink.

"He also talked about me killing you, boss, so him and Cat Tracker can take over," Chip threw in.

"You dirty, *rotten* — !" Warton Bendigo could take no more. He raised the engraved Colt and fired. "Shotgun" Holder quickly pulled back both gun hammers on his double-barrel.

"Kill these *sonsabitches*!" Warton shouted, his voice choking with rage as the Colt bucked in his hand.

CHAPTER 16

Warton Bendigo and Morton "Shotgun" Holder both fired as one at Dow. The half-breed ducked out of the way as the room exploded with gunfire. But Dow was too quick for them. Having sensed trouble when he'd first walked in and seen Holder in the corner with his double-barrel, he'd deliberately positioned himself near the window.

As both pistol and shotgun exploded, he hurled himself sidelong, crashed through the window and hit the ground outside, running toward his horse.

With Warton Bendigo, "Shotgun" Holder and Chip Bryant all focused on killing Dow as he fled across the rocky yard, it wasn't hard for the half-breed to slip across the floor and out of the room like a waft of smoke. Firing out the window, the three didn't realize Tom was gone until they saw him appear outside at the horses and jump into his saddle beside Dow.

Warton Bendigo turned from the window when his ornate Colt stopped firing and the hammer began falling on chamber after chamber of spent rounds.

"Damn it to hell!" he shouted.

He fanned his free hand back and forth through a thick cloud of gun smoke. He jerked open a desk drawer, pulled out a wooden box of bullets and emptied it atop his desk. "All this shooting, and the only thing we hit is a *water trough*?"

"They can't get far," said Bryant, jerking bullets from his belt and reloading.

"Shotgun" Holder broke open his double-barrel and reloaded as Warton and Chip walked hurriedly out of the office, making their way to the hitch rail.

Other gunmen appeared out of nowhere at the sound of gunshots. They began to gather in closer around Warton Bendigo and watch the two riders race across the flatlands, leaving a wall of swirling dust in their wake.

"Who the hell was that?" asked Lucian Clay, who ran up beside Warton, half of his face still covered with frothy shaving soap, a cloth tucked into his open collar. He held a big Remington revolver pointed skyward in his right hand.

"My *good-for-nothing* sons," Warton Bendigo shouted.

Lucian cut a glance to Chip, who gave him a cautioning look.

"Damn, boss," said Lucian Clay. "What happened?"

"They've gone out on their own and dragged a heap of trouble back on all of us," said Bendigo, staring out at the swirl of trail dust.

Recognizing that the outlaw leader was in no mood to explain anything, Lucian Clay sidled over to Chip Bryant.

In a low and guarded tone, Chip said, "They misused Layla Brooks and tried to kill her. Blinded her, is what we're told."

"Jesus . . . ," Lucian murmured, yanking the cloth from beneath his chin and wiping his half-shaved face with it. In a whisper he said, "Warton cares a lot about that whore. Looks like we've got some work cut out for ourselves, catching those two bummers."

"There's more," said Chip. "The horses they led in here? They stole them from a man you should remember. Will Summers," he said flatly.

"Well now, *Will Summers,*" said Lucian Clay. "You're damn right I remember him. He killed a bunch of my pards."

"I know," said Chip. "It looks like you might get the chance to say howdy to him.

229

'Blue Hand' Berger talked like Summers is headed this way."

Lucian Clay gave him a bemused look as he finished wiping shaving soap from his jaw.

"Damn, Chip, you're plumb full of useful information today," he said.

"I try to help anytime I see the chance," said Chip in a wry tone.

Warton Bendigo shoved the engraved Colt down behind his waist sash and turned to face the gathering men at the hitch rail.

"All of yas, listen up!" he shouted loud enough to be heard across the front yard. "I'm not going to repeat myself. My sons Dow and Tom have brought trouble on us. They stole that fine string of horses from Will Summers, and didn't have enough sense to kill him before they rode away."

Hushed voices commented back and forth among the men. Warton Bendigo looked ashamed.

"All right, I know how bad that is, leaving a living witness behind," he said. "But I might as well admit they did it and clear the air. Summers is coming, is my guess. I want everybody here to be ready for him. Nobody rides into Red Cliffs without being invited."

Lucian Clay stepped forward, his hand

resting on his holstered Colt. He wadded up the cloth he'd wiped his lathered face on and threw it aside.

"I am ready for him, boss," he said. "I've been ready and waiting for that horse-trading snake every since he killed the Peltrys."

"Then this is your lucky day," said Warton, "because I'm sending you after him, and I'm going to pay a hundred dollars to anybody who brings me his head on a stick."

Lucian Clay grinned and rubbed his hands together.

"Boss, I'll scour Red Cliffs from end to end until we find him," he said. "This is what Goose and Mose Peltry would have me do to avenge them. I can see them cheering us in hell right this minute."

Warton gave Clay a look.

"Anyway, that's the deal," Bendigo said. "One hundred dollars for his head!" He raised a finger above his head for emphasis. "Now get your Wind River boys and get after him. Tell them to have their bark on. Kill him as soon as he shows his face along the trail."

"Consider it done, boss," said Clay. He looked at four surly gunmen as they came walking up from the bunkhouse. "Here they come now." He grinned. "These boys always have their bark on."

As Clay walked away to meet the four gunmen, a man named Roy Cary asked Warton, "What about Dow and Cat Tracker?"

"What about them?" Bendigo asked in gruff response.

"What are you offering the man who kills them for you?" Roy Cary asked.

"What the hell is wrong with you, Roy?" Bendigo asked. "These are my sons you're talking about. I'll kill them *myself* when the time comes."

As Lucian Clay walked past Chip Bryant, Chip leaned in close to him and said, "Good luck to you and the Wind River boys, scouring Red Cliffs from end to end. Buffaloes have been born and died of old age crossing this place end to end."

"I'm not worried about it," said Lucian Clay.

"Do we look like *buffaloes* to you?" one of the Wind River gunmen asked in a testy voice, his hand resting on his gun butt.

"Not so much at a distance," Chip replied, standing firm, his hand resting in the same position.

Will Summers had made good time along the trail to where the fading hoofprints of the horse string led on toward the distant hill line. Beyond and above the hill line stood a tall, rugged and seemingly endless mountain range.

Red Cliffs . . . , he told himself, singling out the part of the range known to be a former stronghold of the Crow, the Burnt Leg Sioux and countless other renegade bands and outlaw gangs since the end of the Civil War. Now the Red Cliffs lay under the ironhanded rule of one man. *Warton Bendigo,* he reminded himself, nudging his horse on, past the path turning up toward the miner's shack.

Evening shadows leaned long out of the west by the time he reached the turn toward the watering hole. The dog had gone on ahead of him and disappeared a half hour earlier. But now he saw the dog coming back through the wavering heat. He watched him lope along toward him at a much slower pace until he finally slowed to a walk, his head lowered, his tongue lolling.

Looking down at the dog, then back up at the evening sky, Summers caught the first sight of circling buzzards above the water hole. He nudged his horse on and prepared himself for whatever lay ahead. Yet he still felt a jolt in his stomach when he saw the bloated, half-eaten remains of the Appaloosa mare lying with her belly ripped wide open by the big, greasy carrion hunters.

He noted the bullet hole in the mare's forehead and felt the anger rise inside him. A few feet away lay the ragged remnants of the mare's foal, its empty eye sockets and tongueless mouth gaping skyward.

Summers forced himself to look away from the gruesome scene and drew his bandanna up over the bridge of his nose against the terrible stench. He managed to swallow the boiling anger growing in his chest. It was just more reason to kill the men who did this.

The water had gone bad, he thought, seeing the dark tint stretching across both sides of the rock basin. Leastwise, he wasn't about to drink it, nor was the horse beneath him, he thought. He had a rope. He could pull the dead mare out. But leaving her was the best warning he could give anybody who stopped here.

He tapped his bootheels to the horse's sides and forced it on. He had brought two canteens full of water with him, which he always did traveling these high plains, even in early spring. The water would be warm and stale tasting. But it would have to do for him, the horse and the big cur until he reached Red Cliffs.

He rode on.

When he ran out of light, he made a fire-less camp in a deep-cut gully, sipped a little warm water for himself and poured a small ration into his upturned hat, first for the horse, then for the dog. Afterward, he spread his blanket beneath the purple-gold light of the full moon and stars. He dozed with his back against a rock and his rifle beside him, careful not to allow himself to sleep soundly. Three feet away, the dog lay curled into a ball.

In the middle of the night, the dog stirred and growled so low under his breath that Summers didn't hear it at first. Yet when the dog rose from the ground and stood crouched with his head leveled low and his hackles up, Summers awoke. He eased away from the rock in a crouch, moving silently over to the edge of the gully.

"Easy, Buddy," he whispered, hearing the faint click of a horse's hooves on the hard trail.

He looked out across the shadowy, purple terrain, his rifle in hand, and saw the wispy image of a single rider moving along the trail from the direction of the water hole.

As the rider drew nearer, he saw a familiar slender outline silhouetted against the starlit sky.

"Layla . . . ?" he whispered to himself, not believing his own eyes as the rider drew closer.

Having stepped over beside him, the dog settled down, lowered his hackles and even shook his tail, removing any doubts from Summers' mind.

"Layla Brooks, over here," Summers said in a calm, even tone, not wanting to startle her or spook her horse and send it running on the rutted and rocky trail. He was amazed she had made it this far, the condition her eyes were in.

"Will!" she said, seeing him stand up in the moonlight and step into sight. "Oh, thank God! Keep talking so I can find you."

"I'm right here, Layla, coming to you," Summers said, stepping forward in the moon- and starlight.

"Yes, yes, I see you!" Layla said. She hurried the horse a few steps closer to him, stepped down out of the saddle and led the horse forward.

It took her a second to get her cloudy vision fixed on Summers, but then she appeared to have no trouble locating him, even as she stumbled a little on the rocky ground. The dog stepped over the edge of the gulley and stood to the side, watching, wagging his tail.

"Right here, Layla, keep coming, straight ahead," Summers said, continuing to talk in order to help her find him until she stood in his arms.

"Oh, Will," she said, "I hope you're not angry at me." She clutched him to her in an almost desperate embrace. "I know it was foolish . . . but I had to come find you."

"You took a terrible risk, riding out here at night, your eyes the way they are," Summers said.

"Yes, you're right. I know I did," Layla said, still holding him tight, excited that she had found him. "When Vera told me where you were headed, I had to come. I rented a horse from the livery and headed right out. Vera tried to talk me out of it . . ." She paused, smiling to herself. "But she knows how stubborn we doves can be when we get our minds set on doing something."

They turned each other loose but stood close, face-to-face in the moonlight. Summers brushed a strand of her hair from her bandaged cheek.

"You should have listened to her," he said. "This is no place for you."

"Yes, it is," Layla said. "My place is by your side. I know you followed those men out here because of what they did to me. I couldn't just sit there in town doing nothing while you're out here putting your life on the line."

Summers wasn't going to tell her that he had not come out here on her behalf — well, not entirely, that is. He was after his horses, something he would have done to begin with had it not been for needing to help her.

"It's going to get dangerous when I try to find a way into Red Cliffs without getting shot at," he said. "First thing in the morning, you're going back to Wakely."

"I can't go back to Wakely, Will," she said quietly but firmly. "I have no water. The only water hole back that way is bad. The next water is on the other side of Red Cliffs. That's the only direction I can take now." She stared at him with resolve.

Summers paused, knowing she was right. He was also curious as to how she knew so much about the trail to Red Cliffs.

Reading the question in his eyes, Layla said, "I have traveled this trail many times, Will. Warton Bendigo used to send for me. He and I were close, right up until I took up with Lee Persons last year."

Summers knew what *close* meant; he didn't have to ask. But this put a different turn on things — or did it?

"Layla . . . ," he said, letting out a breath.

"It was Bendigo's sons who did this to you."

"No, they wouldn't have done this," she said after a few seconds of consideration. "They wouldn't dare. Warton Bendigo would tear their hearts out if they ever laid a hand on me."

"Not if you were dead," Summers replied. "Whoever did this had no intention of leaving you alive."

"I — I can't believe that, Will," she said, rubbing her temple as if it hurt trying to remember. "If only my memory would come back to me. I try . . . but it's blank."

"You've got the rest of the night to try," Will said, quietly but firmly. "Come morning, I'm taking you back, while I've got enough water to get us there if we keep it rationed short."

"But, Will, your horses," she said. "You're too close to turn back now. The horses' tracks won't last forever. You can't put it off any longer."

Summers managed to hold his tongue. She was right. He was too close to turn back now. But she left him no choice. He pictured the Appaloosa mare and her foal lying dead and picked over by vultures. He pictured his own silver-gray dapple, the three dark bays, the paint horse, the black Morgan cross. He was starting to wonder if he'd ever

239

see them again.

"Get a little rest," he said. "Then we're leaving. We'll travel by moonlight — cheat the sun as much as we can."

CHAPTER 17

An hour later, as Summers resaddled both horses and readied them for the trail, he looked over to where Layla lay resting on his blanket.

"Get up, Layla," he said. "It's time to go."

She didn't answer.

"Layla, get up," Summers said again, his voice quiet but loud enough to be heard.

The dog stood up from the dirt, walked over and poked his nose down against Layla's back. He gave one short bark and stood back.

Still no response.

Summers walked over and stooped down beside the blanket, a curious look on his face. He shook Layla's shoulder gently.

"Layla . . . ?" he said. "Are you asleep?"

She stirred slightly, raising a weak hand and holding his forearm.

"I'm . . . not feeling . . . so good, Will," she said, her voice sounding shaky.

Summers stared at her for a moment. They had talked some more after she had lain down to rest on his blanket. She'd finally agreed that perhaps it was best if she went back to Wakely.

"Is it your wounds bothering you?" he asked.

"No," she said in a raspy voice, "it's my stomach. It hurts something awful." She hugged an arm across her stomach. "And I'm burning up inside. I feel like . . . I've been poisoned."

Summers felt her forehead. It was hot, but not overly hot. He ran a hand inside her dress onto her shoulder. It felt the same.

"What have you eaten before leaving Wakely?" he asked.

"Just stew . . . and some biscuits," she said. "That's not it. It was the water . . . I shouldn't have drunk it."

Summers looked at her, stunned.

"You drank water from the water hole after seeing it was bad?" he asked.

"I was . . . so thirsty," she said. "I rode around to the other side, away from the mare. I only . . . drank a little. I couldn't stand the thought of what was in it."

"Jesus," said Summers. "It only takes a little. You've poisoned yourself."

She managed to grip his arm more firmly

and stared up at him with her right eye.

"Will, am I going to die?" she asked.

Summers didn't answer. Instead, he looked all around in the grainy moonlight as if searching for something that could help her.

"Will," she repeated, "am I going to die . . . from drinking bad water?"

What next? Summers thought, cursing to himself.

"No, not if we get you somewhere quick enough," he said.

"Help me . . . back to Wakely," she said weakly.

"I'll get the horses," Summers said.

But before he could stand, Layla's grip tightened on his forearm as Summers saw her whole body tense up in a hard stomach cramp.

"Oh God, Will, please hurry!" she shouted in pain when the cramp let up enough for her to speak at all.

"I will," Summers said. But instead of rising he took her hand from his forearm and held it firmly. He looked off in the direction of Red Cliffs, then back toward the water hole and trail to Wakely. "How far is it to Warton Bendigo's from here?"

Layla gripped his hand tighter for a second as her stomach cramped again. When the pain passed, she let out a long breath, then collected herself.

"It's closer . . . than Wakely," she said.

"Will Bendigo's men let us pass, if I take you there?" he asked, the concern showing on his face in the light of the full moon.

"He told me I'm . . . always welcome there," she said. "But what . . . about you?"

Summers had already reached down, scooped her up into his arms and started toward the horses.

"I'll take my chances," he said. "The main thing is to get you there — get you some help."

In a moment, Summers had sat her atop his horse and climbed up behind her, the reins to Layla's rented horse in hand.

"You're always . . . taking care of me, Will," Layla said in a pained tone. "I don't know what I would do . . ." Her voice trailed away.

"*Shhh,* don't talk now, Layla," Summers said. "Just try to rest some. We've got a long night ahead of us."

He nudged the horse forward and rode up out of the gulley and back onto the rocky trail, leading Layla's horse behind him. The dog ran ahead of them as if he knew where they were headed.

As first light streaked on the horizon, a trail guard, Conn Alvarez, stood atop a boulder and looked down on the narrow path over a hundred feet below.

"Clinton, Nettles, both of yas come look at this," he said over his shoulder to the two other men sitting close to a small fire, tin cups of coffee in their hands.

They stood and hurried over beside him, and looked down. Immediately, they spotted a man and a woman riding the same horse. The woman lay sprawled in the man's arms.

"What the hell is all this?" Ellis Nettles murmured aloud, staring down in the gray swirl of morning. "That looks like the whore Warton Bendigo was sweet on last winter."

Beside him, Dade Clinton said, "If the boss ever heard you call his woman a whore, he'd most likely carve your tongue out and nail it to a post."

"I meant no harm," said Nettles. "I know Layla Brooks, and I have nothing but respect for her. I'm just calling her what she calls herself."

"Both of you quiet down," said Alvarez, noticing that the man had raised an arm and was waving it back and forth slowly. "Let's hear his story."

"I've got Layla Brooks here," the man called out to them. "She drank some poisoned water . . . she needs help, fast, else she's not going to make it."

"Damn, it's Will Summers," said Nettles. "Warton's offering a hundred dollars for his head on a stick!" He started to jerk his rifle up to his shoulder.

But Alvarez shoved the rifle down.

"Boss will have *your* head on a stick if we let something happen to Layla Brooks," he said. Turning back to the trail below, he called out to Summers, "Ride in, but stop at the first stand of rock, where we can see you clearly."

"Whoa, Conn," Clinton said, "you're just letting them ride in?"

"What the hell else do you propose we should do?" said Alvarez. "Boss told us Layla is always to be let in. Look how many times we've let her in before."

"You'll be the one who answers for it," Dade Clinton warned him.

"That's right, I expect I will," said Alvarez, stepping back from the edge of the boulder. "Both of you be ready to put a bullet in Summers if he tries anything shady.

I'll ride down and see what this one's up to."

"What about the hundred dollars?" Nettles asked.

"If he's telling the truth, the woman *is* sick, and I'm taking them both to Bendigo," Alvarez said. "If the *boss* says kill him, I'll kill him, and we'll split the reward money three ways. Otherwise, we can kiss the hundred dollars good-bye."

Nettles and Clinton looked at each other with sour expressions.

"Are you going to cover me?" Alvarez asked, stopping before walking on to his horse.

"Yeah, go ahead," said Dade Clinton, "we've got you covered."

Alvarez hurried on over to his horse and climbed atop it as the two others kept watch on Summers.

"Remember," said Alvarez, turning his horse to a path leading down the steep hillside, "one false move out of this horse trader, blast him straight to hell."

On the trail below, Will Summers sat waiting in his saddle, Layla slumped against him. When Conn Alvarez's horse stepped down into sight around a stand of rock, Summers raised his hands chest high in front of the woman and sat quietly until Alvarez sidled up close to him, pulled the Colt from Summers' holster and looked it over.

"You're riding Arlo Hughes' cayuse; you're carrying his shooting iron. I take it your paths have crossed recently?"

"I don't know the man who wore this gun and rode this horse, but he won't be needing them again," Summers said.

"Oh? He's dead, then," said Alvarez.

"He is," Summers said flatly.

"What happened to him?" Alvarez asked, pulling his own Colt out and cocking it as he shoved the gun he took from Summers down behind his belt.

"This woman needs help to stay alive, mister," Summers said. "Let's not waste time talking about who's dead or how they got that way."

"We will if I say we will —"

Layla whispered in a barely audible voice, cutting him off, "Conn . . . get me to the house . . ."

Alvarez gazed down at her face, seeing the bandages, the dust and the painful expression on her face. Then he looked at Summers with resolve as he reached over and drew Arlo Hughes' rifle from the saddle boot and laid it across his lap. He gestured Summers ahead of him on the trail toward the ranch house.

"Let's ride, horse trader," he said. "You stay in front of me where I can see you."

Summers only nodded and nudged his horse forward. He saw the dog's paw prints now and then in the dirt, yet he saw no sign of the dog itself. But Summers knew the big cur could take care of himself.

They rode in silence for the next hour, eventually watching the ranch house rise into sight as if it grew up out of the rocky ground.

At the crest of a low rise a mile from the front yard, Summers gave a sharp jerk on his reins and caused his horse to veer sideways. At the same time he pulled Layla's rented horse between himself and Conn Alvarez.

It took only a split second for Alvarez to see the move and jerk his own horse around, his hand going to the butt on his holstered six-shooter. But by then it was too late. As the dun stepped out from between the two men, Alvarez stood looking down the barrel of another big Colt that Summers had carried across his lap, behind Layla Brooks' back.

"We stop here," Summers said. "Lift that gun with two fingers and let it fall. Do the same with your rifle. My Colt and my rifle too."

Alvarez did as he was told, but with a look of bitter contempt on his face.

"*Your* Colt, *your* rifle," he said. "You mean *Arlo's* Colt and rifle. I've heard things about you, Summers. Now I see with my own eyes what kind of snake you are." He spit in disgust. "What kind of world has this turned into when a no-good —"

"Hey, *hey,*" Summers said, stopping him. "This is not the time or place to go into all that."

Alvarez shut up and sat staring with the same look of disgust on his face.

"Get your horse over here beside me. Take Layla from me," Summers said.

"Take her from you?" Alvarez asked in confusion, even as he nudged his horse closer.

"That's right, take her," said Summers. "It was no trick. She *is* water-poisoned, and she needs help. Tell Warton Bendigo this doesn't change anything. I came to get my horses. I'm not leaving without them."

Layla stirred against his chest as Summers handed her over into Alvarez's gloved hands, all the while keeping the gun pointed at Alvarez.

"What's going on . . . Will?" Layla asked

in a faint voice as the two made their transfer.

"This man is taking you to Bendigo for help," Summers said. He stared at Alvarez, the Colt cocked and pointed at his heart.

"I'll tell him you asked for the horses," said Alvarez, adjusting Layla onto his lap. She slumped against his chest.

"*Asking* is not what I've come here to do," Summers said. "I know it was his sons who stole them. They beat this woman, raped her, shot her —"

"No, Will," Layla interrupted. "It wasn't Dow or Tom. It couldn't be . . ." Her weak voice faded away.

"Get going with her," Summers said with force, ignoring Layla's defense of the Bendigo brothers. "Anything Warton Bendigo needs to settle with me, I'll be here somewhere inside Red Cliffs until I get what I came for."

"He won't stand for this — you being inside Red Cliffs, stolen horses or not," Alvarez said. "This is *our* place. Most likely Warton will say, 'Let the killing begin' when I tell him you're prowling around out here."

"Then let it," Summers said, leveling his Colt toward Alvarez and taking close aim as if he was about to shoot him in his head.

"Damn it, you're loco, horse trader!" Alvarez said, ducking his head away and booting his horse toward the distant ranch house.

Summers watched as the cloud of stirred-up dust moved farther and farther away. Wrapping the rented dun's reins around his saddle horn, he stooped down, collected the guns Alvarez had dropped to the ground and swung back up into his saddle.

Now back to work, he thought, turning the horses away from the main trail and toward a stretch of tall pines lining a hillside that reached beyond the big ranch.

His own silver-gray, three dark bays, a paint horse and a black Morgan cross . . . , he told himself, booting his horse up into a trot, the rented dun right behind him.

CHAPTER 18

Warton Bendigo sat at the long wooden table in the yard behind his big stone-and-timber ranch house. Twenty feet away his cook and houseman, Heto Salizar, turned steaks on a grill rack above a bed of fiery coals. Beside the iron grill rack, a stone *chiminea* wavered in its own heat. The smell of biscuits drifted in the air.

Bendigo sipped coffee from a thick mug and sat with his head bowed slightly. Chip Bryant was seated halfway down the long table, knife and fork in hand, awaiting a fresh-cut steak and a ladle of red beans and peppers. "Shotgun" Holder sat across from Chip, sipping his coffee and eagerly anticipating breakfast. Save for the three men, the big table was empty, Bendigo having sent some of his gunmen out earlier to continue searching for his sons.

The three were quiet. Warton had unsuccessfully led his own select handful of men out until long after dark the day before. It was past midnight when they'd ridden back into the yard and stepped down from their worn-out horses.

Reflecting on their efforts the night before, Warton said aloud to himself, "We find them today. We bring them in either faceup and bloody or facedown and bled out."

Chip nodded in agreement. He watched hungrily as Heto Salizar walked up beside Warton Bendigo and set a wide wooden plate down in front of him. Smoke curled up from a sizzling steak cut two inches thick.

While Bendigo stuffed a cloth napkin down inside his shirt collar, Heto hurried over to the grill. He came back carrying two more sizzling steaks and slid them in front of Chip and "Shotgun" Holder.

Heto's young nephew, Pero, walked up carrying a large bowl of red beans and peppers and set it in the middle of the table, a big ladle sticking up from the bowl.

"Eat up, boys," Bendigo said gruffly.

But as the three fell upon their food like wolves, they heard the sound of a galloping horse coming from the side of the house. They looked up as Mitchell Udane rounded the house and slid to a halt a few feet from the table.

"Boss! You better come quick!" Udane

said, excited and out of breath.

Bendigo only stared at him angrily, his knife and fork in hand.

"Alvarez is riding in with a woman in his arms!" said Udane. "Murphy swears it's Layla Brooks!"

Bendigo snapped up from his chair, jerking the napkin from under his shirt collar.

"If this is just Murphy's stupidity, I swear to God . . ." He left his threat unfinished as he walked quickly along beside Udane toward the front yard.

Holder and Chip stood up too, both of them stuffing a forkful of steak into their mouths as they tore themselves away from their breakfast and hurried along, catching up to the outlaw leader.

In the front yard, Murphy turned and handed Bendigo a battered telescope as the outlaw walked up beside him with a look of rage on his face, his big fists clenched at his sides.

"If you're wrong, Murphy, I'll beat your head in with a shovel!" Bendigo said.

"Take a look, boss. It's her, I *swear* to it!" Murphy said quickly, having double-checked and made sure it was indeed Layla Brooks sitting slumped back against Conn Alvarez's chest. "Even with bandages covering her face, I recognize her."

Bendigo looked out through the telescope. He focused in on the woman, and studied her face, straightening up with a jolt of recognition.

"Hell yes! It's her!" he said over his shoulder, still staring out intently. Seeing the bandages on Layla's face, Bendigo cursed.

"If those two rotten, no-good sonsabitches have blinded her —" He stopped himself, realizing that he had run out of threats.

To Mitchell Udane, he said, "Mitch! Go get my horse! Pronto! Chip, Holder, get mounted!" he ordered.

Still working on the mouthful of steak, Chip looked back longingly in the direction of the table, then hurried away with Holder toward their horses standing at the iron hitch rail out in front of the house.

Udane ran back to the front yard leading Bendigo's horse by its reins.

"Shotgun" Holder and Chip Bryant, atop their horses, pounded out behind him in a cloud of dust toward the oncoming Alvarez, his arms around the half-conscious Layla Brooks.

From the shelter of the pine-studded hillside, Summers watched the riders move along at a run.

"Good enough . . . ," Summers said to himself. Wrapping the rented horse's reins around a thin pine sapling, he eased his horse down toward the lower edge of the hillside. He followed the shadowy cover of trees until he was past the ranch house and straight across from the big barn standing twenty yards behind it.

Keeping watch on the gunmen, Summers rode quickly across a two-yard stretch of rough terrain until he knew the house itself provided him cover. The rest of the way he only slowed down a little, knowing that the riders would soon be back at the house. The horses would be taken to their respective stalls.

He circled back behind the barn, found a stand of rock taller than his head and left the horse there, its reins around the sun-bleached remains of a small dead oak.

With the rifle in hand, he hurried in a crouch to the barn and slipped in through a back door. Out front he heard the horses pounding closer to the yard.

He hurried from stall to stall, even looked out into a side corral, yet he saw none of his horses.

On his way out the rear door of the barn, he looked down and saw the line-marked hoofprints leading out the way he had come in. He followed the hoofprints with his eyes until they ran out of sight toward the trees.

"Double Xs . . . ," he murmured. Rifle in hand, he ran in a crouch back to his horse, swung up into the saddle and rode in a wide circle, keeping out of sight from the front yard, back to the treed hillside where he'd left the rented dun.

In the yard, Mitchell Udane looked back at the drifting rise of dust.

"What the hell was that?" he asked, taking the reins to Warton Bendigo's horse as Bendigo stepped down from his saddle and hurried over to Alvarez.

"It's a dust devil!" Bendigo said gruffly. "To hell with it, whatever it is. Get my horse out of here. Clear me a way!" He stood on the ground beside Conn Alvarez's horse as Alvarez handed the woman down to him. He called out to Heto Salizar.

"Heto, run on in, turn down my bedcovers and get some fresh water! And some clean washcloths and bedclothes! Anything happens to this woman, I'm going to blame every son of a bitch ever born!"

On his way to the house, Layla in his arms, Warton saw Udane and Murphy pointing toward a distant rider headed along the lower hill line.

"Look, a rider!" Udane shouted.

Conn Alvarez stared out with them; his hand went instinctively to his empty holster.

"It's Summers," he growled in an angry voice. "He circled around and came snooping here while we wasn't watching. That's the kind of sneaking, low-down coward —"

"He disarmed you, Conn!" Warton called back over his shoulder on his way up the front porch steps with the woman lying wilted in his arms.

"What do you want us to do, boss?" Alvarez called out, still atop his horse.

"Arm yourself, damn it!" Bendigo shouted. "Go after him, if you can keep him from taking your gun again."

"Come on," said Udane to Murphy. "Let's grab our horses and ride. Lucian Clay and some others are out there already. If we run Summers down before Lucian gets to him, we'll split the hundred dollars, fifty-fifty."

"Wait for me," said Alvarez. "I've got a spare gun in the bunkhouse."

"We're not waiting for you, Conn," said Udane. "We need a man who can hang on to his shooting gear."

Out in front of a long-deserted line shack perched on a high-treed hilltop, Dow and Tom Bendigo sat on the stone steps of the front porch, drinking from a bottle of whiskey. In a corral a few yards away, the stolen horses milled in the shade and drew water from a trough fed by a runoff stream. Dow smiled admiringly at the horses.

"I was right about one thing, Cat Tracker," he said. "These stolen horses sure took the old man's mind off me gambling away all that cattle money." He chuckled and took a long swig of whiskey. "He never even mentioned it."

Tom Bendigo only nodded a little and stared off toward the trail leading down the rocky, treed hillside.

Dow saw the wary look on his half brother's face.

"Hey, stop worrying so much about our back trail. No one is going to be looking too hard for us. They know how riled the old man gets, and they know how soon he can get over it." He passed Tom the whiskey bottle.

The half-breed took it, tossed back a mouthful and let out a whiskey hiss.

"Besides," Dow said, "if we had a dollar for every time he's threatened to kill us, we'd both be millionaires." He laughed and reached over for the bottle.

Tom considered what Dow said. He nodded in agreement and handed the bottle back to him, turning his eyes back to the trail and watching a breeze stir the treetops along the hillside.

Dow shrugged and swirled the whiskey remaining in the half-empty bottle.

"I have to say, though, I thought he was all set to put us both in the ground today," he said. "He *meant to . . .* That's why Morton Holder was there with his scatter-gun." He stopped swirling the whiskey and took a drink.

Tom only nodded again slightly, and continued searching the rocks, trees, dips and gullies.

"Yep, the son of a bitch wants to kill his own sons," Dow said after a moment of grim thought. "He just ain't worked himself into it yet." He paused, reflecting on the day's events. "What kind of low, no-good bastard wants to do something like that?"

He paused again, a moment longer this time. "I don't blame him, though. I would kill us both if I was him, wouldn't you?"

The half-breed didn't answer. He was focused on a large pile of downed and weathered pines lying among a clump of land-stuck boulders.

"What the hell are you looking at over there, Brother Cat?" Dow asked, seeing the guarded stare intensity in the half-breed's dark eyes.

Without taking his gaze off the boulders, Tom eased his hand over beside him and closed it around the stock of his rifle leaning against the porch.

"Whoa, I see it too!" said Dow, having turned his gaze out in the same direction. He reached down toward the butt of his holstered Colt. "Is that what I think it is?"

The half-breed offered no response. Instead, he levered a round into his rifle chamber and raised the butt of his gun to his shoulder. He sighted down the barrel and took aim on the cur's large, furry head staring at them from above the downed pines.

"Kill that son of a bitch!" Dow whispered, knowing that his Colt would be ineffective at such a distance.

The half-breed reached his thumb across his rifle hammer and cocked it slowly, quietly.

The big cur stared blankly, his tongue lolling out of his mouth after a long trek up the steep hill trail. The animal was satisfied, having captured his next meal. On the ground, a dead rabbit lay on a brittle carpet of dry pine needles.

Dow sat holding his breath as Tom took fine aim and squeezed the rifle trigger.

As the rifle bucked against his brother's

shoulder, Dow heard the dog let out a sharp yelp; he saw its big head disappear as the echo of the shot resounded out across the hillsides and valleys. In the corral, the stolen horse gave a startled jolt.

"You got him, Brother Cat!" Dow shrieked with joy. "You nailed that son of a bitch!" He jumped to his feet, waving his Colt in his hand. *"Hal-a-damn-lujah!"*

Tom just tossed him a curious look and stood up, dusting the seat of his trousers. He cradled his rifle in the crook of his arm and made his way onto the porch and into the shack.

"Hey, where the hell are you going, Brother Cat?" Dow asked. "Come on, let's go cleave his damn head off and stick it on a corral post." He grabbed Tom by the arm.

The half-breed shook his arm free and stared at Dow coldly, standing firm on the porch step.

"Okay, Brother Cat," said Dow, "stay here if you want to. I'm going to go make sure the scalp-tearing son of a bitch is dead."

Among the downed pines, the big cur licked his forepaw where splinters raised by the rifle shot had struck him. He examined the damage of the sting, but there was no blood. After a few quick licks, he turned his attention back to his meal lying in the pine needles.

Minutes later, when Dow circled below the stand of rocks, he saw the dog devouring the last bites of ravaged carcass. Upon hearing the gunman approach, the dog raised his head and stared blankly as he crunched and chewed a mouthful of bone and meat, his flews red with rabbit blood.

He's alive!

"You damn *son of a bitch*!" Dow shrieked. He quickly raised his Colt and emptied it on the big dog, but the dog only backed away unhurriedly as shot after shot whistled past him.

"I'll kill you, you mangy —" He stopped shouting as his gun hammer fell on spent cartridges. "Damn it to *hell*!" He cursed the empty gun, shaking it violently in his hand.

The dog stared at him and gave one bark, a matter-of-factly bark at that.

"Stay right there, you hairy bastard! Don't move!" Dow commanded, popping bullets from his holster belt with trembling fingers and hastily reloading the Colt. "I'll get you this time!" Loaded, he snapped the Colt up at arm's length. "I'll blow your damn head —" But just as he cocked it, the big dog vanished on the other side of the pines. In frustration and anger, Dow fired three shots blindly. Then he let his smoking Colt slump to his side.

He cursed, ranted and almost sobbed aloud in anger. Searching wildly, he finally sighted the dog again as he made another appearance farther up the hillside. Two shots exploded from Dow's Colt, but now the dog was out of pistol range.

"Damn it, damn it, *damn it*!" said Dow, seeing the big dog duck away again, and reappear a few yards farther up the hill.

As Dow stood, slumped, his smoking gun hanging in his hand, he got the strangest feeling that the dog had only been playing with him, taunting him all along.

As the dog disappeared and reappeared at the top of the hill, Dow shouted out, "Are you fooling with me? *Huh?* Are you?"

From his seat on the porch of the line shack, Tom "Cat Tracker" Bendigo heard his drunken half brother bellowing at the empty hillside.

"Are you following me?" Dow's voice echoed across the rugged and steep terrain. "You *bastard*," he shouted. "I'll get you . . . I'll kill you *yet*!"

The half-breed listened, shook his head slowly, then stood up and walked inside. It was twenty minutes later when Dow came in, drunk, wild-eyed and out of breath.

"Get saddled up, Brother Cat," he said. "We're going after that blasted cur."

Tom gave him a questioning look.

"That's right. You didn't kill him. Hell, you missed him altogether!" Dow sneered. "But I'll kill him, if it's the last thing I ever do . . . after what he did to me!" He gestured a hand toward his slow-healing scalp. "Now, come on, damn it. Let's get a move on."

Tom gritted his teeth. He stood up nonetheless, swiped his hat off the table and jammed it down atop his head.

CHAPTER 19

Will Summers had lost his stolen horses' trail across a stretch of boulders that reached upward layer upon layer, terracing the long stretch of hills west of the Bendigo ranch. In the afternoon he'd had to stop, having no idea which way to continue on. It was as if the string of horses had dropped off the edge of the earth.

He'd stepped down from his horse and scoured the hard ground. *Nothing . . .*

As he'd stood considering his next move, he'd heard the rifle shot echo in the hills above him to his right. For a few minutes he'd waited, his senses piqued, listening intently for more rifle shots — but none came.

It had to be one of Bendigo's men, he reasoned. There were no other resident inhabitants of Red Cliffs. But it didn't matter . . . He let out a tired breath. One shot could have meant anything — a rattlesnake in the trail, he thought. Even if it had meant something, it had come and gone now, and nothing followed.

He had started to step back into his saddle and ride the trail upward to his right, holding Layla's rented horse by its reins, when the sound of pistol fire erupted from the same direction as the single rifle shot.

Uh-oh . . . , he thought. After counting six shots, he swung up into his saddle. He sat stone-still in anticipation, judging what he considered to be the time it took to reload. When three more pistol rounds echoed along the hills, he turned his horse and the rented dun to the left, in the direction of the echoing gunfire.

"It's as good a way as any," he murmured to the horses as they began making the climb on a thin path weaving up the rocky hillside.

An hour later, he stepped down from the saddle on a broad shelf of stone. Walking a few yards, he stopped where a stretch of softer earth ran across the crest of the hill he'd just climbed. Looking down at the dirt, he let out a breath of relief, seeing his stolen horses' trail pointing from right to left in the same direction as the earlier gunfire.

A little luck never hurt, he told himself. He looked off in the direction of the gunshots, adjusted his hat down onto his head and led both horses forward.

When he reached the crest of the hill, he continued to follow the marked hooves as they led him down off the top of the hills, along a narrow trail overlooking a deep valley.

As he rounded the hillside, he stopped at the sight of the big cur streaking in and out of sight through the trees on another craggy hillside in the distance.

He stared in surprise for a moment. Then he backed his horse over behind a rock spill for cover when he caught sight of two riders pounding down the same direction, in pursuit of the big cur.

"Stay with it, Buddy . . . ," he said to himself, speaking to the cur. "Help's coming . . ." He eased the horse forward and rode on once the two riders had moved out of sight.

Across the valley, a mile away, still racing through woodlands and rock otherwise unfamiliar to him, the big cur bounded upward over tops of split and broken boulder. At length, he stopped for a moment, looking back down the rocky hills at the two riders, still a good distance behind him. A strong, familiar scent had led him onto the slope. It had wafted into his nostrils, attracting him like a siren's call.

Halfway up the steep rock-strewn slope, the scent had grown stronger and stronger. Now atop a clump of boulders, his tongue hanging from his frothed and gaping mouth, the cur looked down before him and saw a wildly running stream. For a second he studied the water, watching it roll and wind sharply, cascading down into a broad basin fifty feet below him. Then he turned in the direction of the riders and began barking loudly.

"Look at this, Brother Cat!" Dow said, jerking his horse to a halt. "The dumb bastard is skylighting himself, and barking his fool head off to boot." As he spoke, he drew his rifle from its saddle boot.

With his rifle already in hand, the half-breed only stared at him as if in grim premonition.

"Looks like it's all going to stop right here!" Dow said, booting his horse hard, forcing it to climb at a stiff, awkward run on the brutal terrain.

Tom followed, but he kept his horse checked down on the rocky hillside. He stared up at the dog, seeing it crouched slightly on its forepaws, barking down at Dow as if cursing him relentlessly, daring

270

him to give chase. Which Dow did, in his half-drunken rage.

Tom just shook his head slowly as he watched the big cur turn and disappear out of sight. Dow slapped his horse's rump with his rifle barrel to keep it climbing.

The cur plunged headlong, almost straight down a gravel and dust coyote path. Half running, half sliding and raising dust in its wake, the dog hit the edge of the fast-moving stream, righted himself and shook himself off. He stood for a moment as if in anticipation, staring up toward the edge he'd descended.

In a second, a terrified cry from rider and horse alike resounded out over the cliff's edge, joined by the loud, angry bawl of a mother grizzly as she rose from among the rocks and stood protectively over two cubs huddled beneath her.

"Holy *God*!" Dow managed to scream in the split second before the big sow's massive forepaw swatted him and his horse, sending them both sprawling sideways, tumbling and bouncing end over end down the rocky slope.

As soon as the horse's flailing hooves found purchase, it was up and gone in a flurry of gravel and dirt, its saddle hanging halfway down its side. Dow continued to bounce and roll another ten feet, yelling loudly until he came to an abrupt stop headfirst against a sunken boulder. Tom winced and then smiled faintly at the sound of his brother's head smacking the rock. Dow melted into a limp silence.

The big grizzly sow came down off her hind legs and loped forward a few feet. Upon seeing that the perceived danger to her cubs had passed, she bawled out threateningly, then backed away, as shot after shot from the half-breed's rifle peppered the rocks in front of her.

Along the water's edge, the big cur had already turned away from the sounds above him and loped along at an easy pace. Afternoon shadows had begun to stretch long across the valley and hillside. Darkness would soon be upon the land. The cur watched and searched the looming shadows, his nose and brain working together deftly, searching through a mix of scents that he knew instinctively would grow stronger and closer with the coming of night.

Crossing the valley floor on their daylong search for Will Summers, Lucian Clay brought his men to a halt and looked up toward the far sound of rifle shots following the less audible bawl of the bear.

"What the hell is going on up there?" he asked, speaking to no one in particular.

"It sounds like Summers wants a little bear steak for supper," said Ben Twist, one of the four Wind River Boys, whom Lucian Clay had recently brought into Warton Bendigo's Red Cliffs Gang.

"We'll steak his bear," said Clay, staring off at the hills ahead of them in the afternoon light. "I'm not going back without his damn head stuck on the end of my rifle barrel."

The other three Wind River Boys looked at one another. They sat slumped in the saddles, their wrists crossed on their saddle horns.

One of them, an older gunman named Abel Anders, patted his horse's wet withers with his gloved hand.

"Let me make sure I understand," he said. "All this is worth a hundred dollars? Hell, I won more than that night before last playing poker with these two."

A shaven, round-faced man named Moon Layhee interjected quietly, "Which I will be winning back tonight if we're not too damn worn out to gamble."

"Is not a gamble vit you," said a German gunman named Drate Kunz in a thick accent. He laughed a little at his own joke, but no one else did.

"What did he say?" Clay asked Ben Twist.

"He said it was not gambling, playing poker with Moon here."

"Make him keep his mouth shut 'til he learns to speak English," said Clay. "Foreign tongue offends me."

The Wind River Boys fell silent for a moment. Finally Ben Twist said, "We're all a little tired and testy. You figure on riding back, or riding ahead, see if that's the man we're after?"

"I told you," said Lucian Clay, "I'm not going back without Summers' head on my rifle —"

"Aw, this is bullshit!" said Anders, cutting him off. "This man killed your pals, the Peltrys. So what? I knew some men who knew the Peltrys. They said Mose and Goose were a couple of lunatics. Neither North nor South wanted them on their side —"

His words stopped beneath a blast of blue-orange flame as Lucian Clay spun facing him in his saddle, his Colt out arm's length, blazing and bucking three times while the other three gunmen ducked away in surprise.

After a stunned silence as smoke curled and loomed in the still air, Ben Twist ventured his horse a step forward and looked down at Abel Anders lying dead in the trail.

"Well then . . . ," he said. He looked at the other Wind River Boys, then back at Lucian Clay. "I expect if we had any doubts how you feel about the Peltrys, ol' Abel here just flushed them out."

Smoke still curled up from Clay's gun barrel.

"I told the lot of yas from the outset that I come out here to kill a son of a bitch," said Clay. "I hope nobody thought it was all loose talk on my part."

"I say we ride on, just like you want," Ben Twist replied, with a guarded expression. "I never knew the Peltrys, but I'm sure they were both fine men."

Clay turned his gaze and his smoking gun toward Moon Layhee.

"To hell with poker," said Moon. "I'm on this thing like stink on a rutting monkey."

Clay turned to Drate Kunz.

"Me too, vit vat he said," Kunz added quickly.

"Is he agreeing with me?" Clay asked Ben Twist with a puzzled expression.

"Yes, he is," said Twist.

"Good, then let's keep going," Clay said, flagging the three past him with his gun barrel.

In the front yard of the Bendigo ranch, "Shotgun" Holder and Chip Bryant had both heard the distant gunfire, but the two outlaws had only given each other a look. Holder sat leaning back in a wooden porch chair whittling with a jackknife. Chip stood nearby leaning on a post, his arms crossed, staring out at the hills and mountain lines.

"Somebody's always getting shot; somebody's always getting shot at," he mused sagely.

"Not us, though," "Shotgun" Holder pointed out, then went back to his whittling.

"Not today anyway," said Chip.

Inside the house, Layla Brooks sat propped up in Warton Bendigo's bed with a large feather pillow behind her back. As soon as Warton had carried her inside and laid her on the bed, Heto the houseman had wiped her face and arms with a cool damp cloth. After allowing her a few moments of rest, he'd fed her a small portion of thin beef broth laced with dried medicinal herbs from one of several herb tins he'd brought with him from across the border. She had slept like a stone.

When she had awakened, her bandages were gone except for the one covering her left eye. The vision in her right eye had cleared considerably, even though it still had some healing to do. The buckshot wounds on her cheek and her chin had scabbed over and dried down smaller in size. Beneath the bandage, she could feel the swelling and soreness in her left eye was much less.

Heto had left a hand mirror lying on the stand beside the feather bed. She sat gazing into the mirror, examining the damage to her healing face, when Warton Bendigo came and stood over her.

"My goodness, Layla, you're awake," he said, taking her hand between both of his. "You've had me worried sick. I'd made up my mind, if anything were to happen to you I'd kill every four-legged critter living for miles around, maybe a few two-legged ones too."

Layla gave a thin smile and let him hold on to her hand. Closing her eye for a moment, she reflected.

"To think it was a dose of poisoned water that brought me to you," she said. "Imagine my surprise. I lost consciousness crossing the flatlands and awakened here in your bed."

"Just you say the word, little darling. You'll

awaken every morning in my bed, in my *arms*," said Warton. He raised his left hand from hers and caressed her forehead. "How are you feeling? It seems that Heto's herbs caught it in time."

"They must have," Layla said with a sigh. "I feel so much better.

"I'm thankful for that," said Bendigo.

"Warton, I didn't mean to come to you like this," Layla said. "But I want you to know that I intended to come to you all the same."

"Oh, you did?" Warton said, sitting down on the edge of the bed. "What about that miner you took up with?"

"Lee is dead, Warton," Layla said. "He died weeks ago. I had been waiting for the weather to break so I could come down the mountainside. Will Summers showed up with a mule he'd brought for Lee. I was going to ride down with Will, then head this way."

"So, there is nothing between the two of you?" Warton asked.

"No," said Layla, "no more than what's between any dove and her caller. I paid in kind for the mule he brought Lee. That was all. He was most kind and considerate to me after I was beaten and shot." She looked at him with her right eye.

Bendigo winced and said, "I'm damn sorry that happened, Layla."

Layla shrugged. "I've taken beatings before. I must've gone for my gun. That's probably why they shot me. I suppose that makes it my fault, in a way. A dove should have handled it differently."

"No, you're wrong," said Bendigo. "It wasn't your fault, dove or no dove."

Layla put the matter aside and continued on, talking about Summers. "Anyway, Will took me to Wakely and saw to it I was taken care of. He's a good man, Warton."

"I'm not doubting that he is, Layla," said Warton. "But it changes nothing. My men are going to kill him. We can't just allow folks to traipse in and out of here, especially a damn horse trader."

"He brought me here *to you,* Warton," Layla said. "Doesn't that count for anything?"

Bendigo stared at her closely. He still held her hand, but his grasp felt different now.

"My understanding is Summers came here searching for his stolen horses. And to kill the men who stole them. Which are my two good-for-nothing sons."

"That too, Warton," Layla said, "but he didn't have to bring me here."

"But he did, and here you are," said

Bendigo. "And I never want you to leave." He leaned in closer, hoping he had put an end to the matter.

But Layla would have none of it. She turned her face away from his.

"Killing people is not the answer to everything, Warton," she said.

"I know, but it solves *most* things," Bendigo said with a rare smile. "Killing is something you never have to do twice, not if it's done right the first time."

"And Dow and Tom?" she asked. "Are you going to kill them too, for beating me, for shooting me?"

"I'm going to kill them, yes," said Bendigo. "Will that make you happy?"

"No, Warton," Layla said firmly. "Killing them won't make me happy. If they did this, it was because they were drunk and loco. Anyway, I don't know that they're guilty. I can't remember *who* did this."

"It was them, Layla," Warton said grimly. "Dow admitted it. He even made unseemly remarks about raping you. About *raping you,* Layla!" he said with emphasis. "I can't live with that. I've got to kill the sonsabitches. This is not just another father's idle threat."

Staring into his eyes, Layla could tell that he meant it. She had heard his threats before, but this time they seemed different.

There was resolved finality in both his tone and his demeanor.

"I wasn't raped, Warton," she said. "I was beaten and shot but I wasn't raped."

Bendigo studied her good eye, searching for the truth.

"You weren't? How do you know?" he asked.

"A woman knows, Warton," she said quietly. "I wasn't raped. Does it help you to hear that?"

Bendigo let out a breath after a deep moment of consideration.

"Yes, it helps some," he said. "But they still beat you and shot you —"

She cut him off. "They didn't rape me, Warton. Can you live with the rest of it? If not, I can't stay here with you. I don't want Dow and Tom's blood on my hands."

Warton sighed and said with difficulty, "If letting them live will keep you here with me, I expect I can do it." He paused, then added, "But the horse trader has to die. There's no way around that."

Layla only sighed. She reached up and shoved a strand of gray hair from his forehead.

"Sit here quietly with me for a while," she whispered.

CHAPTER 20

It was after dark by the time Tom "Cat Tracker" Bendigo brought his brother back to the line shack. The two rode double, Dow hanging over the saddle like a roll of limp carpet. Tom rode on the horse's rump behind the saddle. The sudden stop head-first against a rock had broken open some of the stitches holding Dow's scalp together. Most of the ride back he had flopped on the saddle, his arms dangling down the horse's side.

Once the horse was in the yard of the line shack, Dow stirred and tried to right himself on the saddle.

"Wha— what are we doing back here?" he asked, still a little dazed, but starting to come around.

Tom didn't answer. Instead, he slipped down from the horse's rump, reached up and gave a hard shove on Dow's shoulder, sending him backward out of the saddle and sprawling in the dirt on the other side of the horse.

"I — I'm going after that blasted cur, Cat," he said groggily. "I'm going to . . . kill it."

Tom reached a hand down and pulled him to his feet. Dow staggered in place as he wiped his nose and forehead where blood started to trickle down from his loosened stitches.

"I'm — I'm a mess," he groaned. "I remember a bear swatting me and my horse . . ." He struggled to piece fragments of his memory together. "Chasing that damn cur caused it."

Tom stepped back to his saddlebags, pulled out a bottle of whiskey and uncorked it. He took a sip and shoved the bottle into Dow's hand.

"Oh God . . . ! Thank you, Brother Cat," he said, taking a long swig, hoping to feel the effects of it soothe the pounding inside his head. Whiskey ran down both corners of his mouth.

Tom stood staring at him with a questioning look on his face.

"You're damn right we're going after it," Dow said, staring into his brother's dark, expressionless eyes. "As soon as I can get a horse under me." He took another drink and let out a hiss.

Tom still stared.

"There's an old saddle in a corner in there," Dow said, thumbing toward the shack. "Take the saddle off your horse and put it on the silver-gray. You take that old saddle," he demanded.

The half-breed gave him a look.

"That's right, Cat, you heard me," Dow said with force. "I'm hurting here, damn it. I need the best ride I can get . . . just 'til my head straightens out."

The half-breed walked into the shack without a word. Dow slumped down the stone step and sat holding the bottle, his bloody head bowed.

Moments later, the half-breed came back from the corral leading the silver-gray. He stood it beside his tired horse, swapped the saddles and walked back and stood over his half brother. His hand rested on his holstered Colt, and he stared ahead with a dark, unfathomable shine in his eyes.

"Thanks, Brother Cat," Dow said quietly without raising his bowed head. "I'm obliged to you . . . I always am." He held the bottle up to Tom, still without lifting his head.

The half-breed's expression softened a little; his hand slipped away from his gun butt and hung loose at his side for a second. Finally, he took the bottle, took a drink and nodded to himself as if satisfying something in his mind.

"Damn it, Brother Cat," Dow said out of the blue. "Why am I such a no-good son of a bitch?"

Tom only stared down at him, the whiskey bottle hanging from his fingertips.

"Huh? Why is that?" Dow asked. He raised his face up toward the half-breed. His eyes welled with tears. "Why the hell am I so damn loco all the time? There's never a good thought crosses my mind. If I ain't up to no good, I'm not doing nothing at all." He took the bottle from the half-breed. "I am the most wild, loco, good-for-nothing I ever seen . . ."

Tom reached a hand down to him to help him to his feet.

"We both loco," the half-breed said flatly.

"*Jesus*, Brother Cat," Dow said, stunned at the sound of his half brother's voice. "I almost forgot that you *can* talk." He took Tom's hand and pulled himself to his feet.

Tom just stared at him.

"You know what, Cat?" he said. "We're going on back to the ranch." He looked back along the darkening trail they'd ridden in on. "As soon as I've killed that damn mangy, scalp-eating cur, we're going on down to home. String them horses for the trail."

The half-breed looked at him curiously.

"You heard me right," said Dow. "We're going to give them to the old man as a peace offering." He gave a weak, broken grin. "As bad as he hates us, there's still nothing he loves better than stolen horses."

The two walked to the corral together, Dow dusting the seat of his trousers . . .

Seven miles down the hillside, on a level shelf of rock beneath a cliff overhang, Will Summers sat beside a small fire eating a strip of jerked elk he had rummaged from his saddlebags. He sipped hot coffee boiled from a few beans he found lying loose in the saddlebags and ground on a rock with the butt of his Colt. It was weak, yet satisfying.

When he heard a quiet sound from the edge of the overhang, he set his tin cup down and slipped his hand over to his rifle lying on the blanket beside him.

He heard the sound again, this time closer — something or someone moving down a narrow path around the corner of sheltering stone. He swung the rifle, coming up onto a knee and taking quick aim. But then he let out a breath when the big cur loped into the circle of low firelight and came to a halt, its tail wagging slowly, its tongue lolling from his mouth.

Summers shook his head, relieved, and lowered the rifle back to his side.

"You can't be sneaking up on a fellow that way, Buddy," he said.

The dog stood back a few feet, staring at him, his head lowered slightly, awaiting an invitation.

"Come on over here," Summers said, already tearing the jerked elk in half. "Get some of this. It's not good, but it beats starving . . . by a little, I suppose."

The dog stepped forward, caught the piece of elk as Summers pitched it to him and dropped onto his belly as he swallowed the dry hard meat effortlessly.

"I'd offer you coffee, but you wouldn't thank me for it," he said.

He rose into a crouch as he spoke, picked up his canteen and his hat and moved over closer to the dog, placing his hat upended on the ground. He opened the canteen and poured tepid water into the yawning hat brim. The dog stood, drank the water, then plopped back down.

Summers looked him over good, having seen the two riders chasing him earlier and later hearing the gunfire and angry bawl of a bear.

"You look like you've had a rough day," he said, satisfied that the dog was all right.

Buddy looked back over his shoulder as if checking his back trail. Then he looked at Summers and barked and pushed himself up from the ground as if ready to go.

"No, Buddy," Summers said, "not tonight. Let's both get some rest. We'll head out early come morning."

But no sooner had he gone back to his blanket and started to pick up his coffee cup than Summers heard the cock of a rifle hammer and froze. He glanced toward his rifle lying on the ground.

"Grab for it, *horse trader*," said Mitchell Udane. "Save us all a lot of awkward introductions."

"What did you call me?" Summers asked, still frozen in place, judging the distance between his right hand and the holstered Colt on his hip.

"I called you *horse trader*," said Udane.

"Mister, I'm not a horse trader," Summers said, needing to stall long enough to find himself an edge. "You must have me confused with somebody else."

The dog had jumped up off his belly, his

hackles up, a low growl rumbling in his chest.

"Easy, Buddy," Summers said, knowing the dog was apt to leap at the gunmen any second, and knowing that if he did, they would kill him.

"What do you say, Conn?" Udane asked Conn Alvarez. "Have we got this man confused with somebody else?"

"Nope," said Alzarez. "It's him. There's Arlo Hughes' horse to prove it."

The dog had settled a little at Summers' command, but now the growl rose again in his chest.

"Easy, Buddy," Summers whispered side-long.

"Yeah, it's him all right," said Udane, staring hard at Summers. "Horse trader, your head is coming home with us. The rest of you goes to the coyotes. You're worth a hundred dollars from the neck up."

"Yeah," Ed Murphy said with a greedy laugh. "That's forty dollars apiece."

Udane and Alvarez both gave him a strange look. Buddy, who had settled again upon Summers' earlier command, now began to growl deeper, more intensely.

"Stand up, Summers!" Udane demanded loudly, causing the dog's hackles to bristle all the way down his back.

Summers stood and turned slowly. He knew the dog was going to explode any second.

"Shoot that damn dog and shut him up!" Mitchell Udane said to Alvarez.

"With pleasure," said Alvarez. He turned a battered and rusted Dance Brothers revolver he'd taken from the bunkhouse toward the dog.

In that second, as all three men turned a quick glance toward the big cur, Summers made his move.

Summers' Colt — the same one he'd taken from Alvarez on the trail — came up fast and began firing. His first shot hit Alvarez in the cheekbone just as the gunman pulled the Dance Brothers trigger.

The shot ripped straight through Alvarez's face, spraying the other two men with blood and stinging slivers of cheekbone and teeth. The dog sprang forward, unaffected by the loud gunfire. Summers' second shot hit Udane squarely in his chest and spun him around in time to catch the snarling dog in full leap. Udane fell backward with the dog's big jaws engulfing his face and shaking it savagely.

Ed Murphy howled, blood and bone fragments sticking to his face. His rifle flew from his hand as Summers turned the Colt toward him. As Summers fired his third shot, Murphy turned and ran screaming off the edge of the cliff into the deep purple darkness.

Summers and the dog both turned and froze, listening to the fading scream until it stopped suddenly amid the sounds of the breaking and thrashing of treetops over a hundred feet below.

The dog stepped off Udane's bloody chest. Udane gave a sharp gasp. His head fell limply to one side, a wide-eyed look of terror on his ripped and mangled face. The dog shook himself all over, raising himself onto the tips of his paws, and trotted over beside Summers, who walked to the edge of the cliff and spotted Murphy's barely visible body swaying back and forth, impaled on the tip of a sharp pine trunk.

Summers stared down for a moment, his smoking Colt still in his hand. He reached down and patted the big cur atop his bristly head. He replayed the scene out in his mind, the way the dog had charged forward with no regard for his own life, no fear of the guns or the men wielding them.

"Buddy," he said, without looking at the dog, "I don't know who Sergeant Tom Haines is, or was, but he sure taught you how to handle yourself."

Upon hearing the name, the dog pricked his ears and looked expectantly up at Summers, as if awaiting a command.

"Come on," Summers said, not noticing the cur's reaction. "Let's go figure out where they left their horses."

The dog loped ahead of Summers as the two climbed the thin, narrow path leading up around the edge of the cliff overhang. Ten yards up they came to another small flat shelf of rock. In the grainy, purple moonlight, Summers saw the black silhouettes of three horses standing huddled at a short scrub juniper. With his reloaded Colt in hand, he moved forward warily.

"Easy now," he whispered to the horses, running a soothing gloved hand along the first one's side as his eyes searched the darkness for a fourth gunman they might have left to guard the animals while the three crept down to kill him.

He gathered the reins from around the juniper and led the horses down the path beneath the overhang.

As he rummaged through the saddlebags for food, coffee or anything else of use, he stopped and looked at the dog, who sat on his hindquarters watching his every move.

"Come to think of it," Summers said to the dog, "why didn't you hear those three sneaking in on us?"

The dog stared and cocked his head curiously at him.

"It's all right," Summers said. "I should have heard them myself." But he continued to wonder if maybe the dog had heard them. Maybe that's why he had looked back over his shoulder.

The dog barked once as Summers took a piece of hardtack from one of the saddles, sniffed it and turned it in his hand.

"You are a puzzling animal, Buddy," Summers said. He pitched the hardtack to the dog. With only a slight move of his head, the dog snapped the morsel out of the air before it hit the ground.

Summers dropped the saddles from the three horses' backs and looked them over. He cut a length of lead rope from a coiled lariat hanging from a saddle horn, and strung the horses together, leaving a breakaway knot in case one happened to lose footing on the steep downhill trail to the valley floor. When he'd readied the horses, he turned to the dog, who had lain down, now watching Summers from on his belly.

"I hate to disturb you, Buddy," Summers said, "but we've got to clear out of here before any more company drops in uninvited."

The dog rose, ready, like a trooper standing at attention.

"Yep, *real* puzzling," Summers said, confirming his earlier statement to himself.

CHAPTER 21

Morning light spread silvery and thin on the western horizon as Lucian Clay and the remaining Wind River Boys rounded a high turn on their way up the steep rocky trail. They had made a dark camp the night before en route in the direction of last evening's gunfire, and stayed the course as soon as Lucian had awakened them roughly and gotten the three of them under way.

When the trail straightened before them, Lucian stopped his horse with a jolt and sat staring up at the dead body of Ed Murphy hanging above them in a wafting silver mist. Murphy's arms were spread, a look of terror frozen on his lifeless face.

Five feet of blood-smeared pine stuck through his chest where his ribs met. Short and bloody pine limbs littered the ground. Ed's hat lay tipped on its side against the tree trunk. One of his boots had come off, fallen and bounced and landed standing straight up in the middle of the trail, as if the hapless gunman had stepped out of it and left it there overnight.

"Lord . . . !" Ben Twist said under his breath, gazing up at the dead outlaw. "Was this what all the shooting was about last night?"

"Yeah," Lucian said grimly, staring up, "Ed's end of it anyway."

"What kind of sick, crazy bastard would do a man that way?" Ben Twist asked.

"Nobody *done* him that way . . . nobody *could,*" said Clay, still looking up, disgusted with Twist for having to ask. "In a pinch, ol' Ed was a runner. Like as not, this is what his running brought him to, once the shooting started."

"Sumbitch ran off a cliff," Moon Layhee said to Drate Kunz with a bemused look on his face. "Did you ever see such a thing?"

The German gunman only shook his head. He sat staring up in disbelief.

Clay turned his horse off the trail and onto a narrow path leading up the steep slope toward the cliff overhang above them.

"Come on," he said over his shoulder, his Spencer rifle in his hand. "Let's go see who else is dead up there."

Ben Twist nudged his horse along behind

296

him, followed by Moon Layhee and Drate Kunz.

"Maybe we'll get lucky and find the horse trader lying there with his brains blown out."

"Don't jinx us, Twist," Clay shot back to him, sounding cross. "I don't want to find the sumbitch dead. I want him alive and kicking when I level my sights on him." He shook the rifle in his hand.

"I'm just saying, it would save us the trouble," said Twist.

"Huh-uh," said Clay, having none of it. "Any killing he gets I want it coming straight from me."

The three Wind River gunmen gave another quick glance up at Ed Murphy, and then shot each other guarded looks. Ben Twist pulled his Winchester rifle from his saddle boot and laid it across his lap. The other two did the same.

Lucian Clay was piqued at the sound of metal drawn over leather, and of rifles being checked, levers being open and shut. He dropped his horse back, motioned the three ahead of him with his rifle barrel and followed along behind them.

They rode on through the blue-grainy light.

At the top of the path, the riders followed

another stony trail around and down the corner of the overhang. They spread out on the stone shelf, stopped their horses and stared at the two bodies sprawled out on the ground.

"This horse trader is no fool," said Clay, looking at what appeared to have been Summers' campsite.

Twist gave him a questioning look.

"He built his fire small and back out of sight," said Clay, nodding toward remnants of the campfire. "He knows he's in our backyard, and he knows Bendigo has us all out here searching for him. He was out of here last night before the dust settled."

Moon Layhee also nodded toward the small blackened campfire. "I can put my hand in there and tell how long the fire's been put out."

The other two Wind River gunmen gave him a look.

Clay just glanced away and let out a breath.

"It's the truth, I can do that," Moon insisted, not to be ignored. "It's an old tracker's trick they used to use, to see how long —"

"Nobody cares, Moon," said Ben Twist, cutting him short, recalling how quickly Clay had turned and shot Abel Anders for almost no reason.

"He left as soon as the shooting was over," Clay said. He nodded toward Udane's slashed and mangled face. "His dog did that. When you get that dog in your sights, remember what you saw here. Kill him quick before you get the same thing Udane got." He turned his horse to ride away, but as he did, a bullet struck the stone shelf at the horse's hooves, spooking the animal, causing it to rear straight up and let out a loud whinny.

"Who-o-o-a!" shouted Clay, hanging on, trying to collect the frightened horse and keep it in hand.

But the horse would have none of it. As a second bullet whistled past Clay's head, the horse came down hard onto its forehooves and unleashed a powerful kick of its hind legs.

The kick launched Lucian Clay upward, slamming him face-first into the ceiling of the rock overhang. He dropped even harder, still conscious, but feeling enormous pain in his face, knees and chest.

"Holy God . . . ," he groaned, addled by the impact. Pine residue and dirt covered his throbbing face, his chest and the knees of his trousers as he rolled and struggled, trying to right himself up onto his feet.

The three Wind River gunmen scurried down from their horses and dived for cover beneath the overhang. More shots rained down on them from a higher trail on an adjacent hillside.

"Stay down, Lucian!" Twist shouted. He dropped his rifle, ran a few feet, tackled Clay to the hard shelf and dragged him back under the overhang as rifle fire grew heavier. Their horses bolted away and up the narrow stone path.

"Damn!" Moon shouted, firing shots back at the puffs of rifle smoke on the adjacent trail. "We're nothing but sitting ducks down here!" No sooner had he spoken than a bullet punched through his forehead and splattered blood and brain matter on the stone wall behind him.

Pulling Clay back beneath the cliff overhang, Twist picked up his rifle from where he had dropped it and began firing at the streaks of muzzle flashes in the morning gloom.

"Damn it, he's got us pinned down from over there," he said to Clay.

"He won't for long," said Clay, still stunned by the fall, but throwing himself into the fight. "Give me that rifle!"

He yanked Ben Twist's rifle from his hands before Twist could stop him.

"Wait!" he said to Clay, but it was too late.

Clay rose to his feet and walked forward, firing shot after shot as quick as he could lever bullets into the chamber.

"Come on, you *horse-trading son of a bitch*!" he shouted, walking toward the edge of the cliff. "Step out and fight. Don't be a damn coward!"

But instead of drawing more fire, the rifle shots stopped suddenly.

On the adjacent trail, Tom and Dow Bendigo looked at each other.

Horse-trading son of a bitch . . . ?

"Damn it, Brother Cat, that's Lucian Clay. Those are our men we're shooting at!" Dow said in a whisper.

The half-breed only stared at him flatly, as if it didn't matter to him who they shot at.

"Come on, let's get the horses and get out of here before he sees it's us," said Dow.

Standing on the edge of the stone shelf, Clay looked down at the impaled body of Ed Murphy swaying steadily in the morning breeze. He took a cautious step back and looked at the gray rifle smoke adrift along the higher trail across from him.

"I'm thinking I've killed him, Twist," he

301

said over his shoulder. "Either that or he's had enough . . . I've sent him ducking and stooping."

"You think so?" Ben Twist asked, stepping forward, having drawn his Colt when Clay grabbed his rifle from him. He stared warily up along the smoky higher trail.

"Damn right," said Clay. He gave a tight grin and added, "Let's go find his body — slice his *horse-trading* head off."

Dow and Tom Bendigo rode at a brisk pace, pushing their horses and the stolen string horses more than they should have on the treacherous hill paths and rocky trails. But they slowed down to a more suitable walk once they had circled over onto the same trail they knew Lucian Clay and the Wind River gunmen would be riding.

It was midmorning when the two parties converged at a Y in the trail. Acting surprised, Dow jerked his horse's reins hard enough to cause it to rear slightly and come down positioned quarter-wise to Clay and other two riders.

"*Hola,* men . . . ," Dow said, lifting his gun hand in a show of peace, in spite of its being his father's gunmen facing them. "We heard shooting a while back, over on the other hillside. Thought we'd best go take a look."

"Yeah," said Clay, half of his face still blackened from pine soot where he'd hit the stone ceiling. "There was shooting all right. Looks like we've killed that horse trader. Now all we've left to do is cleave his head off and get the hundred dollars your pa put up."

Dow shook his lowered head in regret.

The half-breed sat staring at the black half of Clay's face, as if he was fascinated by it.

"I hate to be the bearer of bad news, Lucian Clay," Dow said. "But we just came from where the shooting was over there, and we saw no body, not the horse trader's or anybody else's."

"What?" Lucian Clay frowned. "We must've killed him. He was firing like a half dozen men. He'd already killed Alvarez, Udane and Murphy. Why would he just stop, real suddenlike?"

Dow shrugged with a thin, smug grin. Tom sat with the same brooding stonelike look on his face. Clay looked back and forth between them for an answer.

"Maybe he ran out of bullets, Lucian," Dow offered.

"Are you funning me, Dow?" Lucian asked, forgetting for a moment who he was talking to. "If you are, you best let me know before I take offense and do something ugly. I'm aware your pa is the bull of this bunch, but I'm not a man who takes to being —"

"No offense intended, Lucian," Dow said, cutting him short. "Maybe the horse trader heard us coming and lit out rather than getting caught in our cross fire."

"But to stop all at once that way," Lucian said. "It makes no sense."

Dow's thin smile had melted away. His expression turned dead-serious.

"See . . . I don't really give a damn why he stopped shooting, Lucian. The fact is, he's not lying back there dead. If you want to call Tom and me liars, go see for yourself. Then keep riding from there all the way to hell far as I'm concerned." He stared hard at Clay.

The half-breed stepped his horse forward, reached out and ran two fingertips down Clay's face through the black soot from the overhang ceiling. He studied it on the tips of his fingers as Clay stared at him in confusion.

"I'm not saying you're lying, Dow," Lucian said at length, seeing that Dow Bendigo was on the verge of getting his bark on over the matter, which meant the big half-breed was also, the two always taking each other's side.

"Oh . . . ?" Dow said.

"No, I'm not," said Clay, backing off from the issue. He thumbed over his shoulder to where Drate Kunz sat leading Moon Layhee's horse by its reins. "We lost a man back there to this damn horse trader, not to mention him killing Alvarez and the others. We even had to chase our horses down afoot, after the gunfire spooked them on us. I expect we're all three strung a little tight over it."

The Bendigo brothers just sat staring flatly at him.

Attempting to lighten a tense situation, Clay looked back past Dow at the string of stolen horses.

"Where are you two headed now?" he asked as if making conversation.

"Home," said Dow. "I'm taking these horses to our pa, see if him and us can't get our minds off of killing each other for a while."

"That sounds like a real fine thing to do," Clay said. "We all know how much the boss likes good horses. Right, fellows?" he said to the two men behind him.

Drate Kunz and Ben Twist continued to stare at Dow, making Dow think they had a suspicion it had been him and his Indian brother on the adjacent trail earlier.

Seeing the look on Dow's face, Ben Twist finally gave in and showed his belly.

"Yeah," Ben said quietly, "we all know how much."

"Ride back with us, Clay," Dow said. It sounded more like an order than an invitation. He didn't want Clay and these men riding over and snooping around, maybe figuring out it was he and the half-breed who'd killed Moon Layhee.

Clay looked at Dow as if considering it, but he knew he had no choice on the matter.

"Yeah, sure, why not?" he said finally. "We can get some grub, some supplies and come back."

"There you are," said Dow. He and Tom backed their horses to the side and made room for the three to move past them. "After you, fellows," Dow said.

When the three were in front of them on the trail, Dow turned his horse in behind them. But after a couple of steps, he noticed that the half-breed wasn't beside him. He spun his horse and saw Tom sitting atop his horse in the middle of the trail.

"What the hell is this, Brother Cat?" he asked, nudging his horse back and stopping in front of Tom, the string of Summers' horses bunching up behind him.

The half-breed jerked his rifle up from across his lap at port arms and pitched it to Dow. Catching it in the same manner, Dow looked at it, and then looked at Tom.

"Are you sure about this?" he asked. "You're not letting the black on Clay's face stir up the Injun in you?"

The half-breed glowered at him, but didn't answer. Instead his Colt streaked up from his holster and spun backward in his big hand. He pitched the gun to Dow butt first.

"Come on now, damn it. Don't go nuts on me," Dow cautioned him. "The horse trader is back there. He *will* be coming. War paint won't stop a bullet — it's been proven."

The half-breed's hand went to the handle of a big knife in his boot well. He swung it up and laid it across his lap. He stared at Dow with a look of finality.

"Damn, Brother Cat," Dow said. "Sometimes you beat all I ever seen."

On a high ridge a thousand yards behind them, Will Summers lay prone, gazing through a battered telescope he'd found rummaging through Arlo Hughes' saddlebags. The big cur lay in the dirt beside him, resting after their long trek. Summers and the dog followed the marked hooves of the stolen horses all the way to the line shack where the Bendigo brothers had taken them the night before.

Summers watched the riders move away, his string of horses tacking along behind Dow on the lead rope. He'd watched the half-breed give Dow his rifle and sidearm before Dow turned and rode away. Now Summers watched Tom Bendigo step down from his saddle after the others had ridden out of sight.

"Curious . . . ," Summers murmured to the dog lying stretched out beside him. He watched the half-breed strip saddle and bridle from the horse and drop both items alongside the trail. He saw him raise two fingers to his cheek. Then he saw him unbutton his shirt, take it off and toss it aside.

"All right, I get it . . . ," Summers said aloud. Tom Bendigo had staked himself out. If Will Summers wanted to take his horses back, he'd have to get past the half-breed to do it. Either get past him or go around, Summers thought. *If this is what it takes, so be it . . .*

Standing and brushing his knees and

chest, Summers closed the telescope and walked back to the horses. He wasn't going to duck around the half-breed — he knew he'd have to look back over his shoulder for him from now on if he did. He stepped up into the saddle, picked up the lead rope guiding the three horses and rode off along the trail, toward the place where the half-breed would be waiting below. The dog loped along beside him, this time not taking the lead.

CHAPTER 22

Summers rode around a turn in the trail almost a full hour later and recognized the half-breed's saddle and tack lying a hundred yards ahead, yet he saw no sign of the half-breed himself. He'd noted before rounding the turn that the dog had cut across the trail and disappeared upward along a rise of rock.

What was this . . . ?

His eyes searched along a wall of rock lining the left side of the trail, which stretched on past where the half-breed had dropped his saddle. The rock wall was a perfect place for an ambush, he thought, searching warily, resisting the urge to pull his horse and the three-horse string far over to the right and skirt the outer edge. Beyond the right edge lay a steep, almost straight, drop two hundred feet down. The tops of pine trees stood pointing up like spear tips.

Summers pictured the dead outlaw, Ed

Murphy, impaled on the top of such a pine. Checking the horses to the middle of the trail, he drew his Colt from his holster, cocked it and laid it across his lap. He rode on, doing so without taking his hand off the gun butt, or his finger off the trigger.

Fifty yards farther along, just as he'd settled himself and taken a deep, soothing breath, he caught sight of dust and small gravel streaming down the rock wall to his left. He instinctively jerked his horse to his right as a loud war cry resounded above him. As he turned quickly in his saddle, his Colt came up at arm's length. Looking up in time to see the half-breed appear on the edge on a ledge ten feet above him, he pulled the Colt's trigger. But not before he saw a flash of sunlight on a streak of steel.

Summers stiffened in his saddle as the point of the half-breed's big knife found its target. It sliced deep into his left shoulder — eight inches of finely sharpened steel burying itself almost to the hilt.

The shot from Summers' Colt hit the half-breed in almost the same spot, but a bullet in his left shoulder wasn't about to stop the big half-breed. He leaped down at Summers like a charging cougar.

Summers felt the big blade twist deeper into his flesh and bone as the impact of the half-breed fell upon him and the two rolled from the horse's back down onto the rocky ground.

Above the trail, Buddy had scouted ahead silently when he had caught the scent of the half-breed and turned and looked back in time to see him standing on the edge of the cliff. Spinning around, the big dog raced along the jagged edge, his paws appearing to barely touch the ground.

Nearing the spot where the two combatants rolled and thrashed in a death lock below, the dog streaked out diagonally off the edge without hesitation. But entering a swirl of dust filled with whinnying frightened horses, the dog let out a sharp yelp as a hoof caught him in midair and sent him tumbling off the right edge of the trail onto the dangerous rock slope.

Sliding, tumbling, the dog caught broken glimpses of the swaying pine tips reaching up toward him. Even in his diminished state — the kick having knocked his breath from him — he spread his forepaws in the loose dirt and gravel. His hind legs kicked and scratched and clawed in desperation, trying to find purchase on something solid, while the pine tops swayed beneath him.

Summers had heard the dog's yelp, but there was nothing he could do as he and the half-breed grappled, kicked and clawed at each other amid the kicking, stomping hooves of the three horses tied to one another on a short lead rope. Summers had the lead rope wrapped around the saddle horn of the cattle-horse that had belonged to Arlo Hughes. The horse seemed determined to keep the other three animals in their place.

Summers felt a wild hoof graze his side as the half-breed's right fingers finally manage to close around his throat and squeeze hard. Weakened by the knife stuck in his shoulder, Summers rolled sidelong and put Tom Bendigo right under the whinnying horse that still tried to kick him.

The half-breed let out a hard grunt as the horse's hoof slammed into him. His grip loosened some, just enough for Summers to shake his throat free and roll away up into a crouch as the half-breed collected himself and crawled after him. The horses had not settled in the least. Summers frantically looked through the thick dust and the kicking hooves for his Colt, which had been knocked from his hand.

Summers finally spotted the gun in the dirt and grabbed for it, but just as his hand started to close around it, Tom Bendigo, who had struggled halfway to his feet, hurled himself into Summers. The two went rolling and fighting once again in the dirt. This time the half-breed also saw the gun. He wanted it every bit as badly as Summers did. He also wanted his knife back. He made a grab for the handle that was still lodged in Summers' shoulder, hoping to pull it out and plunge it deeper, next time in a more lethal spot.

But Summers wasn't giving up gun or knife as long as he still had life in him. With his weakened left hand, he caught the half-breed's wrist and held it back from the knife handle. With his right hand, he struck fast and hard, three short but solid punches to the half-breed's chin, his jaw, his temple.

Tom staggered back a step, shook the punches off and charged forward, this time swinging a powerful roundhouse that slammed Summers hard in his chest only inches from the knife's handle.

Over the edge of the trail, the big cur was also in a fight for his life. He struggling had paid off. His frantically digging hind paws had twisted sideways enough to catch a sliver of the edge for just a second before losing purchase. But in that second he changed position enough to get another dig at the edge. His right hind paw continued digging, getting one grab on the edge, then another, until finally he had enough of his weight raised to where he could pull himself forward.

With both hind paws finally pushing him upward, he pulled hard with his front paws, feeling loose dirt and gravel pass under his flattened belly and fall away into the deep chasm behind him.

Hearing the shinnying, chuffing, frightened horses above him, he sprang to a stand. Without taking a breath or shaking himself off, the big dusty cur raced up over the edge onto the trail, dirt and rock still spilling behind him.

In the thick swirling dust among the horses, Summers staggered against a horse's rump and rolled sidelong away from another hard roundhouse. *Nothing's going to stop Tom Bendigo but a bullet in his brain,* he told himself, making a dive for the Colt still lying in the dirt. But Tom Bendigo saw Summers going for it. He gave Summers a hard shove just as he reached for the dust-covered Colt.

The shove sent Summers tumbling headlong past the gun. He landed facedown in the dirt and turned around just in time to see the half-breed grab the gun and shake dust from it.

Summers sat frozen in the dirt, staring up

at Tom Bendigo standing crouched over him, the cocked Colt in hand.

"*Oh no . . . !*" he said, unaware that he'd even spoken out loud.

"Oh *yes,*" the half-breed said in a deep voice, a tight, cruel grin spread wide across his face. His teeth were bloody, as were his lips. A trickle of blood ran down from the corner of his mouth. Summers noted the two black marks down his jaw where he had painted himself with the pine soot he'd rubbed from Lucian Clay's face.

Summers desperately searched for something, anything to use in order to save his life. He even thought of trying to yank the knife from his shoulder, but there was no time.

"Is this a good day to die, horse trader?" the half-breed asked, his deep voice sounding thick and halting — the voice of a man who didn't talk much, Summers thought, as if that made any difference in the world.

"You tell me," Summers said. He kept his gaze fixed on the half-breed's dark eyes, realizing these were the eyes of the man who would end his life.

"No," said the half-breed, "not a good day for you." He leveled the Colt. He had braced his hand to squeeze the trigger when the big cur streaked into the swirl of dust, racing across the backs of two horses, and dived into Tom Bendigo hard enough to knock him sideways, but not off his feet.

Summers saw the Colt fly from the half-breed's hand. Throwing himself to one side, he caught the gun with both hands and leveled it in his right, his left hand turning weaker still.

Bendigo stood with his right hand clutching the cur by his throat. The big dog had slashed the half-breed's face trying to get his fierce jaws locked on him, but Bendigo was the stronger of the two. He held the animal at arm's length, the helpless cur kicking and thrashing wildly, but losing strength fast. Summers knew the half-breed's move all too well. He would grab the dog by its hindquarters and slam it down over his cocked knee, breaking its spine.

No, you won't!

The Colt bucked in Summers' hand. The shot hit the half-breed in the center of his chest. Bendigo staggered back a step but didn't fall. He still held the squirming dog.

Summers fired again; the bullet hit less than three inches from the first one. Still the half-breed only staggered in place.

"Damn it, *die*!" Summers shouted, firing again. This time he aimed for the center of his head, seeing the dog kicking less, silent, unable to growl.

The half-breed's eyes drew inward, as if trying to see the gaping bullet hole between them. Buddy fell to the ground, gasping and gagging. Tom Bendigo slumped backward against a horse and rolled to the ground as the horse shied away.

Summers lay staring up for a moment, out of breath, the handle of the half-breed's knife still standing in his shoulder.

When the big cur walked over and licked his face a moment later, Summers sat up and touched the knife handle. A warm, fresh trickle of blood ran down his shoulder. He looked around. This was not the right time or place to try to pull the knife out and start it bleeding even worse, he thought. He picked up the Colt that he had dropped beside him and pushed himself to his feet.

He looked at the dead half-breed lying faceup in the dirt and saw the top of a letter sticking up from his trouser pocket, a gold watch chain hanging over the pocket's edge. Out of curiosity he stooped down and pulled out both letter and watch, examining them. He shook the folded letter open and read it to himself. Then he folded it, stuck it in his own trouser pocket and shook his head.

"I know somebody who'll want this more than anything in the world," he said to the big cur, who had now recovered from being choked and stood beside Tom Bendigo's body, licking a paw as if nothing had happened.

Vera Dalton drove Dr. Chase's buggy across the last stretch of flatlands before reaching the trail into the Bendigos' front yard. The guards at the top of the pass had received orders from Warton Bendigo himself to let her in, knowing she had traveled here to check on Layla Brooks' condition.

When she heard the single, hoarse bark of a dog, she looked over to her right and saw the cur loping toward her. Beyond the dog, she saw Will Summers sitting slumped in his saddle at the bottom of a thin hill trail, the three-horse string standing bunched beside him.

When the dog saw the buggy start toward him, he turned around and loped back toward Summers, looking back over his shoulder to make sure Vera still followed.

"Oh my, Will Summers!" she said, when she stopped the buggy and saw the knife handle and the slow seepage of blood that had covered the left shoulder of his shirt. She examined their surroundings, knowing what would happen if any of Bendigo's men saw him.

"Dr. Dalton," Summers said in a weak voice, keeping one hand on his saddle horn to steady himself. "I hope you have every tool it takes . . . to get this knife out of me."

"I do," she said, raising her hands, showing him that she carried the tools she needed. "First, let's get you somewhere out of sight." She hopped down from the buggy, unwrapped the lead rope from the saddle horn and looked up at Summers. "Any reason why you need four horses?" she asked.

"Force of habit, I suppose . . . ," Summer said, shaking his head slowly. "I can't seem to turn loose of them."

"You need to, though," said Vera.

Summers nodded and said, "Turn them loose. Mine are waiting for me at the Bendigo spread."

She quickly loosened the hackamore rope rigging that held the three horses together. She shooed them away, swinging the length of coiled rope back and forth to get them moving.

"Get going! All of you. Go find yourselves some wild cousins!" she said as the horses turned their rumps to her and trotted away. "I hope you all fare better than the horse I saw lying in the water hole."

"That was one of mine," Summers said, watching her as he struggled to keep himself upright.

"I'm sorry," she said. "Here, let's get you down and into the buggy before someone comes along and sees you."

"I can get down on my own," he said quietly.

"Yes, and I bet it feels *real good* doing it," she said, reaching up, helping him anyway.

Moments later, Will Summers sprawled in the seat beside her, the horse tied behind the rig, Vera drove the buggy up onto the hill trail a short ways and cut over into a small clearing.

"This will have to do," she said, tying the buggy horse's reins and stepping down from the rig.

As she led him to a rock and sat him down, Summers looked at her curiously.

"What are you doing out here anyway, Doctor?" he asked.

"I promised Layla I'd ride out in a few days and check on her eyes," she said.

"You rode all this way to check on her?" Summers asked.

"Of course," she said. "You sit right here. I'll get my bag and some bandages and be right back."

When she came back carrying a canteen of water, a leather medicine bag and some bandages, Summers started in again.

"That's a long ride, coming all this way to see how she's doing," he said.

"It's what Dr. Chase would have done," she said. "I'm not a doctor, but I'm trying to keep things going the way I know he would want me to."

"You're not a doctor?" questioned Summers.

"No, I'm not" she said, "and it appears I may never be." He could tell by the pained look on her face that she didn't want to talk about it. So he decided to drop the matter until she had removed the knife from his shoulder.

When she'd finished examining the knife from every angle and laid out a clean cloth on Summers' knee, she turned his face away and said, "This might take a few minutes. Look over that way."

"Anything you say —"

His words stopped as he felt a sharp, hard jerk down deep inside his shoulder. Behind the sharp flash of pain, he felt a flood of relief and a surge of warm blood.

"There," she said, picking up the bandage from his knee, "you can look back now."

Summers stared back at the wound; instead of seeing the knife blade, he saw Vera's bloody hand pressing the bandage to the spot where the knife had been.

"You tricked me," he said. "Is that what a doctor would do?"

"I learned it from a doctor," Vera said, still pressing, checking the blood flow and pressing again.

"He would be proud of you," Summers said.

"Yes, I believe he would," Vera said quietly. She placed Summers' right hand on the bandage. "Hold this," she said.

Pressing the cloth against his wound, he watched her unbutton his shirt and pull it back off his left shoulder, then his right, placing her hand on the cloth as she did so.

"Now to get you cleaned up and bandaged," she said.

"I don't how I'm going to repay you," Summers said, even though he had money in his pocket.

"I'm used to not getting paid," Vera said, "at least not for the doctoring. Nobody pays doctoring." She smiled. "But everybody pays a dove."

Summers reached down and pulled the folded letter and the watch he'd taken from Tom Bendigo's pocket and handed them to her.

"Vera," he said, "I think Dr. Chase wanted your days as a dove to be over."

Vera held the watch in her bloody hand while she opened the letter and read it. Summers watched her eyes well as she clutched the letter to her bosom.

"Oh my goodness," she said, "where did you get this?"

"I took it off Tom Bendigo," Summers said. "How he got it is anybody's guess."

"Will, you have no idea how much this means to me," she said tearfully.

Summers reached out with his right hand and brushed a strand of hair back from her cheek.

"Oh, I think I might at that," he said.

Chapter 23

Warton Bendigo stood watching from the front yard as Dow, Lucian Clay and the remaining Wind River gunmen, Ben Twist and Drate Kunz, rode in from the hill line. He searched for his son Tom, but only for a moment, his eyes wandering to the string of stolen horses.

Summers' horses . . . , he reminded himself. For two cents, he'd shoot every one of them and be done with the matter. In fact, he might just do that very thing, he thought.

"Heto," he said over his shoulder to the houseman who stood by awaiting his order, "bring me my gun, pronto!"

"La pistola de su oficina, señor?" Heto asked in his native tongue.

"No, not the pistol from my office, *damn it,*" Bendigo said gruffly. "Bring my rifle from the hall rack. I'm going to shoot these four-leggers soon as they're in the corral."

"Sí, jefe, en seguida," Heto said. He and

his young nephew grimaced at the thought of shooting the horses, but Heto hurried away toward the front door to do as he was told.

Inside, Layla had gone into Warton Bendigo's office to look for him when she heard voices in the front yard. She walked over to the window to catch a glimpse outside. She saw Dow and the others riding closer in a rise of dust, the string of Summers' horses riding abreast of Dow on the lead rope.

She recoiled at the sight of Dow Bendigo, but she caught herself and held her feelings in check. *You're a dove . . .* , she reminded herself. *You can handle this . . .*

All right, she thought, taking a deep, cleansing breath. She knew what she had to do. She touched her fingertips carefully to her scarred but healing cheek. It was time for her and the Bendigo brothers to face each other and settle this thing between them. She turned away from Warton's office window and closed her eyes for a moment to compose herself.

It had to be this way . . . , she told herself.

In the clay-tiled hallway, Heto took a Winchester repeating rifle from an ornate Spanish gun rack and checked it to make sure it was loaded. He shook his head gravely and crossed himself as he turned to walk back out front. When he looked up, he saw Layla Brooks walking down the hallway and he forced a stiff smile.

"La señorita se siente mejor?" he asked.

"Yes, I feel much better, Heto, thank you," Layla said.

"Ah, *bueno, bueno,*" he said. Nodding with his stiff smile, he turned and rushed away out the front door and down off the porch.

Layla walked on down the hallway into Warton Bendigo's bedroom and closed the door. She picked a horsehide chair cushion up from a wooden chair against the far wall and sat down. Hugging the cushion to her bosom, she gazed out the window with her right eye at the hill line and overshadowing mountain range in the distance beyond the barn and the surrounding flatlands.

In the front yard, Warton Bendigo took the Winchester from the houseman and levered a round into the chamber as the riders drew closer to the house. Dow saw the rifle in his father's hand and brought the riders to a halt thirty yards away.

"I want to know right now, are you still harboring a mad-on at Brother Cat and me?" Dow called out.

Lucian Clay and the two Wind River gunmen sidestepped their horses away from Dow, just in case.

"I'm still mad enough to kill you both," Warton called out in reply, not wanting to look weak in front of his men. "So it's best you leave me simmer awhile longer."

Dow let out a breath and said, "All right, if that's the way you feel."

"That *is* the way I feel," said Warton. He half raised the rifle, gestured it sidelong and said, "Now get over away from Summers' horses."

"Why, what are you talking about?" Dow asked.

"I'm shooting the lot of them," said Warton. "They've been nothing but trouble ever since you two stole them and brought them here. Get over! If I shoot you, I don't want it to be by accident."

"Damn it . . . ," Dow murmured under his breath. But he started to turn loose of the lead rope.

"Wait, boss!" Lucian Clay called out to Warton Bendigo, seeing what was going on. "Ain't you even going to tell him first?" he said to Dow.

"Hell no," Dow said stubbornly. "Let the old bastard find out after he kills them."

"Let me find out *what*?" Bendigo called out, lowering his rifle an inch.

"Boss," Clay said to Warton, "he said he's giving you these horses . . . making you a gift of the whole —"

"Shut up, Clay, you *son of a bitch*," Dow said angrily, cutting him off. "I know how to speak for myself."

"Then start doing it," said Warton, "or get the hell out of my way . . . I'm turning these cayuses into dog meat." He raised the rifle again.

"All right," Dow called out, letting loose a breath of exasperation. "Brother Cat and I talked it over. Want you to have Summers' horses." He held the lead rope forward in his gloved fist. "Call it our way of making up with you."

"Yeah?" Warton Bendigo said, sounding a little suspect of his sons' intentions. "Why now? You no-good sonsabitches have never given me anything but a hard way to go."

"Yeah, well," said Dow, "a hard time is about as much as you ever showed us."

Warton Bendigo stood in silence for a moment. Again the rifle lowered an inch.

"Bring them horses on in here. Let me take another look at them," he said.

Dow led the string forward to the yard. Lucian Clay and the Wind River gunmen

329

followed at a cautious distance.

"Where is your brother?" Warton asked when Dow stopped in the front yard. He ran a hand along one of the dark bays' withers with renewed interest now that the horses were being given to him.

"Brother Cat got a wild hair, Pa," said Dow. "He staked himself out to kill the horse trader when he comes along."

"Damn, he's starting that nonsense again?" said Warton, shaking his head. "That's what he did to the teacher that time I tried sending yas to school."

"Well, he's doing it again," said Dow. "He saw the war paint on Clay's face and got restless."

"War paint . . . ?" Bendigo eyed the black pine soot on one side of Clay's battered and bruised face.

"It's not *war paint,*" Lucian Clay said, "but it's a long story." He looked embarrassed.

Bendigo stared hard at him and said, "You and these Wind River men were going to bring me Summers' head on a stick, remember?"

"I remember, boss," said Clay. "It turns out Summers is not an easy kill."

"An *easy kill*? Is that what it takes for you and these jackasses?" Bendigo fumed.

Ben Twist and Drate Kunz sat staring coldly at Warton Bendigo.

"That's not how I meant it, boss," said Clay. "We'll get Summers next time out."

"My son Tom will have him skinned and gutted before you three get back out there," said Bendigo. "Now get out of my sight," he added with disgust.

As the three rode away toward the bunkhouse, Dow sat grinning at his father.

"Are we settled with each other?" he asked. He handed Warton the lead rope to the horses.

"No," Warton said firmly, "not until you settle things with Layla Brooks." He gestured a nod toward the house. "She's in there, right now, in my bedroom."

Dow gave a worried look at the house.

"Jesus . . . ," he said. "I suppose she's been filling your head against Tom and me."

"No," said Warton. "In fact, she said you were lying about the two of you raping her. Said neither of you would do such a thing. Said you were just trying to rile me."

"She said all that?" Dow looked at him closely.

"That's right, she did," said Warton. "I want you to go to her and see to it this thing gets straightened out. She's going to be living here. I want you to make her feel

331

welcome . . . see to it she's happy here."

Dow ran the possibilities through his mind — him and Layla Brooks under the same roof? Her not telling his father anything he'd done?

Oh yeah . . . , he thought. *I'll make her feel welcome.* He would see to it she was happy, every chance he got.

"I will go to her, Pa," he said with intention. "But not this evening. I'm plumb worn out. Let me get fed and washed and get a good night's sleep first."

Warton Bendigo stared at the failing evening light. *All right,* he thought. He needed to talk to Layla first anyway.

"Tomorrow it is, then," he said, raising a finger for emphasis. "Don't you let me down on this. I'm thinking about marrying that woman . . . That would make her your mother."

My mother . . . ? There was a name for what that would make him, Dow thought, stifling a grin. He pictured him and Layla Brooks alone, in the empty bunkhouse, the barn loft, on a cot, a blanket, wherever he could grab her and pin her down . . .

He nudged his horse forward, touching his hat brim.

"That will be wonderful, old man," he said in earnest, riding away.

■ ■ ■ ■

In Warton Bendigo's bedroom, Layla Brooks looked up with her good eye as the outlaw leader walked in and closed the door. She still sat in the wooden chair near the window on the far wall, holding the horsehide cushion in her lap now.

"Are you feeling better? Seeing better?" Warton asked. He crossed the room and stooped down beside her chair. He tossed a glance out the window, then looked back at her.

"I feel much better. And yes, I'm seeing a little more clearly every day," she said. She reached out her hand and cupped his cheek. "See? There you are." She smiled with a tint of regret. "I wish I could say my scars were getting better."

"They will in time," Warton said. "Anyway, they'll never be looked at or mentioned. Not here. If anybody ever speaks of your scars, we'll see how far his tongue pulls before it rips off."

Layla forced a smile.

"Anyway," said Warton, "Dow is here. He wants to talk to you and make things right." He stared at her. "If that doesn't suit you, say the word and I'll put a bullet in his head."

"No," Layla said, "I'll talk to him. We need to clear the air between us. I want a fresh start for you and me, Warton," she said.

"We're getting there, Layla," he said. He took her hand in his. "I told him to come see you tomorrow after he's rested up and made himself more presentable. Does that suit you?" He wasn't going to mention that it was Dow's idea instead of his own to wait until the next day.

"Yes, tomorrow is good," Layla said, looking a little relieved. "I'll feel even better tomorrow, after another night's rest."

Warton squeezed her hand a little and gave a suggestive smile.

"Another night or two of rest, there's no telling what we'll be doing in here, eh?"

Layla smiled, but said nothing.

"I'm afraid I have to ride out and take care of some business tonight." Warton stood up and looked down at Layla. "I'll be back here tomorrow, first thing, I'm hoping."

Layla looked at him curiously.

"It's Tom," said Warton. "Dow tells me he staked himself out along the trail." He gave a slight shrug. "It's something his ma's people do when there's an enemy they want dead."

"I know what it means for an Indian warrior to stake himself out, Warton," Layla said. "But Tom Bendigo is as much white as he is Indian."

"I know," said Warton, "but now and then he sees something that sets him off, makes him go a little loco. He starts thinking he's a Great Plains warrior — he's a mean sumbitch, my son. We always let him go 'til he gets the killing out of his system."

Layla gave him a pointed look with her right eye.

"He's staked out there somewhere waiting to kill Will Summers, isn't he?" she asked.

"Now, Layla, it's nothing to worry yourself with," Warton said.

"I want to know the truth, Warton," Layla said. "Is he waiting out there to kill Will Summers?"

"Yes, he is," replied Warton. "If he hasn't already killed him, he's going to. But it doesn't matter, Summers was a dead man the minute he stepped foot inside Red Cliffs. That's just how it works."

"Will Summers only came here to get his horses back after Dow and Tom stole them from him," Layla said. "He's done no wrong. I can't abide him dying this way."

"You've got to get over it," Warton said. He kneeled down beside her and took her hand. "Things will be better when I get back tomorrow. If Summers isn't dead when I find Tom, I'll call everybody off. Everybody except Lucian Clay, that is. Fair enough?"

"Why not Lucian Clay?" she said.

"Summers killed the Pelty brothers and some other pards of his," said Warton.

"You can stop him, Warton," Layla said.

Warton stood back up and let out a breath.

"We'll see," he said.

But she could tell by his tone and demeanor that he had no intention of putting a stop to anything.

CHAPTER 24

It was in the dark just before morning when the buggy rolled to a halt alongside the trail leading to the Bendigo spread. The big cur had jumped aboard the rig an hour earlier, and now leaped down to the ground as if rejuvenated and ready for anything. Summers stepped down with this left arm in a sling Vera had made for him. He walked to the rear where his horse stood hitched to the buggy. Vera watched him in the moonlight and shook her head.

"Will Summers, as your doctor I have to warn you against doing this," she said, keeping her voice lowered in case anyone might be in hearing distance.

"I appreciate you concern, Doctor," Summers said, trying to ignore the pain in his stiff shoulder. "But if I don't do this now, I may never have another chance."

Watching from the edge of the hills, they had seen Warton Bendigo's face in a torchlight as he and a group of riders took the train away from the ranch earlier in the night. If Summers' hunch was right, the men would be riding out to look for the half-breed, who hadn't shown up as he should have. The riders had a long way to travel to get to where the half-breed had stayed behind to make his stand. If he played his hand right, Summers would be in and out with his horses before anyone knew it. If he ran into Dow Bendigo, well . . . he'd kill him, simple enough, he thought. He owed him that much for the Appaloosa mare.

"What do you want me to tell Layla?" Vera asked.

"Tell her whatever she does, I understand," said Summers, unhitching his horse from the rig. The big cur sat in the dirt watching his every move. "I hope I'll see her in another place, at another time, when things are different."

Vera smiled slightly. She sat looking back, watching him collect his horse, swing up into the saddle one-handed and adjust his hat atop his head.

"I'll pass along the message," she said. She watched him nudge his horse forward and stop beside her. "And if I don't see you again, I want to tell you just how much you've done for me, bringing me this letter." She patted the pocket of her coat where she'd put the folded letter and Dr. Chase's gold watch. Her voice cracked a little with emotion.

Summers smiled down at her in the moonlight.

"I'm proud to be the first to officially call you *doctor,*" he said. "I'm also obliged to you for yanking this pigsticker out of my shoulder." The handle of the knife stuck up at the edge of his boot well.

"Be careful, Will," she said quietly as he turned his horse toward the shelter of the hill line.

"Yes, Doctor," he said. He smiled and tapped his heels to the horse's sides. The big cur shot ahead a few yards and moved along at an easy gait, like some shadowy spirit prowling the moonlit night.

Man, horse and dog traveled up high enough onto the stretch of hill line to not be seen by anyone on the flatlands below. He knew Vera would take the buggy on to the ranch and with no delays arrive at daylight. Traveling the hills, he should be there around the same time. But he would circle as wide as he had done before. He would round up his horses from the barn or corral, wherever they might be, string them and get them out.

It wouldn't be easy keeping out of sight, making his way out of Red Cliffs, possibly with the Bendigos trailing him. He knew the odds were against him making it out alive. But he had played long odds before and managed to come away the winner, he reminded himself. Besides, what choice did he have? Give up his horses without a fight?

What kind of horse trader would do that?

He pictured the horses as he muttered to himself. His own silver-gray dapple, three dark bays, a paint horse and a black Morgan cross. He thought about the Appaloosa mare and her dead foal bobbing in the water hole, buzzards picking their innocent remains.

No kind of horse trader that he ever knew . . . , he finally answered himself, feeling his right hand clench into a fist around his reins.

As dawn glowed on the western sky, Summers and the dog stopped on the treed hillside adjacent to the Bendigo ranch house. For the last two miles, he had been led by the glow of an oil lamp that traveled throughout the house, then stopped and burned softly in a window. Behind the house, the barn and the bunkhouse lay in shadows. Had there been someone inside either building, this was the time of morning to expect them to be up and around, he thought.

Summers stepped down from the horse and leaned against a tall pine, his rifle in his right hand. The dog sat close to his side, quiet and serious, as if knowing that one false move might well be a fight in the making. Both man and dog watched the dark house, the dark outbuildings and the dark trail as all of these became more defined in the encroaching dawn.

"Here we go," Summers whispered to the dog as he saw the black silhouette of the buggy rolling into sight along the trail to the front yard. He leaned his rifle against the tree, reached down and slipped his left arm from inside the sling and worked his fingers open and closed. Surprisingly, his arm was not as weak as it had been — but Vera had warned him against depending on the arm for anything of life-and-death importance. It was a warning he intended to heed.

He looked at the dog and said, "Buddy, you're sitting this one out."

The dog appeared anxious, wagging his tail restlessly.

"No, Buddy, *stay,*" Summers said. He

held a flat palm out toward the dog. "Stay and watch after the horse," he whispered.

The dog whined quietly, but seemed to understand Summers' command. He dropped his back half to the ground and sat staring in the grainy light of dawn.

Summers looked at the cur, considering things. He thought about tying him to a tree, but if he did, and something went wrong, the poor dog wouldn't stand a chance. He had to trust the dog. That's all he could do.

"Stay," he said again as if to make himself perfectly clear. The dog cocked his head and stared at him, as if to say he'd gotten the message the first time.

Summers picked his rifle up from against the tree and eased away quietly on foot, knowing he'd have one of his horses beneath him on his way back from the ranch. He looked back every few steps to make sure the dog was obeying his command. The big cur sat staring quietly in the misting light.

By the time Summers had crossed the grasslands and brush between the hill line and the barn, the morning light had grown to the point that he could clearly see Vera rolling up to the front yard in the buggy. Crouched, he hurried along to the back edge of the barn, looked around the corner and saw his horses, all six of them, standing at rest, bunched together in a corner of the corral. The black Morgan cross raised its head slightly and gave a quiet chuff toward him. "Easy, fellow," Summers whispered even though he was too far away to be heard.

He slipped along the barn to the rear door, tested it for creaking and when he didn't hear any to speak of, he opened it just enough to squeeze inside.

He found the lead rope he had made himself hanging from a peg on a barn post and lifted it off, hooking it over his right forearm. Before leaving the barn, he eased to the front door and looked out through a crack toward the bunkhouse for any sign of Dow or Bendigo's men.

Nothing. Good . . . , he thought, turning back to the rear door and slipping out as quietly as he'd slipped in.

He heard the faint sound of voices from the front yard — Vera bidding someone good morning in English, then a man replying in Spanish.

"So far, so good," he whispered to himself.

He hurried as much as his one good hand would allow, stringing the hackamore-fashioned lead rope from horse to horse, rubbing the horses soothingly as he worked to keep them calm. When he had them all strung together, he walked out of the corral and into the wild grass and brush, still hearing Vera's voice and the voice in Spanish coming from the front yard. *No problems . . .*

Inside the house, Dow stood at the door to his father's room and knocked quietly. He heard the bed rustle as Layla sat up.

"Who is it?" she asked.

Dow grinned to himself. *She knows who it is . . .*

"It's me, your soon-to-be stepson," he said quietly. "Let me in. The old man wants us to talk things out between us."

"At this hour of morning?" Layla asked.

"We're all early risers here," Dow said. He waited, listened, heard her get up and walk across the floor in her bare feet. But he didn't hear her unlatch the door.

"Well, are you going to let me in?" he asked.

"It's not locked," Layla said.

"Oh, really?" he said. He shoved the door with one finger and watched it open on its own.

Layla sat in the chair by the window in a thin, cotton nightgown. Her left eye was still covered by a bandage, but the bandages had been removed from her chin and her cheek.

She held the horsehide cushion against her bosom, covering herself.

"Warton wants us to talk?" she asked, as if she'd heard nothing about it.

"I told him I wanted to tell you how sorry Tom and I are about everything that happened." He paused. "So, here it is. I'm sorry for the beating, the buckshot and all that."

"I'm a dove, Dow," Layla said, playing it off with a shrug. "I know how to take a beating."

Dow nodded and said, "All right, then." He gave a shy smile. "I suppose I should thank you too, for not telling him we poked you that night. When he thought we raped you, he was ready to kill us both. This time I believe he would have, had he got his sights on us."

"You don't have to thank me, Dow," Layla said. "I told him that for a reason."

"I know," Dow said. "You wanted us to all get along now that we're going to be one happy family, eh?"

"No, that's not why," she said, catching the suggestion in his voice. "I lied to him for the same reason I lied to Will Summers and the sheriff in Wakely about not remembering anything that happened," she said. "Because I didn't want them killing you. I made up my mind —"

"Yeah . . . ?" Dow said, with a wide grin, barely paying attention to her. He stepped forward, unbuckling his gun belt and letting it fall to the floor. "I can see we're going to be close."

"Because nobody is killing you *but me*!" Layla shouted, swinging the cushion from her bosom. The engraved Colt from Warton's desk exploded in a streak of blue-orange flame. "How dare you rape a dove!"

Dow arched forward onto this tiptoes and looked down at the hole in his lower stomach and the stream of blood spurting from it. His right hand slapped the empty holster on his hip, his eyes widened in stunned surprise.

A second shot exploded. Blue-orange fire streaked again across the dim-lit room. It struck him in his chest. He fell to the floor with the impact. But he grappled for his discarded gun belt, got it, jerked his Colt from it and fired as Layla sent a third shot streaking across the room.

In the brush surrounding the backyard, Summers spun around at the sound of the first gunshot from inside the house. He saw the second flash of blue-orange flame in the rear window. Knowing that Layla was inside, and that Vera had just arrived, he swung up one-handed atop the first horse in the string, his own silver-gray, and batted his boots to its sides.

His rifle and lead rope in his right hand, Summers raced along a path through the side yard to the front of the house, the six horses sounding like a whole posse arriving. At the front door, Vera and Heto the houseman stood looking scared and bewildered.

"Who's in there?" Summers asked, jumping down from the silver-gray's bare back and running onto the porch.

"No one but my nephew and me . . . and the *señorita*!" said Heto, his eyes even wider now at the sight of the rifle in Summers' hand. "*Mi jefe* and his hombres are gone looking for his son!" he exclaimed in mixed language.

"Someone locked him out, Will," Vera said quickly. Inside, two more shots resounded.

Summers shoved Heto aside, shouldered the door and felt the latch split loose from the jamb. He shouldered it again and it flung open. On his way through the house, Vera and Heto right behind him, one more shot exploded, followed by the thump of a body hitting the floor.

"Stay back," Summers said over his shoulder, going to a door where smoke seeped out all around its frame and curled up onto the ceiling.

Heto and Vera ducked to one side; Summers grabbed the knob and threw the door open. He stopped suddenly and stood slumped, his rifle hanging in his hand.

"Oh no . . . ," he said quietly.

Behind him, Vera eased into the room and at the body of Dow Bendigo lying sprawled on the floor facedown in a spreading puddle of blood. She looked over at Layla lying facedown by the wooden chair, a sliver of smoke looming above a gaping exit wound in the back of her head.

Summers stepped forward and kicked the gun away from Dow's hand just in case. Then he stepped over to Layla, Vera right beside him. Heto stood watching from the doorway, his nephew appearing from their bedroom and hovering at his side.

The two stooped down over Layla. Summers reached down with his good hand and with Vera's help turned her over onto her back.

"Oh, Layla . . . ," Vera said in a sorrowful tone.

"He killed her?" Summers said, not wanting to look at Layla's face right then.

"No," Vera whispered. "From the looks of it, I'm afraid the poor thing killed herself."

From the doorway, Heto's nephew whispered something near his uncle's ear.

"Señor . . . Señorita! Por favor!" said the frightened houseman. "Pero tells me they are coming back. He sees them from his window!"

Summers and Vera looked at each other.

"They'll let you pass," Summers said. "Go on, get out of here."

"What about you, Will?" she said. "I can't leave you here to die." She shook her head. "I won't do it."

Summers just stared at her and let out a breath.

"At least keep your head down until it's all over," he said. "I don't want to worry about shooting you."

CHAPTER 25

Warton Bendigo and his men heard the gunshots from across the flatlands and kicked their horses up into a run. "Shotgun" Holder rode a little behind the others, carrying Tom Bendigo's bloody body across his horse's rump.

"What the hell is this, boss?" Lucian Clay asked, riding alongside Warton Bendigo.

"I'd say somebody knew we were gone for the night and figured we wouldn't make it home this early."

"Yeah, I'd say that's it," said Clay, grinning, slapping his reins to his horse's withers to speed it up even more. "If it's Summers, I'm killing him before we can all say 'howdy-do.' "

"Nobody kills nobody until I see what's going on," said Bendigo. "Layla's there. First I make sure she's all right."

"Dow's there too," Clay called out to him above the pounding on their horses' hooves.

"That's what worries me," said Warton Bendigo. "I still don't trust that low-down bastard. The only good son I've got is the one flopping on the back of Holder's cayuse."

They raced on toward the front yard, the rest of the gunmen strung out behind them in a rise of dust.

Summers tried working his sore shoulder a little just to see if he could depend on it for anything at all. *No good . . . ,* he told himself right away, feeling the sharp pain deep down inside the still-fresh shoulder wound. On the way from Warton Bendigo's bedroom, he had stopped at the gun rack in the hallway and taken out a double-barreled shotgun and a bandolier full of store-bought loads.

He stood five yards away from his string of horses in the front yard, the loaded shotgun in hand, his rifle leaning against the front porch, his Colt standing ready in his tied-down holster.

He thought about the big cur waiting up on the hillside with his horse. He was glad that he hadn't tied the dog to the tree, for just this very reason.

He had played this hand straight, he thought, feeling more and more likely that it was just about over for him. He watched the horsemen draw closer. He saw the bloody body of the shirtless half-breed slung across the rear of a horse. *Yep, this is it,* he told himself. He'd done his best and now it was time to die. He watched the riders slow and fall abreast, traveling the last few yards to the house, the dust rising and drifting on the dawn air.

A man can't always pick the way he dies, he reminded himself. *He can only hope to pick the way he lives . . .*

Where had he heard that? Hell, it didn't matter. It made sense anyway — just one of those things that's supposed to make dying easier. Well, it didn't work. He took a glance toward the string of horses at the hitch rail. He let out a tight breath and took a step forward as the riders stopped and Warton Bendigo and Lucian Clay stepped down from their saddles and walked into the yard.

"Well, well, horse trader," said Bendigo. "You've had quite a ride on my ticket."

Summers didn't reply, he only stared.

"We found Tom where you left him," Bendigo said. "Is that his knife in your boot?" He looked down at Summers' boot well.

Summers only nodded, the shotgun poised and ready. He would shoot until their bullets stopped him. There was no other way to play it.

"Give it to me," Bendigo said in a strong tone.

Summers shook his head *no.*

Bendigo was a little surprised, but he caught himself before it showed.

"It doesn't matter," he said. "I'll take it off you later.

Bendigo looked at the string of horses and shook his head in disgust.

"Those damn horses meant all that to you?" he asked. "You threw your life away for them?" He gave a short, tight grin. "I expect if you had to do it over now, you'd have stayed clear of Red Cliff, said 'to hell with the horses,' eh?"

Summers shook his head *no* again.

Bendigo and Lucian Clay looked at each other.

"If he's not going to talk, we should just as well get on with —"

"Dow is dead," Summers said flatly, cutting off Clay.

"What?" shouted Bendigo in disbelief. "You killed him? You've killed *both my sons*?" His hand spread and tightened above his holstered Colt.

"Layla killed him," Summers said.

"Layla killed Dow?" said Bendigo. "She

wouldn't! They were going to talk!"

"Layla's dead too," Summers said flatly.

"Oh no, oh God, no!" Bendigo said in a shaky, broken voice, refusing to believe it. He stared at Summers as if he were lying.

"It is true what he says, Señor Bendigo," Heto called out from the open front doorway. He stood with Layla's body lying limp in his arms.

"Noooo!" Bendigo screamed, bounding up onto the porch and grabbing Layla's body from him. He carried her back and forth for a moment, unsure what to do with her. Vera ventured out of the house and ushered him to a long, cowhide porch sofa and helped him lay her down gently, blood dripping steadily from the back of her head down onto Bendigo's boots.

"She's — she's still warm," he said. "Maybe there's something you can —"

Vera shook her head, stopping him.

"She's gone, Mr. Bendigo," she said gently.

"Both my sons . . . the woman I love," Bendigo said, breaking down right in front of his band of outlaws. "Dead, all three of them," he lamented.

"Yes," said Vera, "and killing Will Summers won't bring any of them back."

"No, it won't. You're right," he said, rubbing his hand back and forth across Layla's warm, bloody forehead, as if cleaning off the blood would help things, would somehow change what was now and forever carved in stone. "Enough killing," he said without looking up from Layla's partially bandaged face.

A tense silence set in. Summers looked around, wondering if fate had suddenly declared this thing over. Maybe so, he thought, but he didn't trust it yet. Fate had lied to him before.

"Speak for your damn self, Bendigo!" Lucian Clay bellowed, reaching for his Colt as he stepped sideways for a clearer shot at Summers.

Here we go . . .

Summers swung the shotgun into play with both hands, though his left arm didn't offer much help. But the blast exploded true and deadly. It picked up Lucian Clay and slammed him backward. A few stray buckshot pellets flew past Clay and peppered the other gunmen's horses, sending them into a kicking, bucking, rearing, twisting frenzy.

Chip Bryant drew his Colt but turned it loose as he struggled with his reins, trying to pull his rearing horse back to earth. Summer had swung the shotgun toward Bryant.

But seeing Bryant's gun leave his hand and his horse touch down and bolt away across the flatlands, whinnying wildly, Summers swung the shotgun toward Ben Twist instead. Twist's rifle was up, taking awkward aim, as his horse stepped high and sidelong in the dirt.

The second blast of the double-barrel picked Ben Twist up out of his saddle and hurled him away, spinning him like a broken pinwheel. The horse wasn't hit, but it went crazy all the same, slamming sideways into another gunman's horse as Summers ducked away with the empty shotgun and took cover behind Vera's buggy at the hitch rail. While he hurriedly took two fresh loads from the bandolier and reloaded the shotgun, he watched "Shotgun" Holder shove the dead half-breed from behind his saddle, turn his horse and ride away.

"Summers, you son of a bitch!" Rowe Jolsyn shouted, jumping down from his horse and walking straight across the yard, firing shot after shot from a big Remington.

Summers jumped out from behind the buggy rig with the shotgun reloaded. A bullet from the Remington grazed his left shoulder as he pulled one of the double-barrel's triggers. Jolsyn's face and chest appeared to explode as the hard blast of the shotgun hit him and sent him flying backward in a red mist. Summers heard a pistol shot explode from the porch and he spun the shotgun toward it, his left arm ready to collapse from weakness and pain.

Yet he saw no one firing at him on the porch, only Warton Bendigo lying limp across the body of Layla Brooks, his arms spread out as if protecting her. His smoking Colt lay an inch from his hand. Smoke wafted away from the bloody bullet hole in the side of his head.

Summers swung the shotgun away from the porch toward the four remaining gunmen who sat atop their settling horses, guns in hand, staring in disbelief at Bendigo's body.

"Damn!" one said, backing his horse away. "Everybody's killing themselves!" He raised his gun in a show of peace, turned his horse and batted his heels to its sides.

Summers watched the other horsemen turn and bolt away, one of them jumping his horse over the half-breed's body instead of veering around it.

"Dr. Dalton," he said, turning around to the porch as he spoke, "are you all right?"

"Yes, I — I think so," Vera said, almost surprised that no harm had come to her. She looked on at Summers and said, "But you're hit, you're bleeding."

"It's just a graze," Summers said.

"In the same shoulder," Vera said with a sigh. She stepped off the porch and walked out to him. "I'll get my bag and get a bandage on it."

Summers didn't appear to hear her as he slumped and let the shotgun fall from his hand.

"I have to admit, that turned out better than I expected," he said, letting out a tense breath.

It was noon when Summers and Vera Dalton rode away in the buggy rig, his left arm back in the sling, the string of horses hitched behind them and trotting along at an easy gait.

A few yards ahead of them, the big cur loped along, scouting the hills to their right and the trail ahead.

"You know, I almost forgot Buddy was waiting up on the hillside," he said.

Vera turned her face and looked at him.

Summers shrugged with his right shoulder and said, "I told him to stay, and he did. I went to get my horse and there he was, just like I left him, only he seemed like he'd been real worried until he saw me coming." He smiled. "But with all the shooting, he never broke ranks, I'll give him that."

They rode on a ways; then Vera said, "That was a nice spot where we buried Layla, don't you think?"

"Yeah, I wish I could have dug the grave," said Summers, "but I suppose she would understand why I had the Mexican and his nephew dig it."

"Yes, she would," Vera said. "You know, when you both came to Wakely, I thought the two of you were, you know, *together*." She looked at him.

"No," Summers said. "We just knew each other. We fell in with each other because her man died and she needed help to town."

"Oh, I see," Vera said.

A silence set in as the buggy rolled along the rocky trail.

"She used me," Summers said. "But that was all right. She was just scared, and she used me to take her to Wakely, then on to Red Cliffs. I don't think she was water poisoned. She wanted to get to Red Cliffs and she knew I'd have to take her if she was poisoned."

"That doesn't bother you, her using you that way?" Vera asked.

"No," said Summers. "To be honest, I used her too. I used her to get inside Red Cliffs once we got there. She told me

Bendigo's guards would let her in. I took advantage of it."

"I see," Vera said. After another pause she said, "Well, what's done is done. I wish I could have seen it coming, her killing herself. But I suppose once she had it in mind to do it, nothing was going to stop her."

They rode on quietly, contemplating everything that had happened.

That night, when they had made their way out of Red Cliffs without any guards showing up to stop them, they rode a few miles farther and pulled off into a path beside a clear, running stream to camp for the night.

Vera changed the bandages on his wounds and boiled a pot of coffee from beans she carried in her supplies.

While they sipped coffee, Vera said boldly out of the blue, "Will Summers, have you ever slept with a doctor?"

"Well . . . I have never seen one that would have led my urges in that direction." He paused, then looked her up and down, and added, "Until *now,* that is."

"I'm going to sleep with you tonight, Will Summers," she said. "And if it works out well for both of us, I'll do the same tomorrow night, and the night after, and so and so on, until we decide we've both had enough." She smiled. "How does that sound to you?"

"That sounds real nice, Doctor," he said. He leaned back against a rock and watched her spread a blanket on the ground in the silver-purple moonlight. He sipped the coffee and looked over to where his horses milled and grazed in clumps of sweet, wild grass.

There they are . . . , he told himself. All of his horses. His silver-gray dapple, three dark bays, a paint horse, a black Morgan cross . . . and a cattle-horse that once belonged to an outlaw named Arlo Hughes.

He looked back at Vera, watching her step out of her clothes and stand naked in the moonlight for a moment, before lying down on the blanket and pulling another blanket over her.

Seven horses in total . . . , he reminded himself. The same number he'd started with. He smiled to himself, pitched out the remaining drops of coffee and crawled over to the blanket.

And they are all fine horses . . .

ABOUT THE AUTHOR

Ralph Cotton is a former ironworker, second mate on a commercial barge, teamster, horse trainer, and lay minister with the Lutheran church. Visit his Web site at www.RalphCotton.com.

CPSIA information can be obtained
at www.ICGtesting.com
Printed in the USA
FFOW03n0622030214
3392FF